FAR EAST EXPERTS ON
DEALING WITH THE CHINESE

"A VALUABLE, IN FACT, ESSENTIAL GUIDE for any Western traveller to China/Hong Kong/Taiwan. Its clear and concise prose leaves the reader well prepared and eager for an encounter with the Chinese—on their turf! This is a very practical aid for any sensitive visitor to China who wishes to be polite, respected, and to successfully fulfill the goals of his visit. I would highly recommend this book to any traveller, especially businessmen and women, to China."

–David B. Warner,
  Vice President and General Manager,
  China/Hong Kong/South Asia,
  The First National Bank of Chicago

"LEADS THE READER THROUGH BOTH THE LOGISTICAL AND CULTURAL HAZARDS THAT AFFLICT SO MANY FOREIGNERS VENTURING INTO CHINA. His insights will prove as valuable for the experienced China hand as for the first-time visitor. Especially useful are the concise 'recaps' at the end of each chapter and the guidance provided for American organizations preparing to host a Chinese organization in the U.S."

–Arthur Rosen,
  President Emeritus
  National Council on U.S.–China Relations

"WISE, CHARMING, PRACTICAL AND COMPREHENSIVE, *Dealing with the Chinese* is the definitive guide to bridging U.S.–China cultural barriers. Seligman's witty and measured style bears witness to his own mastery of the formidable patience, fairmindedness and good humor necessary to successful dealings with China, whether the purpose be business, political or scholarly exchange or simple curiosity. No neophyte should go to China unarmed with this book."

–Judith Shapiro,
  co-author, *Son of the Revolution* and
  After the Nightmare

"An indispensable reference guide for anyone seriously interested in penetrating the important China market. Skim it, return to it, digest it—but keep it close at hand. Like China itself, this excellent book is meant to be savored and explored in depth."

–David S. Tappan, Jr.,
  chairman and chief executive officer
  Fluor Corporation

SCOTT D. SELIGMAN is Vice-president and Creative Director of China for the public relations firm Burson-Marsteller and was previously director of development and government relations and Beijing representative for the National Council for U.S.-China Trade. He is also co-author of *Chinese at a Glance: A Phrase Book and Dictionary for Travelers.*

DEALING
WITH THE
CHINESE

A Practical Guide to
Business Etiquette in the
People's Republic
Today

SCOTT D. SELIGMAN

Illustrations by Edward Trenn

A Warner Communications Company

Copyright © 1989 by Scott D. Seligman
Illustrations copyright © 1989 by Edward Trenn
All rights reserved.
Warner Books, Inc., 666 Fifth Avenue, New York, NY 10103

A Warner Communications Company

Book Design by Richard Oriolo
Cover Design by Victoria Fishetti
Cover Photo by Bradley Olman

Printed in the United States of America
First Printing: July 1989
10 9 8 7 6 5 4 3 2 1

Library of Congress Cataloging-in-Publication Data

Seligman, Scott D.
  Dealing with the Chinese / Scott D. Seligman.
    p. cm.
  Bibliography: p.
  Includes index.
  ISBN 0-446-38994-3 (pbk.) (U.S.A.)
       0-446-38995-1 (pbk.) (Can.)
       1. China—Social life and customs—1976- 2. Business etiquette—
  China. 3. Corporations, Foreign—China. I. Title.
  DS779.23S45 1989   89-5685
  306′.0951—dc19   CIP

Acknowledgments

The author wishes to express appreciation to nine very special people who have, over a period of more than sixteen years, done the most to shape my thinking about the profound differences—and striking similarities—between Chinese and Westerners, and without whom this book could not possibly have been written:

LISA CHANG AHNERT, my very first Mandarin teacher and a good friend who helped me begin to understand what it means to grow up Chinese.

ROBERT C. ATMORE, former executive secretary of Princeton-in-Asia, who took a chance on me and gave me my start in the Orient, who helped me to make some sense of my experiences there, and who has been a constant source of guidance and support in the years since.

I-CHUAN CHEN, my former colleague at the National Council for U.S.-China Trade (now the U.S.-China Business Council) and a Confucian gentleman and scholar in his own right, who consistently provided penetrating insights into cultural differences.

LAN-FENG CHEN, my colleague at Tunghai University who more than anyone else helped me understand Taiwan, Chinese culture, and the Chinese language.

LI WENDA, former advisor, Beijing Office of the U.S.-China Business Council, who provided me with a first-rate, firsthand education on *guanxi*, *houmen*, and the nuts and bolts of getting things done in the PRC.

CHRISTOPHER H. PHILLIPS, former president of the National Council for U.S.-China Trade, who helped sensitize me to some of the finer points of protocol and etiquette involved in international commerce.

IVOR N. SHEPHERD, chairman of the Department of Western Languages and Literature at Tunghai University,

Taichung, Taiwan, who helped shape my earliest perspectives on Chinese institutions and showed me how foreigners can operate within them.

ROGER W. SULLIVAN, president of the U.S.-China Business Council, who has taught and guided me, helped me think more clearly and analytically about China, and whose own love for—and wry perspective on—the Chinese is infectious and always thought–provoking.

RUTH WEISS, a veritable font of captivating anecdotes, who provided the invaluable perspective on China and the Chinese that only a foreigner resident in the PRC for the better part of the twentieth century could possess.

Thanks are due also to the following people for their unselfish assistance in the creation of this book:

ED AHNERT, for sharing some tips on his personal experiences negotiating with Chinese corporations.

CAROLYN BREHM, for contributing a number of important insights on dealing as a foreigner with the Chinese on their own turf, and for offering up some excellent case examples in lurid detail.

SIMON CHEN, for providing guidance as to the differences in customs and etiquette between people in Taiwan and those on the China mainland.

MARSHA COHAN, for sharing her perspective on the Chinese attitude toward laws and regulations.

JANE BLUTHE DRISCOLL, for moral support and helpful suggestions throughout the writing and editing process.

ELLEN ELIASOPH, for sharing her perspective and extensive experience in negotiating dozens of contracts with Chinese units and for conducting a very thorough and beneficial critique of the manuscript.

JEAN HOFFMAN, for imparting some of the juicy details only someone with a great deal of negotiating experience with the Chinese could know.

DALE HOIBERG, for offering insights and criticisms from his own China experience that helped to make the manuscript more accurate and up-to-date and for hunting through numerous reference works to track down the quotation that opens this book.

SARA KANE, for doing a superb job of copyediting the lion's share of the manuscript.

JENNIFER LITTLE, for suggesting countless reference sources and cheerfully fielding nearly as many inquiries.

CHRIS LONSDALE, for contributing useful tips on the very latest changes in the social life of the PRC.

STEPHEN MARKSCHEID, for offering constructive commentary on the manuscript and reminding me of some superb anecdotes that help to illustrate the points made.

BILL NOONAN, for imparting a non-China hand's perspective on the usefulness of the book for a first-timer in the PRC.

JEFFREY SCHULTZ, for giving the benefit of his own years of experience doing business with the Chinese, and for astute suggestions on how to improve the first draft.

LIDA WAGNER, for looking over portions of the manuscript and offering useful suggestions on content and style.

入境而問禁
入國而問俗
入門而問諱

"If you enter a region, ask what its prohibitions are;
if you visit a country, ask what its customs are;
if you cross a family's threshold, ask what its taboos are."

–From *Li Ji (The Book of Rites)*,
one of the five Confucian classics,
ca. 500 B.C.

Contents

Foreword

A few years ago I was asked to participate in a group effort sponsored by the U.S. government to develop a set of guidelines for negotiating with the Chinese. That the government saw the need for such a book and recognized China's formidable skills in negotiating was encouraging. But it quickly became apparent that a major point was being missed. The organizers of the meeting said they wanted a short, easy-to-understand book that government executives could read on the plane. I remember thinking at the time that negotiators who believed that all they needed was a simple set of guidelines they could master while on the plane were sure to fail in China. *Dealing with the Chinese* is not short, nor does it oversimplify. In eminently readable style it presents a wealth of information and advice on everything from how to behave at a banquet to how to succeed in complex negotiations. But don't wait until you are on the plane to read it. Use that time to reread it.

Scott Seligman has done a great service not just for business executives but for all who visit China or whose work brings them in contact with Chinese groups and organizations. He is the first author I know of who has gathered in a single book all the key points and insights necessary to begin successful communication with the oldest and perhaps most sophisticated living culture in the world. I say "begin" because, as Mr. Seligman would be the first to acknowledge, learning to understand China and master its "2,500 years of interpersonal relationships" is the task of a lifetime.

Any newcomer about to enter even the most exploratory negotiations with the Chinese should read the book with care and take it along on the trip for ready reference. Much of Mr. Seligman's advice you will remember and confirm for yourself as you gain experience with the Chinese. But other seemingly esoteric pointers, such as who faces the door and where to put the interpreter at a banquet (illustrated in Seligman's helpful charts), is not the kind of information you are likely to remember unless you are a lot more protocol-conscious than most Americans. You will need to have the book handy and consult it frequently, because after reading it you will know why you cannot leave banquet arrangements entirely to your staff or the restaurant manager. If such seemingly routine details are not handled correctly you could inadvertently embarrass or cause undue discomfort to your Chinese guests, and that could turn an otherwise successful negotiation into a costly failure.

This is not just a book for neophytes. Experienced "China hands" will also learn a great deal from reading it. Even the most experienced China expert will want it as a reference to review the "Dozen Notes on Business Meetings" or the "Seven Points on Negotiating." And the next time you find yourself sitting in a hotel room in China wondering how you are going to salvage what appears to be a total waste of a trip, reread "Getting Things Done in China," particularly the "Tactics for Getting to Yes" and "Ten Tips on Getting Things Done."

Why hasn't someone written a book like this before? After all, it has been almost eighteen years since Henry Kissinger made his famous flight from Pakistan to Beijing to arrange President Nixon's historic China visit. I think the simple answer is that other authors have tried but none has possessed Scott Seligman's unique combination of knowledge, experience, humor, and uncanny ability to see the world through the eyes of a person from another culture. He speaks Chinese fluently, but so do many other Americans today. What distinguishes Mr. Seligman from the others is that he can trade jokes and local slang with taxi drivers and hotel room attendants and, with equal facility, deliver an eloquent toast or come up with the appropriate literary allusion in meetings with senior Chinese officials. And both groups will remember him fondly and respect him as a most unusual and civilized foreigner.

If you read this book carefully, consult it frequently, and follow Mr. Seligman's advice, maybe some of his extraordinary success in dealing with the Chinese will rub off on you.

Roger W. Sullivan
President
US-China Business Council

Introduction:
The Scrutable Chinese

You are the chief negotiator on your company's China team, visiting Beijing to try to secure agreement on a joint venture that will ensure your firm's entry into the vast and potentially lucrative PRC market. A successful agreement will probably earn you a promotion back home. Talks have been going on for the better part of a week, but are stalled on what seems to you to be a relatively minor point. Suddenly your Chinese counterpart rises and expresses theretofore unseen exasperation and hostility. "Your insistence on this point is unfriendly," he intones angrily, "and shows us that you are not sincere in your intentions to conclude an agreement with us." Adding, "we have nothing further to discuss with your company," he turns on his heel and leads his team out of the room. What did you do wrong? Anything? And what do you do now?

Or perhaps you are the guest of honor at a banquet with the vice minister of an important Chinese government agency. It is the first time you have met the man, and you are eager to make a good impression on him, since his support will be crucial to the success of an agreement your company hopes to conclude. The waiter brings a plate of food to the table, and the vice minister enthusiastically piles your tiny dish high with sea slug, which he assures you is a delicacy in China and very good for you. You look at the dull, brownish rubbery substance and feel an unmistakable gag in your throat. What do you do? Can you refuse it without causing offense?

At the same banquet, the vice minister raises a glass of fiery *maotai* liquor and challenges you to down a similar glass in one gulp. Everyone at the table exhorts you to try, and you get the distinct impression that a refusal will call your virility into question. But you're quite sure that the 106-proof beverage will burn a hole in your stomach. Is the contract worth a night of severe discomfort in your hotel room? Do you have any other choices?

Or maybe you are hurrying down the stairs of a department store in Taipei and you suddenly lose your footing. You slip down most of a flight of stairs and find yourself on your backside looking up at a crowd of a dozen or more Chinese shoppers. No one lifts a hand to help you, and as you study the faces in the crowd, you detect unmistakable mirth on many of them. As the laughter continues, you feel like killing someone. Why did this happen? And what does it mean?

These are just a few examples of cross-cultural situations that simply cannot be taken at face value if they are to be interpreted properly. If you ever find yourself in one of them, you may feel absolutely certain that you have been wronged or embarrassed, or you may feel completely perplexed at a sudden turn of events. Sometimes it's only a minor misunderstanding, but other times a lot rides on your ability to divine what is going on and formulate an appropriate response.

That's exactly what this book is all about. Why do the Chinese do as they do? What do their sometimes bewildering actions or pronouncements really mean? How can you figure out what motivates them when they conduct business discussions? What are the predictable areas in which their cultural norms are most likely to collide with those of Westerners? And how can you learn to deal effectively with them?

Anyone engaged in business with the Chinese, or considering doing business in China should find this book useful. This includes people traveling to the PRC for brief negotiations as well as those posted in China for extended periods, whether as business representatives, technicians, diplomats, or scholars. The casual tourist, even on a short stay in China, is also likely to find the book worthwhile, and will probably understand a good deal more of what goes on around him or her as a result of reading it.

Most of the examples in the book concentrate on life in the PRC, but anyone planning to travel to Taiwan, Hong Kong, or Singapore on business or pleasure should also find this book of interest, since the similarities among Chinese in the PRC and these other places greatly outweigh the differences. And finally, the book should also prove useful as a guide for people who will be involved in hosting visiting Chinese groups in their own country.

The book is divided according to substantive areas, with some general discussions of cultural differences and intercultural relationships (Chapters 1, 4, and 6, for example) as well as specific points relating to important situations such as meetings, banquets, gift-giving, negotiations, and hosting. The most important points to remember about each major topic are summarized in a recap section at the end of each chapter.

My own credentials for writing a book like this consist primarily of experience in China, Taiwan, and Hong Kong that spans more than sixteen years, including four years of residence during the seventies and eighties in Taiwan, Hong Kong, and Beijing. My first attempts at divining Chinese customs and motivations were made in the early 1970s in Taichung, Taiwan, where I taught English and psychology to college students and learned the rudiments of Mandarin at the same time.

My experience with PRC Chinese began with my employment by the National Council for U.S.-China Trade (now the U.S.-China Business Council). I had the good fortune to join the Council in 1979, the year in which the United States officially recognized the People's Republic. I began by organizing and escorting Chinese purchasing delegations visiting the United States as well as American trade groups conducting technical seminars and negotiations in China. Then, in 1981–82 I was detailed to Beijing, where I managed the Council's newly established office, advising American compa-

nies on their China business activities and meeting regularly
with PRC government and corporate officials to try to identify
and qualify opportunities for the Council's members.

What has always intrigued me more than anything else
about the Chinese has been the sometimes profound and
sometimes minimal cultural differences between them and the
Westerners with whom they do business. How we perceive one
another, and how we can learn to bridge the gaps and
communicate clearly has always held a strong fascination for
me. This interest led me quite naturally in 1985 into a position
on the China team of the public relations firm of Burson-
Marsteller, which has a unique presence in the PRC. In the
past few years we have worked to promote the corporate
reputations and products of many multinational companies to
an increasingly sophisticated Chinese market.

A final credential to which I'd like to own up is an abiding
love and respect for the Chinese people. I say this not to warn
the reader of a potential bias in favor of the Chinese in the
following pages, but rather to mitigate against what might
otherwise seem at times to be quite the opposite. This book
may appear in places to be rather critical of the Chinese and
their practices. In its pages I certainly don't spare them their
lumps when and where I feel they deserve them, for it seems
to me that to do any less would be to write a book that is less
than candid, and hence not as useful to the reader. But in
truth, I couldn't have lasted in this business this long if I were
not energized and charmed by my interactions with Chinese
people.

One of the old saws concerning writing about China—at
least China in the late twentieth century—is that the situation
usually changes before the ink has had a chance to dry on the
page. This has been the consistent finding of all who presume
to commit to paper their observations about Chinese politics,
for example. Movements have come and gone with great
rapidity in the last three decades, and no matter what one
writes, one's words are invariably overtaken by events. Those
who try to provide guidance on doing business in China
frequently find that even before the page proofs come back
from the publisher, the cast of characters has changed, or a

new law, regulation, or policy has been promulgated that makes an entire chapter irrelevant, if not inaccurate.

This constant and rapid evolution is much less the case in the area of protocol and etiquette, which is considerably less vulnerable to the winds of change than business or politics. China may be changing rapidly, but patterns of interaction among people have by and large been affected as little by the 1949 revolution as they were by the upheavals of 2,500 years of history. Beneath a relatively thin veneer of socialist ideology and communist practices, Chinese interactions are really governed by patterns laid down and developed through the experience of thousands of years. Business practices may become more sophisticated, but the underlying principles of human interaction tend to change only very little.

Manners change, too, of course, but they do so somewhat more slowly than other things. And one of the happy characteristics of etiquette is that one is seldom faulted for conservatism. Following traditionally acceptable practices could conceivably cause you to appear old-fashioned, but it will never put you at risk of committing solecisms.

In preparing this book, I've taken care to ensure that it is as up to date as possible. The majority of situations, attitudes, and practices discussed are undoubtedly timeless as far as the Chinese are concerned. The use of *guanxi*—connections— isn't likely to lose its tremendous importance in the foreseeable future, nor are the Chinese likely to abandon their concept of face. And I'd give odds that a dozen years from now, business meetings in China will be conducted in a fashion quite similar to the format used today.

Nonetheless, the reader is strongly encouraged to use the book as a guide rather than a mandate or prescription. If a suggested path of action doesn't get the desired result, or if an interpretation of someone else's behavior doesn't seem to ring true, by all means try something else. Good etiquette is generally just good common sense anyway. The purpose of this book is precisely to shed some light and to contribute some insight as to exactly what it is that constitutes "good common sense" when dealing with the increasingly scrutable Chinese.

DEALING WITH THE CHINESE

1

Protocol and the Larger Picture

2,500 YEARS OF
INTERPERSONAL RELATIONSHIPS

Though keenly aware of their need to learn from the West in technological areas in which their country lags behind the rest of the world, the Chinese people have never felt the need for instruction from anyone in the area of decorum and protocol. Since Confucius first codified the universe of possible interpersonal relationships and their associated duties nearly 2,500 years ago, the Chinese have had an established set of principles governing etiquette on which they have always been able to rely.

China has traditionally been a highly homogeneous society with little tolerance for deviation from generally accepted norms of behavior. To most Chinese there are proper and improper ways for people to behave toward one another, and you will seldom hear any argument as to exactly what these are. Precisely because they tend to share a set of assumptions about how to act, the Chinese are fond of lecturing one another about what constitutes proper behavior in a given situation. There are few if any gray areas.

This being said, however, it is important to point out that the Chinese generally hold only other Chinese to these exacting standards. Disparagement that may readily be directed toward an erring fellow countryman is not likely ever to be leveled at a foreigner. The body of knowledge concerning proper behavior is greatly revered and not considered to be easily acquired; no one who was not raised Chinese can reasonably be expected ever to master it completely.

The Chinese are probably correct in this last assertion. As a Westerner, you'll never be as Chinese as the Chinese; in fact, you'll never be Chinese at all, no matter how much you understand about them. But this does not mean that it doesn't pay to try to learn their ways. Even if you accept the fact that a foreigner will never really "measure up" to the often subtle standards of protocol held by most Chinese, there are nonetheless considerable benefits to be derived by trying to master the art.

THE ADVANTAGES OF
LEARNING CHINESE WAYS

Learning Chinese customs is worthwhile for a number of reasons. First of all, it is useful because imitation is the sincerest form of flattery, even to the Chinese. You'll score a lot of points with a Chinese friend or business associate if you remember to use both hands when you offer your business card or to turn your chopsticks around and use the thicker end when serving food to others during a meal. Even if you never become a latter-day Confucius, you'll ingratiate yourself by demonstrating a sincere desire to make your counterpart comfortable with you. The Chinese are quite simply delighted when foreigners try to speak with them in their own language or deal with them according to their own rules.

Then too, there is the benefit of understanding more clearly what is going on around you. Even if *you* don't play by Chinese rules, *they* always do. They will give signals that express how they feel throughout their interaction with you.

Since these are, for the most part, not the same cues commonly understood by Westerners, many of them will be incomprehensible to the uninitiated. It's up to you whether you choose to acquire the tools to interpret them or not.

Knowing the meaning of these cues can give you a distinct advantage in business and even social situations. It can help you understand if you have offended, pleased, flattered, or amused someone, backed someone into a corner, or caused him or her to lose face. It can help you divine the nature of the relationship between two Chinese people—who defers to whom, who outranks whom, and who really makes the decisions. And it can help you determine what you need to do to keep things moving in the right direction.

Dealing with the Chinese does *not* necessarily mean playing only by their rules, however. Intercultural communications is a two-way street, and there should always be give and take on both sides. In fact, it's a mistake when visiting China to attempt slavishly to do as the Chinese do and forget your own cultural values. You'll be uncomfortable and unsure of yourself, a fact you are unlikely to be able to conceal from your hosts. And you'll be ceding all advantage to your counterparts, who, after all, will always understand the rules better than you do.

What you are left with, then, is a tightrope of sorts. It's advisable to learn how to see relationships and obligations through Chinese eyes, because understanding how they view a situation provides definite advantages. It's also flattering to attempt to do as the Chinese do, and they will certainly appreciate the gesture. But it's equally important to remember who you are and what cultural baggage you bring to the party. The Chinese may not be interested in changing the way they do things, but unless they are provoked or they feel that something important is at stake they can generally be counted on to try to make you comfortable with them. It's precisely the converse—learning enough about them to make them comfortable with you—that is to be strived for here.

TAIWAN, HONG KONG, AND THE PRC

Although this book is written specifically with the People's Republic of China in mind, most of what is contained herein is applicable to Chinese living elsewhere in the world. Chinese people reared entirely in foreign cultures, such as American-born Chinese, are quite likely to have more in common with their fellow countrymen than they do with mainland Chinese. But it is probably fair to say that the similarities among the vast majority of Chinese in the world far outnumber the differences.

The bulk of the Chinese people who live outside of the PRC today are relatively recent emigrants—by Chinese standards, anyway—whose families left the mainland within the last one or two hundred years. A high percentage live in Taiwan, Hong Kong, Macao, and Singapore, as well as in Malaysia, Indonesia, the Philippines, and other countries of Southeast Asia. Many others live in the United States, Canada, Australia, and Europe. Asian Chinese in particular tend to share more cultural values with their compatriots on the mainland, and those in Hong Kong, Macao, and Taiwan—all areas that are historically part of China—probably share the most. What differences do exist are far more likely to stem from politics than from culture.

For example, an average person in Taiwan would be unlikely to be bound by any government restrictions concerning the nature or value of gifts that he may or may not receive from a business associate, but his or her behavior after a gift is offered—obligatory refusal and repeated protestations—might well be indistinguishable from that of a mainland compatriot. Seating arrangements at a banquet in Hong Kong might owe a little less to strict organizational protocol and a little more to informal friendships, but the order of the dishes and the ritual of toasting might well be lifted right out of Beijing. And the setting for a business meeting in Macao or Singapore might be a modern office rather than a stuffy meeting room, but the guest of honor would still very likely be placed on the host's right—just as he or she might in China or indeed, in Hong Kong or Taiwan.

This is not to say that communism has not made its mark on Chinese social attitudes, or that people in the PRC don't do some things differently. The Cultural Revolution of 1966–76 had devastating effects on interpersonal relationships that are felt even to this day. Chinese in the PRC who lived through this period tend to be less trusting and friendly toward people they do not know and less likely to express unorthodox political opinions in their presence. And while the Chinese have historically been a group-centered people, the amount of social control held by one's work unit over one's life in the PRC is unprecedented in Chinese history, except perhaps by that once enjoyed by the patriarch of the extended family.

Throughout this book, differences that the reader is likely to encounter in Taiwan, Hong Kong, and Southeast Asia will be pointed out. What is perhaps most surprising is how few significant ones there really are.

2

Getting in Touch

I once received a telephone call from someone at a company that had not done any business in the PRC, but was interested in developing some. It was clear from the sound of his voice that the man was extremely frazzled and frustrated. He had been put in charge of developing the China market and was eager to succeed. He had done his research and determined which Chinese organization would be the most fitting business partner for his firm. He had drafted a telex to that unit putting forth an abbreviated version of a business proposition, and had sent it off to China. When he received no response, he reconfirmed the telex number and tried again. And again. When I spoke with him four telexes later, he was just about to wash his hands of the whole deal.

We'll never know for sure exactly what the problem was, but I'd put money on something approximating the following scenario. All of the telexes were of course received by the Chinese unit; after translation they made their way to the desk of someone fairly responsible in the organization—probably a manager or a director. The name of the company wasn't familiar to the manager, so he asked around a bit but found no one in the unit who had ever heard of this company.

Perhaps one of the unit's translators consulted a reference book on U.S. business but couldn't identify the company because it wasn't around in 1963 when the book was published or because of an error in spelling. Or perhaps no one even took the matter that far. In any event, when it was clear that no one had ever heard of the company, the leader decided not to risk taking any further action. And once that decision was made, repeated telexes were just a waste of time, money, and paper.

The difficulty here was that since no one had any knowledge of the foreign company, no one could vouch for its worthiness as a business partner. The Chinese don't like doing business with strangers, and ventures and transactions in which precious foreign exchange is at stake are no place for taking unnecessary chances.

There were probably a couple of reasons why the company didn't receive any response at all. First, a negative response is considered impolite; silence communicates the same thing as an overt rebuff, and it is less awkward for all concerned. And second, Chinese generally do not feel strong social obligations to people or organizations they do not know. The telex was sent by a stranger, and one has no obligation to a stranger. Simply put, the Chinese probably didn't feel they owed anyone an answer.

One thing the company might have done differently would have been to use an intermediary. That is, some individual or organization known to the Chinese unit who might make the formal introduction and, in so doing, vouch for the reliability of the company. It might be a consultant or consulting firm, a business partner, or simply an acquaintance. Going through a middleman can build confidence with the Chinese, who, after all, are still relative newcomers to the modern international business scene and who remain somewhat unsure of themselves in that world. Intermediaries are very valuable in interpersonal relationships as well; someone who has been introduced by a trusted friend is generally deemed automatically worthy of trust.

As doing business in China gets more "normal," however, the need for go-betweens is diminishing. Now it's easier than ever to make contact yourself. To avoid a nonresponse like the one above, however, it's best in your initial overture to present a lot of information about your company and the venture that you propose. Send materials that describe your company and its history, and literature about its products or services. Provide references if you can, something to help the Chinese counterpart understand that the firm is a worthy partner. Also be as specific as you can about the type of business arrangement you wish to discuss, and how and where you propose to meet.

It is probably fair to say that the same thing would not have happened in Hong Kong or Taiwan, because these areas tend to be a great deal more sophisticated in international trade, as any examination of their impressive trade statistics will prove. But even though a Taiwanese businessman would likely have answered the first telex, that doesn't mean that he wouldn't have been far more comfortable with more detailed information about the U.S. company, or with the blessing of a trusted intermediary. The fact remains that the Chinese strongly prefer to do business with "old friends." And though this status can be attained relatively quickly and easily after the initial ice is broken, without it the going is nearly always rough at first.

COUNTERPART ORGANIZATIONS

Business relationships with the Chinese tend to be institutional relationships. That is, individuals—even if they are instrumental in forging the association—may come and go without affecting its basic nature. If General Electric signs an agreement with the Beijing Engine Works, any GE representative is likely to be received courteously by that Chinese unit; it doesn't have to be the senior vice president who negotiated or initialed the agreement. Indeed, that particular person may have long since passed from the scene. What lives on is the relationship between the corporations. Personal relationships live on, too, of course, and individuals who switch units carry with them all of the contacts from their previous working lives. But what is important to note here is that institutional relationships are not predicated on personal relationships alone.

It might have occurred to you that in the example given the failure of the American businessman to direct the telex to any particular individual at the Chinese company was a mistake. In fact, it wasn't. Unlike in the West, you do not need to deal with an individual to do business in the PRC; indeed, no single individual is really supposed to be able to make major business decisions by him or herself, anyway. Leadership is collective, and it is the unit—not any individual—that holds ultimate authority.

This is why a Chinese business letter is far more likely to bear the official seal of the unit—usually a red, circular stamp—than it is the personal signature of the writer. It's also why an invitation to visit China will generally be issued by an organization and not by an individual.

None of this means that individuals are not important to business. Organizations are nothing more than collections of individuals, after all, some more talented and powerful than others. It is always a good idea to cultivate friends in whatever organization you happen to be dealing with. Ultimately, it is individuals who make judgments as to whether others are trustworthy as business partners, and whether particular deals are advantageous.

Whether you are visiting China on business or pleasure, your invitation is still generally issued in the name of a Chinese organization. Normal procedure is for Chinese embassies and consulates to grant visas to foreigners when they produce invitations from recognized Chinese organizations. Not all Chinese organizations are empowered to issue such invitations; they must be government organizations of some stature—e.g., a ministry, a corporation, a municipal or provincial government, or a travel service. This counterpart is known as the host organization, or *jiedai danwei*. Invitations are not issued lightly because there are certain responsibilities that go with being a host unit.

The host organization, in essence, vouches for you in China. As a foreigner you have little legal status; it is traditionally the host that is responsible for finding you accommodations, arranging internal travel for you, getting permission for you to visit various institutions (e.g., certain areas of the country, libraries, museums, or industrial facilities). The host

unit is also responsible to other Chinese units should you do
anything to wrong them while you are in China. And your
ability to get difficult things accomplished often depends on
nothing more than the amount of clout that your host
organization has in the Chinese bureaucracy.

This point was driven home to me once a number of years
ago when I was asked to arrange accommodations for a visiting
VIP from the United States. I received telexes from the United
States every other day requesting that I move mountains to
arrange accommodations in the Beijing Hotel, at the time the
finest hotel in the capital, and at which rooms were notoriously hard to reserve. In those days no Chinese hotels would
ever deal directly with foreign guests; they did business only
with Chinese organizations. So I spent my time impressing on
the host unit the importance of this guest, and the correspond-
ing importance of booking the Beijing Hotel for him.

I might as well have saved my breath. The municipal
government unit responsible for assigning hotel rooms in
Beijing—it was not up to the individual hotels—was singularly
unimpressed with the eminence of this foreign visitor. I
learned soon enough that rooms at this premier hotel were not
allocated according to the importance of the *guest* but rather
the importance of the *host*. It was the relationship between the
host organization and the municipal authorities that counted.
And unfortunately for me and for the visitor, this particular
Chinese host organization didn't hold a tremendous amount
of sway in the pecking order of the PRC bureaucracy. The
quest was doomed to failure before it had even begun.

I hasten to add here that the hotel system has changed a
good deal in the last dozen years; the many Chinese-foreign
joint venture hotels that have sprung up in Beijing and most
other cities and tourist areas in China are run like hotels
abroad, and reservations are made on a more-or-less first
come, first served basis. Such hotels may even deal directly
with foreign guests. But the underlying principle still stands:
the amount of prestige—and hence, pull—that a host organization has in China is of vital importance in getting things
accomplished. And, aside from personal or institutional relationships, nothing much else is.

The obvious conclusion to draw here is that your counterpart organization should be selected carefully. For most business purposes, and even for tourism, it is no longer the case in China that one government unit holds a monopoly. In the late 1970s, for example, a company wishing to purchase textile products from China had no choice but to deal with the lone organization in Beijing that made all major decisions concerning prices and quotas. Now, throughout the provinces, there is a broad array of potential suppliers who may make many such decisions themselves.

A foreigner exploring business possibilities in China should therefore consider the power and prestige of the potential counterpart organization in his or her overall deliberations. Having a heavy hitter with a stake in making the deal work on your side is a tremendous advantage in overcoming the inevitable obstacles. On the other hand, if you deal with an unimportant unit with little clout, every minor difficulty has the potential to become an insurmountable stumbling block.

DELEGATIONS

Because their society is so thoroughly group-centered (see Chapter 4), the Chinese are most at ease when dealing with foreign guests in well-organized groups. If you visit China as part of a group, regardless of how you and your comrades see yourselves—as a cohesive team, a loosely affiliated assemblage, or even an unrelated collection of individuals—the Chinese will see you as a delegation. And delegations have a whole life of their own among the Chinese.

Delegations are groups of individuals who bear some relationship to one another—perhaps they all work for the same company, or are all members of the same profession. They are presumed to have a shared purpose, even if it is only to visit Buddhist temples or sample China's finest cuisine. Delegations are well-organized in that they are generally expected to have some structure, with a leader who makes decisions for the group and some sort of protocol ranking of members. This latter requirement—the need for some ordering of group members—is not so important in tour groups, but it is of some consequence among business delegations.

Above all, delegations are expected to act as groups, and not

as random collections of individuals. Nothing confuses and
confounds the Chinese more than many voices in a delegation, each expressing a personal opinion as to what the group
should do or where it should go. Since consensus is an
important component of Chinese group process, they also
expect it from foreigners. The delegation is presumed to speak
with one voice, and it is the voice of the delegation leader.

Some foreign groups lend themselves to this sort of organization more easily than others. Company delegations fit
relatively easily into the mold, with the senior officer invariably assuming the duties of the delegation leader. When many
different companies are represented in a single industrial
delegation, the choice may be harder, and in some cases it
may even be totally arbitrary. The selection of the leader is the
province of the group members themselves, however; the
Chinese will not force their own selection on a group. But if
the identity of the leader is not made explicit to them, they
may make an inappropriate assumption based on title, or even
based on any list of delegates they have ever received.

You can always tell who it is that the Chinese *think* is in
charge. The person understood to be the delegation leader is
the person offered the seat of honor to the right of the principal
Chinese host in a business meeting or a banquet. It is he or she
who is approached when the Chinese have a question to ask
the group. Apart from speaking for the group, the delegation
leader is also presumed responsible for enforcing discipline
within the group if it is ever necessary, and for making
summary decisions when consensus is difficult to reach.

There are other specific roles in a delegation apart from
leadership. When Chinese travel abroad, one person is often
designated as liaison to the foreign hosts. This may be the
interpreter, whose linguistic facility makes communication
easier, but it may also be someone else. It is, however, always
someone of rank lower than that of the leader. The liaison isn't
responsible for making decisions, but he or she does communicate the wishes of the group to the hosts and vice versa. This
person negotiates for the group, passes on requests, expresses
criticisms or dissatisfaction, and, in essence, acts for the group
leader in any potentially difficult or contentious situations.

Naturally, the liaison person must get instructions from the leader and clear any course of action before proceeding. By working in this way, the leader is never put in an embarrassing position vis-à-vis his or her hosts, and no loss of face is ever risked. Negative responses, if they must be expressed at all, are expressed through the liaison.

Organizations who host delegations are expected to assign similar roles to their own individuals. A principal host is assigned to receive any given visiting delegation, and a liaison person is designated as well. Any potentially controversial issues should be negotiated through liaisons, and never raised among leaders until they are fully resolved to mutual satisfaction. Leader-to-leader discussions are expected always to be cordial and correct; while liaisons must handle the thorny issues, the leaders remain free to exchange compliments and accolades.

RECAP:
SIX POINTS TO REMEMBER

1. The Chinese dislike doing business with strangers; it's often helpful to be introduced properly by an intermediary known to both sides.
2. Alternatively, you should provide in your initial approach as much information as possible about your company and what you hope to accomplish.
3. Business relationships are institutional in nature and are not necessarily predicated on close personal ties. It's always a good idea to cultivate personal friends in the bureaucracy, however.
4. It's generally necessary to have a host organization in order to visit China. Such organizations should be selected carefully, since your ability to get things accomplished in China often depends on their clout.
5. Foreign delegations visiting China are expected to speak with one voice and act as cohesive groups, never random collections of individuals.
6. Delegations have definite structures, and individual members are often assigned specific roles such as leader, interpreter, and liaison. Host organizations also assign similar roles to members of their own staff.

3

Meeting and Greeting People

Many Occidentals who have had little contact with the Orient share a common fear that the cultural gaps between China and the West are so vast that bridging them successfully will take a colossal amount of practice and time—if indeed it can be done at all. Such apprehension probably stems far more from the reputation of the Japanese, whose differences from the West are really quite a bit more profound than are those of the Chinese. In many respects the Chinese actually have more in common with Westerners than either does with the Japanese. Though they employ their share of subtle signals that may be difficult to divine, the Chinese are most often friendly, earnest, and enthusiastic communicators.

Count on your Chinese counterpart to be genuinely interested in finding common ground and in learning from you. The fact that you are a foreigner will work in your favor. With few exceptions, the Chinese have a natural friendliness toward foreigners, and a natural curiosity about what it is that makes you different from them.

Establishing effective working relations with the Chinese does not require a mastery of the Chinese language, though some knowledge of it—even a few well-chosen words—can generally get you further. The Chinese are flattered when foreigners make an attempt to learn their language, and a phrase or two will certainly earn you high marks. But whether or not you should attempt to conduct a relationship in Chinese depends mostly on your level of prowess. If your Mandarin is reasonably good, it's perfectly all right to rattle on in it, though you should be sensitive to the fact that you may be depriving a Chinese friend of a rare opportunity to practice English with a native speaker. If, on the other hand, you have only a few Chinese phrases at your command, best to spare everyone the trouble, especially if your counterpart speaks some English. My rule of thumb has always been to speak whichever language makes the conversation flow most easily.

BREAKING THE ICE

The Chinese prefer to be introduced formally to people whom they do not know; they are somewhat reluctant to strike up chance conversations with strangers. This goes for fellow Chinese as well as foreigners. It's for this reason that they tend to be somewhat uncomfortable attending Western-style cocktail parties. If you meet someone by chance, you have no way to know anything about the person—what kind of a family he or she comes from, what type of work he or she does, or whether he or she is someone worth knowing.

If, on the other hand, a friend introduces you to someone, the new acquaintance has been stamped with a seal of approval and is automatically deemed worthy of respect and friendship, unless and until he or she proves otherwise. It's as though you have little responsibility to pay any heed at all to strangers, but an implied obligation to be friendly and solicitous to those to whom you have been officially introduced.

While it is always best to have someone present you, this is not absolutely necessary, and it is permissable to introduce yourself. If you can cite a common friend at that point, so much the better. But even a simple Ni hao ma? ("How are you?") and a handshake are enough to get you started. Stand up when you are being introduced or are presenting yourself,

and keep standing for the duration of the introduction. Say
your name and the name of your company or organization if
it's relevant, and specify the country that you come from.
Speak slowly and distinctly. Present your business card if you
have one, being sure to use both hands while doing so to be
especially polite. And when you receive someone else's card,
spend a few seconds reading it over. This not only helps you
remember the name; it also signals respect for the other
person. It's demeaning to put someone's card directly into your
pocket without looking at it first.

Initial encounters with the Chinese often follow strikingly
similar patterns. When they meet Chinese people for the first
time, for example, foreigners visiting China have an excellent
chance of being asked one or more of the following "top ten"
questions:

What country are you from?
How long have you been in China?
Have you visited China before?
Do you speak Chinese?
What cities in China have you visited?
Do you like Chinese food?
How old are you?
Are you married?
Have you eaten yet?
What's the best way to learn how to speak English?

Note that most of these are earnest questions designed to seek
out common ground. Most Chinese know relatively little
about the world beyond the PRC, so they will first seek to
engage you in conversation concerning something about
which they have some knowledge.

Upon learning where you are from, a Chinese will often
offer an observation about your country—usually a compli-
mentary one. It may be fairly banal, e.g., "Canada is a very
large country," or "We Chinese have a friendly relationship
with America." Or it may be a comment about a friend or
relative who has visited or studied somewhere in your country,
or even perhaps a personal account of a trip there.

Don't be surprised if even in an initial encounter you are

asked a question or two that you deem to be very personal. A Chinese might inquire how much you earn, for example, since salary is no secret and is not considered to be a private matter in the PRC. Or you might be asked the cost of something that you own or are wearing. If you are single, you might be questioned directly as to why you have not married. Or if you are childless, a Chinese might wonder aloud why you choose not to have children. Handle these as best you can; if you object to answering them directly you can dismiss them with a little humor; a Chinese will rarely pursue the matter if politely rebuffed in this way. If all else fails, you can explain that in your country one does not normally divulge this type of information.

Be aware, too, that the knife cuts both ways. Westerners often get too personal too quickly for Chinese tastes, too. Asking a lot of questions about someone's family, for example—other than the basics of whether someone is married and how many children the person has—can be perceived as inappropriate by a Chinese whom you meet in the course of doing business. Bringing up political issues in such a way as to make the Chinese feel pressed to express an irreverent personal opinion is another taboo.

You may find the way in which the Chinese deal with compliments rather curious. Accepting them outright is not considered good etiquette; a Chinese is expected to deflect compliments and pretend he or she is unworthy of receiving them. The Chinese use a number of phrases when flattered, but one of the most common—and by far the most instructive—is *nali*, a word with the literal meaning of the interrogative "where" that has come to mean something like "it was nothing." It's as if to say that the kind words you have just uttered couldn't possibly be directed at me; *where* is the person to whom you are referring?

FORMS OF ADDRESS: NEGOTIATING CHINESE NAMES

Should you ever have the occasion to meet with Zhao Ziyang, the head of China's communist party, remember, please, that under no circumstances should he be addressed as "Mr. Ziyang." The first thing you need to remember about Chinese names is that the surname comes first, not last. More than ninety-five percent of all Chinese surnames are one syllable— that is to say, one character—in length; some of the most common examples are *Wang, Chen, Zhang, Li,* and *Lin.* The remaining few, which are seldom encountered, are two characters in length. Most given names are two syllables long, though a large minority have only one. Thus in the case of the party leader, *Zhao* is the surname and *Ziyang* is the given name. He is properly addressed as "Mr. Zhao."

When speaking Chinese, the surname invariably comes first. But this rule can change if you are speaking English and dealing with Westernized Chinese. Chinese people who are longtime residents of foreign countries, or even some who live in China who have frequent contact with Westerners, occasionally opt to reverse the order of their names—placing the given name first—in order to conform with Western practice and make it easier for their hosts. So don't be completely surprised if you receive a business card on which someone has thrown you a curve ball and placed his or her given name first. It's rare, but it does happen.

In point of fact, you will seldom really need to concern yourself with a Chinese person's given name at all. Unlike in the West, where you may call someone by his or her first name shortly after meeting for the first time, in China almost no one is called by the given name alone, except by close relatives or extremely intimate friends of long standing. Even good friends are far likelier to call a person by his or her *complete* name—e.g., *Chen Lanfeng* or *Liu Fuqun*—than by the given name, *Lanfeng* or *Fuqun,* sans surname.

What people call one another is very important to the Chinese, and it is advisable to get straight how you will address someone very early in a relationship, generally during your first meeting. For business purposes it is traditionally acceptable to call a Chinese person by the surname, together with a title like "Mister" or "Miss" or even "Director" or "Manager." Thus "Mr. Wang," "Director Liu," or "Ms. Zhao" would all be acceptable forms of address, and there's no problem with mixing an English title and a Chinese surname in just that order. If you use Chinese, however, remember that the title *follows* the surname. So, for example, "Mr. Wang" would be rendered as *Wang Xiansheng* and Director Liu would be called *Liu Zhuren*. Among the more commonly used titles are:

Mr.	先生	Xiansheng	Director	主任	Zhuren
Miss	小姐	Xiaojie	Manager	經理	Jingli
Mrs.	太太	Taitai	Minister	部長	Buzhang
	夫人	Furen	President	總經理	Zongjingli
Ms.	女士	Nüshi	Factory Manager	廠長	Changzhang
Comrade	同志	Tongzhi	Mayor	市長	Shizhang
Chairman	主席	Zhuxi	Governor	省長	Shengzhang

FIGURE 1. Commonly used titles in Chinese. When speaking Chinese, the surname precedes the title. So, for example, "Director Liu" would be rendered as *Liu Zhuren*.

Unfortunately, it isn't quite as simple as it might seem. Though nearly all of the titles listed in Figure 1 are in everyday usage in Hong Kong, Taiwan, and among Chinese throughout the world, a few of them were not used commonly in the PRC until quite recently. In particular, *xiaojie* for an unmarried woman and *taitai* or *furen* for a married one fell into disuse on the mainland after 1949 because they carry vaguely feudal associations. Even *xiansheng* for "mister" was used infrequently, being reserved only for exceptionally high-ranking people or revered prerevolutionary figures such as Dr. Sun Yat-sen, the founder of modern China.

When these terms were dropped by the communists, nothing very serviceable was ever introduced to take their place. Among themselves, Chinese in the PRC have always been able to fall back on *tongzhi*, meaning "comrade," and avoid the problem entirely. But this has never been a real option for foreigners, since strictly speaking most of us are not, after all, exactly fellow socialists.

The traditional titles have always been fully understood in the PRC even when they were not commonly used. And now, precisely because they were never effectively replaced, they are making a decided comeback. Though they may sound a bit stilted to uneducated Chinese, they are not in any way considered offensive. And you now hear them more and more frequently among urban and educated Chinese.

Another solution to the problem of what to call a Chinese is to use the functional title of the person. To call someone *Zhao Jingli*, or "Manager Zhao," for example, is to use a polite form of address that recognizes his rank and position in the balance. Interestingly, when addressing people who bear the "deputy" title—deputy general managers, vice ministers, deputy bureau directors—you omit the "deputy" or "vice" appellation and simply use *buzhang* or *jingli*. It's more polite than specifically acknowledging the person's status as number two in the organization. And a good form of address for service people—waiters, store clerks, and hotel employees, though not for government functionaries—is *shifu*. The term originally meant "master" (as opposed to "apprentice") and is very refined.

An even more gracious solution is to use the functional title and drop the surname altogether. To call Minister Li *Buzhang*, meaning "minister" (the government position, not the religious one) to his face is to use an extremely courteous form of address. In fact, using third person forms of address to refer to a person with whom you are talking, as in "Would the Professor like some tea?" or "Perhaps Madame Wang is too cold in this room," is especially deferential. This is as true in Taiwan and Hong Kong as it is on the mainland.

Another popular solution is to use a nickname. The endearing terms *lao* meaning "old" and *xiao* meaning "young" are commonly attached to surnames in China. They are said before, rather than after, the family name; thus *Lao Wang*, or "Old Wang" and *Xiao Huang*, or "Young Huang" are frequently heard. Even though they make explicit reference to age, they sometimes have as much to do with position as maturity and are not at all offensive—old age, after all, is revered in China. And in a country where there are only a few hundred surnames in common usage—*Zhang*, *Wang*, *Li*, *Chen*, and *Lin*, the top five, are claimed by tens of millions of people each—there is often a need to differentiate among people in the same group. The chances of any given organization employing more than one person named *Wang* or *Li* are overwhelming; the use of these nicknames thus helps distinguish among them. The nicknames may also be cute monikers having little to do with the person's given name. The only caveat of which you should be aware is that these are fairly familiar forms of address, best used only when you know someone reasonably well.

Age differences are important to the Chinese, and in social relationships what people call one another is often governed by the relative ages of the individuals involved. Within their families Chinese are often known by names that indicate their order of birth; thus, the youngest male in a brood of four children is likely to be known to all as *xiaodi*, "youngest brother," and he might call his three elder sisters *dajie*, *erjie*, and *sanjie* ("eldest sister," "second elder sister," and "third elder sister"). Or the sons may be referred to as *laoda*, *lao'er*, and *laosan* ("eldest," "second-born," "third-born") all the way to *laoyao*, which means "youngest." You often call a close friend by a similar name, determined by how you would relate to the friend had you been born into his or her family; just add the surname. So, for example, you might call a close male friend who is slightly older *Chen Dage*, or *Chen Xiong*, both of which mean "elder brother Chen." It is considered a friendly and courteous gesture.

When meeting the parents of a friend of your approximate age, it is not considered polite to use the terms *xiansheng*, *taitai*, or *furen* (see above) because using such terms would be considered too formal. The titles of choice, used without surnames, would be *bobo* and *bomu* (or possibly *shushu* and *ayi*, which are used in their place in certain regions of China), meaning "uncle" and "auntie," respectively. Don't fear appearing impertinent by such an ostensibly brazen insinuation of yourself into a friend's family structure; the Chinese take the use of these titles as high compliments, and will think you very polite for knowing how to use them properly. They are part and parcel of the inclusive nature of China's social structure.

In Taiwan, Hong Kong, Southeast Asia, and, indeed, among Chinese all over the world, you can use the term *taitai* to refer to your wife, since it means "wife" as much as it does "married woman." *Xiansheng*, too, can mean "husband" in addition to "mister." But when these terms fell into disuse in the PRC after 1949, the term *airen* came into vogue to describe one's spouse—of either sex. *Airen* literally means "lover," and many Chinese living outside of the mainland get gooseflesh when they hear this term used, since it was customarily used to describe extramarital relationships. It is now rapidly falling into disuse in China. As a foreigner, it's now probably wisest to stick to traditional titles whether you are on the mainland or elsewhere.

OFFICIAL
WELCOMES AND SEND-OFFS

When foreigners arrive in China, it is the responsibility of the Chinese host to meet them at the port of entry, usually the airport. If you are a seasoned China traveler and you know where you are going, this custom may be dispensed with, but if you are a tourist or a member of a small group, the host unit will generally send one or two low-ranking representatives to meet you and escort you to your hotel. If you arrive as a member of a large group or an important government or business delegation, a more formal welcoming party will almost certainly be sent.

The rank of the person sent to meet you will depend on who you are. If you have an important position in your company or organization, someone of approximately equivalent rank will probably be sent from the Chinese side. A head of state would rate another head of state or at least a vice premier; a corporation president might draw a vice minister, depending on the size and importance of his company. To send anyone of significantly lesser rank would be to offer an insult, since it would be a gesture that could cause the visitor a loss of face.

Consider the true story of a diplomat at the U.S. Embassy in Beijing who was meeting with a PRC official in charge of planning the trip to the United States of a cabinet-level minister. When the two began discussing the logistics of the visit, the American was unexpectedly lectured by his Chinese counterpart about the importance of sending an individual of sufficient stature to Dulles Airport in Washington, D.C., to greet the minister upon arrival. The Chinese, it eventually became clear, had been seriously offended during the previous visit of a minister to the United States because the host department of the U.S. government had been able to muster only a deputy assistant secretary to do the honors at the airport. This lapse was viewed as a slight, and the official charged with planning the trip was simply trying to head off a similar unpleasant situation.

The welcoming party, like the delegation itself, generally includes an interpreter and a designated liaison from the Chinese host organization in addition to a high-ranking official. The liaison officer is in charge of communicating with the visitors and serves as the channel of choice for any requests, complaints, or suggestions the visitors care to offer during their stay. Depending on the nature of the trip, the liaison officer may accompany the group throughout its visit to China, or else he or she may simply be in charge of the visit to one city.

Formal delegations are sometimes greeted officially in lounges maintained at Chinese airports especially for this purpose. This ceremony, reserved for people of fairly high rank, may also be skipped entirely, however, and in fact is becoming less common, especially when visitors arrive late at night from far away. Formalities are kept to a minimum; they usually involve the serving of tea, the collection of luggage, and a quick exchange of pleasantries. Then the honored guests are squired off to their hotels to rest or to prepare for the activities to come.

The same basic rules apply to seeing visitors off. The polite

thing to do is to escort them as far as possible. One gauge of
how well a visit has gone, in fact, is the status of the official
selected to see a group off at the airport. If the same person
who received the group—or someone of equivalent or higher
stature—is sent, it's a good sign that all went well. If, on the
other hand, an official having significantly less prestige is sent
out to head up the send-off party, or if no one is sent at all (and
no plausible explanation is given), it is a clue that something
may have offended the Chinese hosts.

Strictly speaking, it is not absolutely necessary to reciprocate
in this fashion when you are in the position of hosting PRC
guests in your own country. Indeed, in most circumstances it
is not necessary to follow Chinese practices when interacting
with Chinese in your own country. The Chinese themselves
have a proverb, *ru xiang sui su* ("enter village, follow
customs"), that is the rough equivalent of the English "When
in Rome, do as the Romans do." They do indeed expect things
to be different abroad.

This being said, however, airport rituals are still an area
where following the Chinese practice can really pay off. The
Chinese put tremendous stock in official meetings, greetings,
and departures—that's why high-ranking officials are willing to
spend hours traveling to and from airports for this purpose, and
it's also why they often feel insulted when the same respect is
not accorded them.

Chinese who have traveled abroad before or had frequent
contact with Westerners generally understand that this is an
area where cultural practices differ. They are far more likely to
forgive a foreign host for failing to perform these ceremonial
duties than their less sophisticated countrymen might be. But
it is far better to start out *any* visit on the best possible footing
and endeavor to live up to the Chinese's highest expectations.

You will score points even among well-traveled Chinese,
who may appreciate the gesture even more because they know
it is offered out of deference to them. In the case of a visit to
a company headquarters by a Chinese minister, that means
moving mountains to get the company president—or at very
least a high-ranking senior vice president—to find the time to
make the trek out to the airport.

NONVERBAL COMMUNICATION

After dealing with the Chinese for any length of time, you may find that they have some habits that offend or puzzle you.

First of all, due perhaps to the density of China's population, the Chinese conception of the proper social distance between people in a room is somewhat closer than that common to many Western cultures. Don't be surprised if you find a Chinese friend standing a bit too close to you for comfort, or breathing directly into your face when talking with you. You may even notice that as you step backward to adjust the distance to a more suitable level, your Chinese counterpart advances proportionately. I haven't ever found an effective way to extricate myself from this *pas de deux*; during conversations with certain Chinese friends I occasionally find myself in constant backward motion.

Traditionally, Chinese were seldom demonstrative with members of the opposite sex in public; even husband and wife seldom touched when walking together on the street, or elsewhere in the public eye. This is changing rapidly, on Taiwan as well as the mainland. While older or more conservative people may still share this prejudice, younger Chinese can now frequently be seen holding hands and even embracing in public places. Foreigners should keep in mind the traditional viewpoint when traveling in China or Taiwan; you may hold hands with a foreign companion of the opposite sex, but should avoid more passionate forms of contact. And when dealing with the Chinese, you should not touch a member of the opposite sex except for a handshake. Other types of physical contact can easily be misinterpreted.

You may find it surprising that it is perfectly acceptable among the Chinese to be physical with members of the same sex. It is common for someone of the same sex to be seen touching a friend, leaning on a friend, or even holding hands walking down the street, though generally nothing much more intimate than this. You often feel yourself nudged through a door or tugged down a street by a Chinese friend. Among the Chinese on the mainland and elsewhere in Asia there is no taboo against this type of contact among people of the same sex; only Chinese who have been somewhat Westernized may feel a bit self-conscious in such situations. And you should also be aware that ninety-nine percent of the time there are absolutely no sexual overtones to this type of physical contact among the Chinese.

The situation in Taiwan and Hong Kong is somewhat different. In Hong Kong, by far the most Western-oriented of the three areas, Occidental standards are better guides. You are less likely to see two males holding hands on the street in Hong Kong, and far more likely to see affection expressed between males and females in public. Taiwan is somewhere in between; in Taipei and some of the major cities, more Western rules apply; the countryside bears more of a resemblance to the traditional mainland culture.

Handshakes are the accepted form of greeting in China, even among Chinese. Often, when you are introduced to a group of people, you will be expected to shake hands all around—a bit like hockey teams do at the conclusion of a game. Unlike the Japanese, the Chinese do not greet with a bow at the waist, though if you look carefully you may notice a vestigial nod of the head that takes place when people are introduced to one another or when a handshake occurs.

Some Chinese habits may appear offensive to foreigners. Belching and expectorating on the street, for example, are seen in China as natural if somewhat inelegant functions; they are not viewed as disgusting, especially by less-educated Chinese. Though the government is trying to discourage such habits as spitting and littering by fining violators, it is still not uncommon to see people do these things. Passing gas is considered improper in polite company in China, and urban Chinese mothers will shame their children for doing it. But among less-educated or less-sophisticated Chinese it can occur unabashedly in public.

Many Chinese smoke cigarettes, and some of the brands available in China are quite harsh by Western standards. There is little realization that smoking in certain places is offensive to nonsmokers, and there are virtually no areas off-limits to smokers. It is unusual for someone to ask a Chinese not to smoke during a meeting or banquet or in a public place. If you need to do this, it's a good idea to couch it in terms of an allergy; this makes it easy to understand.

Visitors to China, especially to the more remote areas, should also expect to be stared at occasionally. Gazing at someone is not viewed by the Chinese as an aggressive action, or even a particularly objectionable practice. If you are unusual in any way—because you are blond, or tall, or wearing odd-looking clothing, or obviously handicapped in some way—Chinese are very likely to stare. They may even point you out to their children or friends. Being stared at as you stand in a department store trying on a piece of clothing can leave you feeling more like an animal in a zoo than an honored visitor, but you should keep in mind that they mean no harm by this. It's simply a cultural difference.

Conversely, sometimes in private situations Chinese will avoid meeting your eyes, even during conversation. This is usually a sign of shyness or embarrassment, and it should not be confused with insincerity. In addition, Chinese sometimes do not smile when they are introduced to strangers. This should not be taken for dissatisfaction, anger, or unfriendliness; it has far more to do with being socialized to keep feelings in rather than express them.

Another puzzling and often misinterpreted piece of public behavior is the Chinese propensity to laugh at a mishap. Many foreign visitors to China who happened to trip on a curb or lose their footing on a slick floor have been infuriated to find themselves sitting on the ground, surrounded by giggling Chinese bystanders who appear to make no effort to help them up. What you need to know about such situations is that you are not really the butt of a joke; laughter, in addition to being a response to a humorous situation, is also one way the Chinese have of dealing with uncomfortable circumstances in which they are uncertain how to respond. And if no one steps forward to help it is probably only because of hesitancy to approach a foreigner, or fear of taking responsibility in what could prove to be a dicey situation.

Finally, you should know how to interpret a very typical Chinese reaction—the sucking in of air between clenched teeth. It generally follows a request that a Chinese finds difficult to satisfy. It is used to buy a little time while reflecting, but if you hear it it's sometimes a good idea to jump in and modify or even retract the plea. Not to do so would likely place your Chinese host in the difficult position of having to say no to you.

The knife cuts both ways. Some of the things you may do quite naturally can drive the Chinese up a wall. Many an American businessman has mortified a Chinese acquaintance after a long separation with a bear-hug greeting at their reunion. The slap on the back or fanny, the mock punch, and other types of rough handling common among American men in particular are simply not done in China, especially among relative strangers, and the Chinese don't know how to react to them. Some Chinese, particularly older ones, can also be strongly offended when guests touch members of the opposite sex in suggestive ways. You must also not be physically demonstrative with those who are much older or who rank much higher than yourself.

Bear in mind also that postures can be important. Don't slink down in your chair or put your feet up on the table when you are meeting with a Chinese, lest he or she feel you are not being properly respectful. And never, never point to something with your head or your foot, still less use your foot to manipulate something; using a body part other than your hands to make such a gesture is considered uncouth. When handing an object—like a teacup, or a business card—to someone else, especially someone of higher rank, use both hands, not just one. This is a symbol of respect.

Then there is a whole set of gestures that simply are misinterpreted because they are different. "Come here," signaled in the West by curling your index finger upward in your own direction, is not understood by the Chinese; they communicate the same concept by extending an outstretched hand face down and waving it up and down. To many Westerners that gesture looks like a good-bye wave. A shrug of the shoulders doesn't mean "I don't know" to the Chinese; it just looks like bad posture. Don't try to give the "OK" sign with your thumb and forefinger forming a circle; you'll just get a blank stare. And few obscene gestures you may care to direct at someone who offends you will be understood per se, though the anger that engenders them will probably still be communicated.

There are, however, some universals. Nodding your head for agreement and shaking it for disagreement, for example, are completely understood by the Chinese, though "no" is also often expressed with a vigorous waving motion of the hand from side to side in front of the face. Pointing to your chest to signify yourself is also comprehended, though you may also occasionally catch a Chinese pointing to his or her nose instead. "Thumbs up" communicates something positive in both cultures. And clapping your hands is a universal way of applauding; the only twist in communist China is that the objects of applause always clap back at the audience as a reciprocal expression of appreciation. You won't see this in Hong Kong or Taiwan.

It is fair to say that Chinese are far more comfortable with silence than are Westerners. Many business executives who visit China find themselves talking too much at all the meetings, simply because they are uncomfortable with even a pregnant pause. Silence can be a virtue among Chinese, for it often signifies reflection and assessment of a situation. In fact, some Chinese accuse Westerners of being far more apt than they themselves to say things spontaneously that turn out to be ill-advised or incorrect.

Silence can also be a sign of politeness, a signal that you have the complete attention of your Chinese listener, who is waiting for you to continue. But it can also be a ploy, used frequently by Chinese negotiators to buy time and, in so doing, ferret out the position of their counterparts.

Communication among Chinese is often far more subtle than among foreigners. What is left unsaid is easily as important as what is expressed directly, and silence at a well-chosen moment can speak volumes. This is not to say that lengthy periods of no conversation are desirable or even common. To the extent that they signify that two people are uncomfortable with one another or can't think of things to talk about, they are of course quite awkward. The natural tendency is to try to make conversation, and the Chinese will do so, too. Just don't confuse such a situation with one in which someone is pausing to mull over a point, waiting for someone else to respond to a question, or deliberately not agreeing with a statement that has been made. Learn also to judge whose silence it really is. If your counterpart owns the floor, it is his or her silence, and you need not concern yourself over trying to break it.

SAYING NO

As discussed earlier, refusing a request made by a guest is considered an unacceptable form of behavior among Chinese everywhere. Being turned down to your face causes you to lose face, and no good Chinese host ever wants to put his or her guests in such a position. This is why you should never press a point that is likely to force your host to say no. If cornered, Chinese people will eventually tell you that no is no; they will wonder all the time why you insisted on pressing the point, however, since the face that's lost in the process is your own.

To save everyone's face, the Chinese have devised a number of methods of refusing without exactly saying no. The most common is to say that to grant the wish would be "inconvenient." Unless you are dealing with a very close friend, don't take this at face value. But neither should you take it as a signal to try to convince the host that the obstacles can be surmounted and it isn't really as inconvenient as it may seem. "Inconvenient" often means that there are political or logistical problems associated with fulfilling a request that the Chinese would rather not have to explain fully. Ultimately, in response to a request or a negotiated demand, "inconvenient" means no, and if you're smart you won't press the point.

Another common tack is to say that a request is "under consideration" or "being discussed." This response can occasionally be taken at face value, but it generally means that something is unlikely to happen, or at very least that there is no way a "yes" response can be given at the time. Saying something is being considered puts the whole problem off; it gets the host out of a tight situation in the current meeting by excluding the topic from further discussion. Still another way of handling an ungrantable request is not to deal with it at all. In both cases the hope is that you will read the handwriting on the wall and back away quietly, never raising the point again.

Another favorite way out is to blame someone else for the roadblock. Accomplishing anything in the PRC generally takes cooperation among different government units; if you don't want to grant a request, it's always pretty easy to find a scapegoat somewhere else in the vast bureaucracy.

Finally, a Chinese may even tell an abject lie to avoid saying no, inventing a story that has absolutely no truth to it just to get out of the uncomfortable position in which he or she feels placed. A colleague of mine once requested and received permission to visit a Chinese arms factory, but as the day of the visit approached the host organization had second thoughts about the propriety of allowing a Westerner in to view such a sensitive installation. Rather than own up to the truth, the Chinese escort officer simply told the foreign guest that the factory was closed on the appointed day. Although this was a case of a Chinese lying to cover up his unit's own mistake, lying sometimes isn't as dishonorable as it may seem on the surface. Equally often the reason for all the machinations is in fact to spare a *guest* a loss of face.

ON THE TELEPHONE

Doing business with the Chinese is generally accomplished through face-to-face meetings, but you are often in the position of making at least some arrangements by telephone. Making a phone call in China can be an arduous process. In Taiwan and Hong Kong, where the phone systems are far more developed, getting a connection is easier and etiquette is more refined. In China, though, you're really in for an ordeal.

First of all, the telephone infrastructure in China is rudimentary, to say the least. In offices many people may share one telephone, frequently located down the hall from where they actually do their work. Private residential phones are rare; if you have access at all to a phone at home, it is generally a common telephone used by your entire building or street. Typically one person in the neighborhood is charged with answering and paging the called party. In both settings getting calls is somewhat inconvenient and leaving messages highly unreliable if not impossible.

Then again, there are too few telephone lines for the volume of calls made, resulting in perpetual busy signals at certain times of the day and week. On Saturday morning, for example, it is often nearly impossible to make a call to certain exchanges in Beijing, since most everyone is on the phone making arrangements for Sunday activities. You commonly dial a number more or less continuously to maximize your chances of getting through. And the equipment is sufficiently unpredictable that it is not uncommon to be cut off randomly in mid-sentence. It's thus best not to dawdle on the phone, but to communicate your message quickly and hang up. Or to send a letter or a telex, even locally—it is surprisingly effective.

Until a few years ago it was hard even to get ahold of a telephone directory in the PRC, and it's still common for people there to carry little books listing names, addresses, and phone numbers of friends and contacts. Don't forget to get the phone numbers of people you hope to meet again, since there's no such thing as directory assistance, and since it may be next to impossible to locate them by calling the main number of their work units and asking for them by name. Switchboards are notoriously unresponsive in the PRC; information is seen as valuable and not to be shared indiscriminately with anonymous callers.

Chinese telephone etiquette leaves a good deal to be desired. The standard greeting you get when a phone is answered is the word *wei*, which doesn't really mean much of anything; it's basically an attention-getter. The word *wei* may shift in meaning, depending upon how and when it is used in the conversation. At the beginning, *wei* means nothing more than "I'm on; now it's your turn to talk." In Beijing people have been known to *wei* each other back and forth a dozen times or more until one gives in and starts talking. When the conversation does begin it's a good idea to verify that you have reached the organization you intended to dial, since Chinese generally do not furnish any identifying information upon answering the phone. *Wei* may also be used to mean "Are you still there?" or "Keep quiet for a moment, I'm about to say something important."

There is a certain suspicion that pervades telephone calls in the PRC, and unless you are known or immediately identifiable to the person who answers, you'll get little information until you have told a good deal of your own story. That includes whom you work for and why you are calling as well as the person with whom you wish to speak. If you fail to provide any of these specifics, you will be questioned about them. Typically you will be asked *Ni naiwei?* meaning, literally, "Who are you?" or *Ni nali?* or *Ni Nar?* meaning "Where are you?"

Neither of these questions should be taken at face value; both are ways of asking the same thing, which is really "What organization do you represent?" A Chinese at work doesn't really care about your individual identity, still less where you happen to be located when making the call. He or she is trying to establish through this line of questioning what your work unit is, and what issue you are calling about. That's all that really matters. So as much of an assault as it may be on your sense of self, the proper way to identify yourself on the phone in China is by naming your organization: "I am IBM" or "I am the Royal Dutch Embassy" are the type of responses that are expected.

Your impulse at this point may be to try to brush off the excessively curious person who has answered the phone, and insist on talking with the individual whom you are calling. Sometimes this works, but more often you have to go through a certain amount of interrogation before the person is willing to call your party to the phone. It's common to provide a summary of what has led up to the call, and many people refuse to settle for much less.

If, for example, you are calling to see if any decision has been made concerning the time and place for an upcoming meeting, you may have to point out to the person who answers the phone that you first spoke with Mr. Wang last Thursday, when he promised to check with Manager Zhu to see if a conference to discuss a long-term purchase agreement for high-quality fasteners could be set up for this Tuesday afternoon, when your boss would to be in town.

Once all of this is made clear, and the person on the other end of the line is satisfied that he or she has gleaned all of the information needed from you, you will either be connected with the person you are seeking or you'll get an answer about the meeting. Although you may wish to hear confirmation directly from your contact person, this is not really necessary; in China, people speak for their work units, and they generally don't speak at all if they aren't sure where the unit stands. So if someone presumes to tell you that a meeting has been okayed, it undoubtedly has.

If the person you are seeking is out, leave a message at your own risk. Often office mates discourage you from leaving word and suggest that you call back later. This absolves them of any responsibility for transmitting the message. If they are willing to take your name and number, there is still a chance that the party will never find out that you called, or at least not find out until he or she happens to return to the office, or happens to ask if anyone called.

Again, probably due to the rudimentary nature of Chinese telephone equipment, phone conversations in the PRC—and to a lesser extent in Taiwan; Hong Kong is different—tend to take place at deafening decibel levels. Chinese are accustomed to poor connections, so they generally yell into the telephone, even when lines are reasonably clear. This, coupled with the fact that phones are generally located in fairly public areas, means that you can rarely hope to have a truly private phone conversation in China. It's thus always a good idea to assume that someone else is within earshot, both on your own end and on the receiving end.

Then too, many a hotel operator in China stays on the line far longer than is absolutely necessary to make the connection. This may be espionage conducted by the Public Security Bureau, but it may also be no more than idle curiosity and maybe a bit of language practice. In any event, it's best to save your very private thoughts and comments for face-to-face meetings and use the telephone sparingly.

RECAP:
A DOZEN POINTS TO REMEMBER

1. Names are very important to the Chinese. Establish how to address someone during your first meeting. Chinese are seldom called by their given names except by close relatives or extremely intimate friends.

2. Chinese surnames come first, not last. Call a Chinese person by the surname together with an English title like "Mister" or "Miss" or even "Director" or "Manager" preceding it. You may also drop the surname altogether and use the functional title only.

3. Formal welcoming parties are sent to airports by the Chinese to meet important delegations and see them off. The rank of the official greeter depends on the importance of the visitors.

4. Don't be surprised to be asked personal questions, e.g., how much you earn or why you have not married. If you are uncomfortable answering such queries, deflect them with humor.

5. A Chinese may stand a bit too close to you for comfort; they are at ease with shorter personal distances than are many Westerners. Other habits that may appear offensive include belching, spitting, littering, or even passing gas in public. Though these are considered impolite, you may experience them among less educated Chinese.

6. Chinese in rural areas may also stare at foreigners. This is not considered impolite, nor is it usually an expression of hostility.

7. Do not touch Chinese of the opposite sex in social situations except for a handshake. Avoid passionate forms of contact in public even with other foreigners. Physical contact among members of the same sex is common in China and generally carries no sexual overtones.

8. Sometimes Chinese laugh at mishaps. This is an uncertain reaction to an uncomfortable situation and should not be confused with humor.

9. Avoid rough handling with the Chinese, even in fun. Keep proper posture and never put your feet up on a table, nor use a body part other than your hands to point a direction or manipulate an object. Use both hands to present a gift or a business card.

10. The Chinese are far more comfortable with silence than are Westerners. What is left unsaid can be as important as what is expressed directly, and silence can be a virtue among Chinese. It can also be a sign of politeness or a ploy to ferret out information.

11. Never force a Chinese to say a direct "no" to you. The Chinese refuse in a number of ways without exactly saying no. Among them are to say something is "inconvenient," "under consideration," or "being discussed."

12. When pressed, a Chinese may even tell an abject lie to avoid saying no. Often the motive is a laudable one, however, e.g., to spare a guest a loss of face.

4

Some Basic
Cultural Differences

INDIVIDUALISM VS.
GROUP-CENTEREDNESS

The single most important and fundamental difference between Chinese and Occidental peoples is undoubtedly the role
played by the individual in the society. In the West, we place
a strong emphasis on personal achievement, creativity, and
initiative. We glory in our individual differences, nurture
them, and value them as the essential features that make us
unique. Indeed, uniqueness is a goal unto itself in the West;
it's vitally important to us that we *not* be exactly like other
people.

Who in the West hasn't been admonished to be your own
person, or to look out for yourself because no one else can be
counted on to look out for you? Who has never been praised
for standing up for what you personally believe in, especially
when the tide of opinion is flowing in the opposite direction?
Among Western peoples, the premium is not on conformity; it
is on individual expression and rugged independence.

In China, on the other hand—and no matter which side of

the Taiwan strait—children are given an entirely different set
of messages. Don't question the world around you or try to
change it; accept it. Submit willingly and unquestioningly to
authority. Your importance as an individual is not nearly as
great as that of the role you play in a larger group.

That "larger group" may have appeared different in ancient
China from what it looks like today. In Imperial China it
would have been one's extended family—grandparents, father,
mother, siblings, uncles, aunts, and cousins of all descrip-
tions, all of whom might well have lived together in the same
compound. In modern-day China the group might be one's
nuclear family, one's class at school, one's military unit, fellow
members of a delegation, or one's *danwei* or work unit (see
below). The situation varies; the dynamics, however, are
much the same no matter what the group is.

Group process in China is not merely based on the authority
of the leaders; there is a real premium on consensus. Matters
are often debated at great length until agreement is reached on
a course of action. And once a decision has been made,
individual group members are expected to embrace it and act
on it. This is one reason you will seldom hear a Chinese make
an irreverent comment, or openly express a view at odds with
that of his or her unit. Toeing the mark is important, and it is
enforced.

In essence, Chinese enter into a sort of compact with their
groups; in exchange for obedience and loyalty, they can expect
protection and support and be confident that their well-being
will be a matter of concern to the group as a whole. Group
membership requires that they subordinate their own wills to
that of the whole and make decisions based on the best
interests of the larger group, not personal selfishness. Chinese
people must listen to those in authority and do as they say. And
their actions, for good or ill, reflect not only on themselves but
also on all of their compatriots.

Consider that fate of former Korean President Chun Doo
Hwan, who in spring of 1988 was forced to resign the few
government and party posts he had retained after he stepped
down from the presidency. Chun's action was necessary not
because he had personally done anything wrong, but rather
because his *brother* was charged with embezzling money.

"Although I exerted myself to the utmost to promote the welfare of the people during my presidential term," Chun was quoted as saying, "I failed to control my brother. It is because of my lack of virtue." He continued: "I feel very sorry for causing trouble to the people with various scandalous actions brought about by my brother's ineptitude."

Though this example comes from Korea—another Confucian society (see below)—rather than China, it might have taken place in Taipei nearly as easily as in Seoul. The principle is the same: you bear responsibility for the actions of members of your family—or your group. Chun's own words contain an apology for "causing trouble" even though it was clearly not he personally who was at fault.

It would be difficult to imagine a similar situation in the West. It would hardly have occurred to former U.S. president Jimmy Carter, for example, to resign because of any of his brother Billy's transgressions. On the other hand, the case should not be overstated. The ideal is one thing; actual practice is another. In truth, many Chinese cadres try desperately to remain in office even after members of their family are caught trading on their positions and engaging in very questionable activities.

For another example, take the case of Chinese tennis star Hu Na, who defected to the United States from the PRC in the early 1980s. The American government, in reaching a decision on whether to grant her political asylum, cited, among other things, the fact that Ms. Hu did not wish to return to the PRC. But the Chinese position was that the young woman's wishes were only one consideration, and a minor one at that; it was also important to take into account the interests and desires of her parents, her work unit, and the government of the society that had given her so much.

The discussion of telephone etiquette in Chapter 3 provides still another illustration of the preeminence of the group in Chinese society. You'll recall that you generally do not identify yourself personally when answering the telephone; what is deemed important is your work unit. The fact that common practice is to answer "I am the Ministry of Foreign Trade" rather than "I am Mr. Wang" speaks volumes about the relative importance of the individual and the group. So does the fact that it is units, and not individuals, that invite foreign guests, arrange activities for them, and sign contracts with them. None of this should be interpreted to mean that the Chinese do not possess unique personalities, however. They most certainly do. The distinction lies in the issue of when and under what circumstances it is permissible for people to express their individual differences.

Although Chinese people must be ever vigilant in fulfilling obligations to fellow group members, it's important to note that as a rule they feel no comparable responsibility toward outsiders. Courtesy and hospitality are frequently not forthcoming when Chinese deal with people with whom they have no connections. Indeed, they are capable of treating one another with indifference that can border on cruelty. The "us-them" dichotomy often surfaces in the work of the government in the form of intractable bureaucratic rivalries that impede progress and innovation. It has sometimes been pointed out that one of Chinese culture's major failings is that its people just don't know how to treat outsiders. Ironically but luckily, foreigners are generally exempt from this kind of treatment, their very foreignness earning them favorable treatment as honored guests.

THE *DANWEI* OR "WORK UNIT"

It is the work unit or *danwei* that tends to wield the most power over an individual's life in China today. Employers in Taiwan and Hong Kong probably hold more sway over the lives of their employees than those in the West, but they do not have nearly as much influence as the *danwei* in the PRC. In China, the work unit has a say in just about any major decision in one's life, and in a great number of minor ones as well.

Chinese typically do not choose their work units the way an individual may shop for an employer in the capitalist economies of the West, except in the case of foreign joint ventures. Typically, once a young person has graduated from school, the local government's labor bureau will *fenpei* or assign him or her to a job in the community. This bureau's responsibility is to coordinate with all the other government units in the area to identify available jobs and establish relevant qualifications and then to attempt to match people with slots.

It is an impersonal and inefficient system. While it can sometimes be manipulated through the use of *guanxi* (see below), the system mostly manages to assign individuals to positions they do not want. Indeed, individual preferences are largely irrelevant to the process. To compound the problem, there has traditionally been almost no job mobility in the PRC—someone assigned to be a factory worker, for example, can for all practical purposes expect to work in the same unit for the rest of his or her working life, though promotions and job changes within the unit are possible.

Switching to another *danwei* is also difficult because it requires that both the old and new unit sign off on the transfer. Someone who is talented may thus find it relatively easy to get a job offer elsewhere, but next to impossible to persuade his or her work unit to grant a discharge. This system is becoming more liberal, however, and switching *danwei* is becoming more commonplace. Job swapping, accomplished through *guanxi* and even through advertising, is on the increase. But organizational change in China is always a painfully slow process.

The influence of a typical Chinese unit extends far beyond employees' working lives and well into their personal lives. Not only does the unit decide what job you do, how much you are paid, and when promotions come; it also may control where you live; how much space you are allocated; whether and when you may travel within China or to other countries, study abroad, or take a vacation. Through your work unit— and only through your work unit—you obtain coupons that permit you to purchase certain scarce commodities: at various times in the last twenty years pork, sugar, eggs, salt, grain, cooking oil, cotton cloth, gas, coal, bicycles, and wooden furniture have all been rationed in the PRC. The unit also controls your access to health care and child care, and pays you your pension after you retire.

Workers must also obtain permission from the unit before they may marry, a decision that has obvious implications for where they live, single people being assigned to dormitories with roommates. Apartments, when available at all, are reserved for those who are married and need the additional space. The *danwei* also has a role in enforcing the one-child-per-couple policy. A good relationship with the decision makers in the unit can pave the way for many comforts and privileges; similarly, the unit can make your life a living hell if you buck the system, and it may discipline you if you break a rule.

The exception to most of these rules is the joint-venture unit. An enterprise that is a joint venture between a Chinese organization and a foreign company operates quite a bit differently from the typical Chinese unit. Here there is a great deal of mobility; jobs are advertised and filled by applicants in a more or less supply-and-demand fashion. Employers find it far easier to hire and fire staff. Subsidies have been reduced to bare bones and are generally limited to housing, medical care, and unemployment compensation. And there are far fewer intrusions into individuals' personal affairs. Though joint-venture employees constitute only a small fraction of China's workers today, the government has said that such enterprises are to be treated as models for future development of state-owned enterprises. Thus the tremendous social control exerted by the *danwei* is quite likely to diminish considerably in the future.

Though there is little direct insubordination in a Chinese work unit, this is not to say that there isn't a good deal of passive resistance on the part of the workers. When decisions come down from above, one is obligated to obey, but one doesn't have to like it. Since socialism traditionally offered workers nothing in the way of material incentives to perform, the work of people in the PRC has historically been uninspired and their performance lackluster. Raising productivity has thus become a key goal of the Chinese regime, and in recent years they have proven themselves willing to experiment with a system of material incentives that owes a good deal to capitalism.

The best example I know of the pervasive control exercised by the work unit is the story of a young American woman who went to Beijing to teach English at a small language institute. After she arrived in China, it became clear to her that the meager salary to which she had naïvely agreed before her arrival was going to be insufficient to meet her expenses. She complained to the school's authorities, who immediately convened a committee to look into the problem. The teacher was asked to appear before the committee and to submit to them a detailed listing of her monthly expenses. The matter was ostensibly resolved—to their satisfaction if not to hers—when the committee members offered her "helpful" suggestions as to ways in which she might economize to stretch the salary she was already receiving.

CONFUCIANISM

The position of the individual in Chinese society cannot be fully understood without a discussion of the teachings of the sage Confucius (551–479 B.C.) and his disciples, which has exerted a potent influence on Chinese culture through the centuries. Confucianism is actually more a system of ethics and morals than a religion per se, and it stresses the obligations of people to one another as a function of the relationships among them.

It would be hard to overstate the contribution of Confucius, who delineated the five important human relationships—those between ruler and subject, husband and wife, father and son, brother and brother, and friend and friend. He taught of a social order that emphasized duty, loyalty, filial piety, respect for age and seniority, and sincerity. Such traits remain valued among Chinese the world over even to this day, despite a brief period toward the end of the Cultural Revolution when Confucius's teachings were severely criticized on the mainland as feudalistic and counterrevolutionary.

Confucius's philosophy can be seen at work in myriad ways in China today. Deference to people in authority and to elders is an obvious one. Chinese are seldom guilty of outright insubordination and are taught to know their places in any given hierarchy. Characteristic Chinese unwillingness to depart from the straight and narrow path set by the leaders—as evidenced in the reluctance to offer an irreverent opinion discussed above—is also traceable to Confucius; to do otherwise would mean to fail in your duty and to be disloyal.

None of the above should be construed to mean that Chinese are not capable of sabotage, subversion, or revenge—their capacity for these things is as great as anyone's. It's just that expressing them directly or overtly would be un-Confucian. Passive resistance can be every bit as effective as the active kind, and it goes it one better in that it needn't involve any disturbance of the surface harmony.

China's bureaucracy probably owes as much to the Confucian heritage as it does to the Soviet Union, on which the government structure of the PRC is largely modeled. Far from the "classless" organization of communist mythology, it is in fact strictly hierarchical, with rank and its privileges defined extremely clearly. People relate to one another not as individuals, but rather according to their relative ranks. Decision making is strictly from the top down, and nothing much is accomplished without support from the higher echelons. Personal loyalty is highly valued, and it is common for high-ranking cadres to install cronies in important positions under their control.

Confucianism is an inherently conservative belief system. It suffers innovation rather badly, and does nothing whatever to encourage it. On the contrary; a hierarchical, vertical system of government where decisions of even minor import must be referred upward is no crucible for revolutionary change. No one is willing to stick his or her neck out, and so new ground is seldom broken, except by those at the very top. Characteristically, the Chinese bureaucracy is notorious for long delays and nearly imperceptible progress.

In Confucius's ideal society, each individual occupies his or her proper place—rank is critical and there is no real equality. In his writings, Confucius speaks frequently of the "superior man," who embodies a number of virtues, most of which are as highly valued among Chinese today as they have ever been. Traditionally, there are eight such virtues: *zhong* (loyalty); *xiao* (filial piety); *ren* (benevolence); *ai* (love); *xin* (trust); *yi* (justice); *he* (harmony), and *ping* (peace). The superior man embodies all of them in some measure.

The superior man is modest, even self-deprecating; he is moderate in habits, generous, and given to compromise and conciliation rather than direct confrontation. He has no need to parade his belongings or his accomplishments before others. He is driven by a well-developed sense of duty. He endeavors to make others comfortable, and is solicitous of guests. He never loses his temper, and remains poised no matter what the situation. A man of integrity, he overlooks deficiencies in others and demonstrates honesty and propriety in all of his dealings.

Confucius and all he stood for took a major drubbing in China during the tumultuous Cultural Revolution period from the mid-1960s to the mid-1970s, when his teachings were widely and vehemently criticized as bourgeois and counterrevolutionary. But more recently there has been a pronounced return to Confucian values. Even the government stepped in with a manufactured propaganda campaign that began in the early 1980s urging people to learn and follow the *wu jiang si mei* or the "five stresses and the four beauties." These are admonitions to stress culture, etiquette, hygiene, order, and morals and to strive for beauty in spirit, language, environment, and behavior.

MIANZI OR "FACE"

Another important cultural concept is that of *mianzi*, which is Chinese for "face." Interestingly, the Chinese term is the exact equivalent of the English word, no matter whether one means by it the area between one's forehead and one's chin, the surface of an object, or the less tangible commodity that is related to a person's dignity and prestige.

The Chinese are acutely sensitive to the regard in which they are held by others or the light in which they appear, and it is very important to be aware of the concept of *mianzi* if only to head off situations in which you cause someone to lose it. The consequences can be severe; at the very least you will cease to receive cooperation from the person; you are quite likely as well to open yourself up to some form of retaliation.

Face is a fragile commodity in China, and there are many ways in which one can cause someone to lose it. One sure way is to dress someone down or insult someone in front of his or her peers. Another is to treat someone as if his or her feelings do not matter, or to deliberately patronize someone. Failing to treat someone with proper respect is a real sin with the Chinese, and it almost always comes back to haunt you. For if you cause someone to lose face you will not only lose the respect of the person you have wronged; you will also lose that of others who are aware of your transgression.

The story in the last chapter of the Chinese minister who was insulted after being met at the airport by a deputy assistant secretary is an excellent case study in *mianzi*. The reason the Chinese were so furious at the treatment the minister received was that it appeared to them for all the world as if the U.S. government was delivering a deliberate slap in the face. Only after it was made clear that the offense had been inadvertent rather than deliberate could the Chinese forgive; forgetting was out of the question.

I can offer another, more personal "losing face" story. I once wrote a business letter to a Chinese minister in an attempt to set up a meeting with him for my boss, who was coming to China the following month. In the letter I mentioned that he would be visiting China at the personal invitation of a vice premier. In point of fact, although the vice premier had indeed suggested to my boss that he lead a delegation to China, the actual invitation had been issued by our host organization, which considered itself the official host and thus interpreted my letter as patronizing.

I was summoned in the very next day by the host unit and summarily dressed down for my perceived offense. I explained that I had certainly not intended a slight and to this day believe that my hosts overreacted to the situation. But offense exists in the eye of the beholder and my intentions were seen as somewhat less important than my crime. The matter was not to end to their satisfaction until I wrote a formal retraction, which of course was a blow to my *own* prestige. The fact that *I* was caused to lose face in the process was of little concern because I was seen as responsible for the whole situation. Having delivered the first blow, I apparently had no right to expect any magnanimity in my host unit's posture toward me. And I got none.

The vehemence of my host unit's reaction surprised me, but it really just underscores how important face is to the Chinese.

When you cause someone to lose it, you can just about count on retribution of one type or another. The Chinese do not usually show anger; to do so would fly in the face of the Confucian virtues. They do, however, get even. And while active confrontation would also be viewed as unacceptable behavior on the part of the superior man, passive aggression is always fair game. The Chinese, in fact, are masters of the art. It can take different forms, but often appears as "inability" to accomplish something they know you wish to get done, or failure to show up at an appointed time with an obviously fabricated excuse. All the while, however, etiquette will never be breached.

One of my favorite examples of "saving face" is a volleyball game in which I once participated at the Chinese Embassy in Washington. The Embassy team played volleyball nearly every day; it was their chief form of recreation and exercise. The American challengers, on the other hand, were a pick-up team that had never really practiced together and whose members varied tremendously in skill. From the beginning it was clear that this was not to be a serious match; it had been billed as more of a social occasion than anything else. But from the start the Chinese played to win, and win they did—the first game was, as I recall, a shutout.

The second game turned out to be quite the opposite. Without so much as a word being spoken among them, the Chinese team members suddenly started to miss shots they had had no trouble making during the previous game. In the end they tallied up a respectable score, but it was the Americans who won—or, as I quickly realized, had been *permitted* to win—the second game. Had it been a legitimate test of skill, the Chinese would no doubt have played mercilessly and the second game would have ended up very much like the first. But it was a social gathering and it would have been unsociable in the extreme to cause guests to lose self-respect—face—in such a situation. Far better to even out the score and let everyone go away feeling like a winner.

The concept of "face" certainly exists in the West as well, but perhaps not to the same degree as it does in the Orient. In the West people tend to be more willing to forgive slights that cause them to lose face. Friendly hazing is, after all, somewhat acceptable in the West. Name-calling, playful dressing down, and sarcastic commentary may occur, but all is seen as good, clean fun. Such behavior, however, seldom occurs among Asians, for whom face is always very serious business.

The Chinese concept of face is also broader and better defined than it is in the West. In English you can *lose* face and you can *save* face; in Chinese, however, you can also *give* face. Giving face means doing something to enhance someone else's reputation or prestige. Complimenting a worker to his or her superior and publicly recognizing someone's contribution are good ways of giving face. Thanking someone who has worked hard on a particular project, even someone of very low rank, is also an excellent example of this. Such actions carry a great deal of weight among Chinese when they come from foreign guests.

My host organization once placed me in the seat of honor next to its chairman during a reception held in Beijing. Though I was flattered by the attention, I did not think much of it until a representative of that organization approached me for a favor a few months later. To ensure my compliance, he was careful to remind me of how much face the unit had accorded to me through that action.

GUANXI OR "CONNECTIONS"

It's often the case that you can't even get to first base in China without *guanxi*, and you can do just about anything—even things you probably ought not to do—when you have it. *Guanxi* literally means "relationships," but "connections" is a far better translation in this sense of the word. It has everything to do with who you know and what these people are willing—or obligated—to do for you.

To the Chinese, *guanxi* is a sort of "tit-for-tat," "you-scratch-my-back-I'll-scratch-yours" kind of arrangement. Someone with whom you have *guanxi* can be counted on to do you favors, bend the rules, and even break them sometimes on your behalf. It is a cultural phenomenon common to Chinese all over the world, and by no means the exclusive province of the PRC. In an economy of scarcity such as that of China, however, the use of *guanxi* can gain you access to goods and services that are otherwise difficult or impossible to come by.

Guanxi is, of course, a reciprocal obligation. You are expected to behave in similar fashion and to deliver favors to those with whom you have *guanxi*. Most often the currency of *guanxi* is not cash. You might be asked to procure airplane or train tickets, admission to a movie or a play, or even a hospital. Or the request might be for foreign electronic equipment, hard-to-get foodstuffs such as fresh fish or fruit, or even an introduction to someone you know who has the bureaucratic power to do an important favor. It may, however, also be a loan of money. In its more advanced form, *guanxi* becomes *houmen*—literally, the "back door," which is discussed in Chapter 10. "Going through the back door" is often the only real way to get some things accomplished in the PRC.

The Chinese tend to extrapolate from their own system and they generally expect foreigners to understand *guanxi* and behave according to its rules. A woman I knew in Beijing once explained to me that she had worked hard to develop *guanxi* within her work unit, and she had established a relationship with someone who had access to the chop—the official seal—of the unit. This person could be counted on to stamp her application to the Public Security Bureau for a passport. Luckily, a former colleague of her father's was well-placed at the Bureau and she was reasonably certain that her father's relationship with this man would guarantee that the application would be approved after it was submitted.

She lacked only *guanxi* at the U.S. Embassy, which would have to issue her a visa before she could leave China and travel to the U.S.—her fondest wish. That was where I was to come in; although she knew I was not a diplomat, she figured that as an American I was very likely to know someone at the Embassy I could pressure on her behalf. When I attempted to explain to her that the U.S. system didn't really work the same way and that I had no particular sway with the U.S. consular officers, it was like talking to a brick wall. I had a dreadfully difficult time convincing her that I wasn't simply shirking what she perceived as my responsibility as her friend and refusing to help.

This same woman once asked a colleague of mine who was leaving for a week in Hong Kong to make a purchase on her behalf. She asked for a Japanese cassette deck, which my associate generously agreed to bring back for her. This was no small favor, for it involved laundering some local Chinese currency and exchanging it for hard, Hong Kong dollars, and it also involved evading Chinese Customs, which assessed excessive duties on such articles.

It turned out that the tape player wasn't even intended for her—it was really for a friend of hers. She was using her *guanxi* with my colleague to do a favor for a friend to whom she herself had an obligation. When the deed was done, my coworker and I were invited to a dinner hosted by the recipient of the cassette deck as a way of expressing her own appreciation. But since *her* parents' apartment was too small to accommodate all the people, the home of *another* friend was borrowed for the purpose. Again, *guanxi* at work.

RECIPROCITY

Closely related to the concept of *guanxi* is that of reciprocity. It is as applicable to interpersonal relationships as it is to business dealings, and what it means is that the economy of favors between two individuals or units is expected to remain in rough balance over a period of time. Reciprocity is the reason that Chinese people feel comfortable presuming on those with whom they have *guanxi*—if they have done a favor for a friend, they feel they are owed a favor in return.

A corollary to this is that you should proceed with extreme caution before putting a Chinese in a position in which he or she is totally unable to return a favor. Giving an extremely expensive gift can place the recipient in an uncomfortable situation. If there is no possibility of the person ever repaying the gift with something of approximately equal value, he or she will always be beholden to the giver.

Sometimes someone seeking a favor will approach even a relative stranger with a gift. Though it is seldom expressed overtly, the obvious implication is that accepting the gift means accepting an obligation to perform the favor. If you do not wish to be beholden to such a supplicant, you should decline the present (see Chapter 8).

The Chinese New Year—called Spring Festival on the mainland—is a common time chosen to settle accounts, and many gifts change hands at this time of the year. People visit friends, colleagues, bosses, and business associates bearing fruit, meat, and other presents that may be very expensive. Sometimes they are repaying specific favors done for them in the course of the previous year; other times it is more like positioning themselves for favors they may need to ask in the future.

Guanxi is not an inexhaustible commodity. A former colleague of mine once treated his organization's relationship with a Chinese official as if it were, and the strategy backfired badly. Because his company had once hosted the official's delegation trip to the United States, my friend constantly asked this person for favors. He was successful up to a point—the point, presumably, at which the Chinese official figured that the obligation had pretty much been repaid. After that, when the requests did not cease, the Chinese official became more remote and less and less available. The relationship ultimately deteriorated to the point that my friend's telephone calls to the unit were no longer returned.

PRIVACY

I count views of privacy as a basic cultural difference not because the Chinese would consider it a particularly important concept in their society, but because Westerners find it to be conspicuously absent. There is no direct translation in Chinese for the English word "privacy"; the notion simply doesn't exist in the same way among Chinese people.

Perhaps the difference is that the idea of being alone and unobserved never had much meaning in a land that has always been overpopulated and overcrowded, where a half-dozen people may live in one room, and where there has never been much mobility. Prying eyes are everywhere in China, aimed not only in the direction of foreigners, but also at the Chinese themselves. Neighbors are *encouraged* to know one another's business and people are generally very much aware of the comings and goings of those around them.

This can be seen as a form of social control, and indeed, it is; suspicious goings-on are noted and reported to the authorities. One of the many unfortunate consequences of the Cultural Revolution, during which people were encouraged to inform on one another if any bourgeois activities were suspected, is that many people in China harbor suspicion of other Chinese they do not know well. Only close friends may be completely trusted.

When foreigners encounter the issue of privacy, it is generally in their apartments or hotels, and then primarily in the Chinese-style hotels where service personnel are everywhere. Until recently it was standard practice in the PRC for hotel staff to enter guest rooms at will, often without knocking first. Many old Chinese hotels did not even have locks on guest room doors, and there was simply no awareness of the fact that a guest might be indisposed to entertaining visitors, or engaged in any sort of private activity. This is not so much of a problem in the joint-venture hotels, and in fact it is much less of an issue than before in Chinese-run hotels in the major cities catering to foreigners. Enough embarrassing incidents occurred that most Chinese service personnel have learned to knock before entering.

PRC guesthouses typically have a service desk on each floor that commands a view of all of the guest rooms. The desk is strategically placed so that all guests and visitors must pass it on their way to the rooms, and it provides an excellent means of keeping tabs on the guests. Similarly, elevators in high-rise buildings in which diplomats and other long-term foreign residents reside are generally operated by service personnel. The fact that an occasional foreign male has been "busted" for inviting a local female into his room for ostensibly nefarious purposes supports the notion that these people are expected to spy on foreign guests and report any suspicious goings-on to the Public Security Bureau.

When Chinese need to be alone, they generally go outside for a walk. There is enough anonymity in the larger cities, especially after dusk, to allow people to be apart with their own thoughts. Where the real problem comes in is when couples wish some privacy to court or to make love. So few single people have access to private quarters that if they can't persuade a roommate to make him or herself scarce for a period of time, they, too, will take to the streets. Public parks in Beijing, Shanghai, Tianjin, Guangzhou, and indeed, in nearly any large city in China are jammed after dark with young couples locked in passionate embrace who literally have nowhere else to go. The irony is that it is only in the most public of situations that many Chinese are able to find privacy.

RECAP: ELEVEN POINTS ON CULTURAL DIFFERENCES

1. Chinese are socialized not to question the social order or try to change it. They are taught to submit willingly and unquestioningly to authority, and that group membership is more important than individuality. The actions of individuals reflect not only on themselves, but on all of their compatriots in a group.

2. The Chinese place a real premium on consensus. Matters are debated until agreement is reached on a course of action. Individual group members are expected to embrace and act on group decisions regardless of their personal views.

3. The *danwei* or "work unit" wields tremendous power over the lives of individuals in China. It has a say in just about any major decision in their lives. It controls your work, where you live, and where you travel as well as your ration of scarce commodities.

4. Chinese do not choose their own work units, and switching among them, though increasingly possible, is still highly restricted. The exception to the rule is joint-venture units, where there is far more mobility.

5. The Confucian system of ethics and morals governs much of the way Chinese interact with one another even today. It emphasizes duty, loyalty, filial piety, sincerity, and respect for age and seniority. Deference to authority and to elders, rank-consciousness, modesty, moderation in habits, generosity, and avoidance of direct confrontation are all highly valued Confucian traits.

6. Confucianism also helps explain China's bureaucracy—strictly hierarchical, with well-defined ranks and privileges. Decision making is strictly from the top down, personal loyalty is highly valued, cronyism is rampant, and innovation largely stifled.

7. Face or *mianzi*, the regard in which one is held by others or the light in which one appears, is vitally important to the Chinese. Causing someone to lose face, through dressing someone down, failing to treat him or her with respect, or insulting someone, results in a loss of cooperation and often in retaliation. If you do so you will also lose the respect of others who are aware of your transgression.

8. In China, face can not only be lost and saved, it can also be given. Doing something to enhance someone's reputation or prestige such as lauding a worker to his or her superior is an example. Such actions carry a great deal of weight among Chinese when they come from foreigners.

9. *Guanxi* or "connections" is a "tit-for-tat" arrangement between people or units that makes the Chinese system go. It gains you access to goods and services otherwise difficult to acquire. The currency of *guanxi* is normally favors, not cash. Chinese generally expect foreigners to understand *guanxi* and behave according to its rules.

10. The balance sheet between two individuals or units is expected to remain in rough balance over a period of time. Try not to put a Chinese in the position of being unable to return a favor, and don't accept presents or favors unless you are prepared to reciprocate.

11. Prying eyes are everywhere in China; local Chinese are watched, as are foreigners. In foreigners' apartments and some hotels, service personnel keep tabs on the guests. Suspicious goings-on are reported.

5

The Business Meeting

Whether you are received by a vice premier or a prison warden, or whether you visit a factory, a kindergarten, a commune, or the Great Hall of the People, you should not be surprised to find a striking similarity in the way the meeting is conducted. Chinese meetings follow a protocol all their own no matter what the setting, and understanding their rhythm can help you to read signals more clearly.

ARRANGING THE MEETING

First of all, setting up a meeting in the PRC often takes more than a simple phone call or telex, and can in fact be quite an involved process. If it is the Western party who requests the meeting, and if that party is not well-known to the Chinese organization with whom the conference is being sought, the Chinese may be loath to agree to a face-to-face parley without further information. Just as Chinese individuals prefer to be formally introduced to new people, Chinese organizations want some background information about their counterparts before they agree to formal discussions. Sometimes they are even required by a government agency to have such information before they may assent to a meeting.

The first order of business is thus to establish your credentials. This may be accomplished through an introduction by a third party known to both parties—either an individual or an organization—or else you can act for yourself. It's best to provide as much background information as possible in the initial overture—preferably in written form. Also provide a description of the topic that you wish to discuss and give the Chinese side some time to study the request.

If it is the Chinese who requested the meeting in the first place, there will be less trouble all around, for the homework will have been done. It is perfectly acceptable in this case to ask the Chinese side for as much advance information as possible prior to the meeting, so you can learn more about what it is they hope to accomplish and prepare your responses.

There are two good reasons why the Chinese prefer—and often insist on—advance information. First of all, they dislike surprises. Knowing up front what the other party wishes to discuss enables them to hammer out their own positions, and to approach the meeting with the confidence that they have the benefit of the collective wisdom of their work units. This approach goes against the Western grain to a certain extent—Westerners often prefer to be present when an idea is first introduced in order to make the best case for it and to gauge the reaction of their counterparts firsthand. But the Chinese don't work that way; if ambushed they will simply listen and defer the matter for later consideration. You'll seldom see a Chinese leader make an off-the-cuff decision during a meeting with a foreigner.

The second reason why it is helpful to "tip your hand" in advance of a meeting is that to do so maximizes the chance of the Chinese side lining up the correct individuals to attend. If a Chinese ministry or corporation is asked to meet with a foreign company and the topic is not spelled out clearly in advance, chances are good that responsibility for attending the meeting and reporting back will devolve on the "external affairs section" of the Chinese organization. This department, staffed by what one wag has referred to as "barbarian handlers," makes no major decisions of its own, performing instead a basic liaison function. While the external affairs section can provide a useful means of identifying the proper decision maker within the organization, going this route can also waste time. A little advance warning can short-circuit the process and result in accomplishing the same thing in fewer meetings.

A Chinese organization will frequently agree in principle to hold a meeting but will resist setting a concrete time for it, or specifying exactly who will preside over it. This is especially true if the request comes well in advance of the desired meeting date, or if the meeting is being sought on behalf of individuals who have not yet arrived in China. China is a place where arrangements are frequently made at the last minute. A Chinese leader who commits to a specific time weeks in advance of a meeting loses the flexibility to engage in other, possibly more important, activities that may present themselves in the intervening period. Then, too, the Chinese feel that until someone actually arrives in town there is no hurry to set up a meeting time; any of a million things could happen to delay or cancel the trip.

This is why it is often the case that you can arrive in China to find that none of the half dozen meetings you requested months in advance has in fact yet been set up. The Chinese penchant for last-minute arrangements can be maddening in its uncertainty. The good news is that these things have a way of working themselves out, and most of the meetings generally wind up getting on the agenda somehow.

It is also why meetings with extremely high-ranking officials in China—vice premiers and their ilk—are almost *never* pinned down until the day of the event. Such meetings also have a way of occurring on the very last day of your visit to Beijing. I've often suspected that keeping these audiences indefinite until the last second serves a number of purposes: it creates suspense and a feeling of gratitude toward the host organization on the part of foreign guests, who perceive the hosts as "coming through at the last minute" for them. It's also a form of manipulation; a way of "rewarding" foreigners for doing something the Chinese desire them to do. And they aren't above doing this to extremely high-ranking guests, including foreign ministers and corporate CEOs.

THE SETUP

It's unlikely that you will attend a meeting in the office of a
Chinese official. Offices are crowded and rather dreary places
in China, and a small room with four desks, uncomfortable
chairs, and one or two ringing telephones is not considered a
fitting place to receive guests. The fact that stray papers bearing
what are purportedly state secrets may be lying around is the
ostensible reason that many Chinese organizations actually
prohibit foreigners from entering working offices.

Most often, meetings are held in rooms set aside solely for
this purpose. They may be located down the hall from the
office or in an adjacent building. They usually are furnished
with the ubiquitous overstuffed chairs and sofas that you see
throughout China—the same type of furniture visible in the
photos of Richard Nixon's reception in Chairman Mao's study
in 1972. The chairs, which line the perimeter of the room, are
generally draped with drab seat covers and antimacassars, and
are interspersed with coffee tables and end tables. Alternatively, there may be an oblong table in the center of the room
with straight chairs arranged all around it, rather like a
Spartan, Western-style conference room.

It is very important to arrive at a meeting on time in the
PRC. Punctuality is considered a virtue on the mainland as
well as in Taiwan, and keeping others waiting is seen as
impolite. If you happen to arrive late at a meeting, be sure to
apologize; this is a signal that you intended no slight by your
tardiness. Nor is it appropriate to arrive too early for a meeting.
A Chinese delegation I escorted around the United States once
arrived fifteen minutes early at the headquarters of a company
with which they had scheduled a meeting; rather than go in
and embarrass their unprepared hosts, they insisted that the
driver cruise around the block until the appointed hour.

Meeting formalities begin with the arrival of the guests at
the site. It is considered very important that guests be greeted
upon their arrival and escorted to the meeting room. The
principal host need not go down to the street to meet the cars,
but he or she must send a representative to do this. When the

guests arrive at the meeting room, it is considered good form
for the host to be present, waiting for them. The highest-
ranking guest should ideally enter the room first; if he or she
does not, there is a risk that the Chinese host will mistake
whoever *does* enter first—whether a secretary or a low-level
functionary—for the head person. Chinese delegations tend to
enter rooms in something approaching protocol order with the
first- and second-ranking delegates leading the way. Only
interpreters typically break rank, since they are necessary to
help the leaders communicate. So, extrapolating from their
own procedures, Chinese will expect the leader to come in
first.

After hands are shaken all around, guests are escorted to
seats. Seating arrangements are not completely rigid, but there
is a certain protocol to where the most important people are
placed. The principal guest is generally escorted by the
principal host to a seat of honor. In rooms where chairs are
arranged along the perimeter, this is the place to the host's
immediate right on a sofa or in chairs at the end of the room
opposite the door. Other high-ranking guests are shown to
seats in the same general area of the room, and the interpreter
sits strategically near the host and the principal guest. The
remaining guests are left to their own devices to seat themselves, though if you hesitate you may be directed to a seat by
a solicitous Chinese host. Only after the guests have selected
seats will the balance of the Chinese participants seat themselves.

If the meeting room has a large central table, the principal
guest may be seated directly opposite the principal host (who
has the door to the room behind him or her) rather than to his
or her right. Other participants fill in the other seats. In formal
meetings and negotiations it is often the case that the Chinese
delegation sits on one side of the table and the foreigners line
the other, with the lowest-ranking delegation members seated
at the ends of the table, furthest from the principals. In less
formal situations, the sides need not be so assiduously segre-
gated.

Many meeting rooms also feature metal or plastic spittoons on the floor near the chairs. Don't be surprised—or
offended—if the Chinese avail themselves of them; spitting,

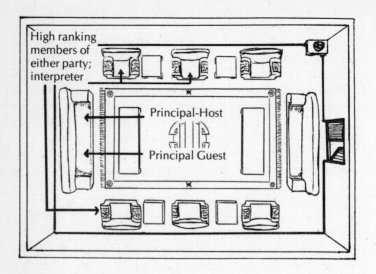

FIGURE 2. The arrangement of a typical Chinese meeting room. The principal guest is seated to the host's right on a sofa or in chairs opposite the door. Other high-ranking guests are seated in the immediate vicinity, as are interpreters.

though considered a bit inelegant, is not seen as impolite in China. Many Chinese will think nothing of expectorating in polite company. In fact, when China's paramount leader Deng Xiaoping, who is known to engage in this habit, visited the United States in 1979, his protocol officer reportedly was careful to caution him to refrain from spitting during his trip. America, he was told, had no spittoons.

THE COURSE OF THE MEETING

Most Chinese gatherings begin with some small talk, especially when the host and guests do not know one another well. The purpose is to get acquainted and make preliminary assessments of each other before any business is discussed. The Chinese are eminently patient in most business dealings, and they recoil from the practice of some Western businessmen that allows for a "lay-all-your-cards-on-the-table" approach to

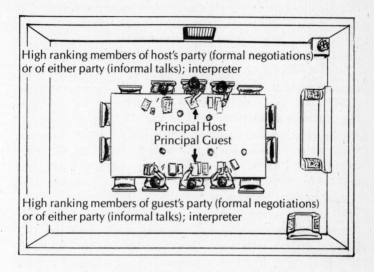

High ranking members of host's party (formal negotiations) or of either party (informal talks); interpreter

Principal Host
Principal Guest

High ranking members of guest's party (formal negotiations) or of either party (informal talks); interpreter

FIGURE 3. A variant meeting room arrangement in which individuals are seated around a large conference table. The principal guest is seated opposite the host, facing the door to the room. High-ranking guests and interpreters are seated in the immediate vicinity.

people one does not know well. Important business dealings are to be undertaken only with those one trusts, and trust is not something that can be established in a short period of time.

It's important, then, not to "come in swinging," but to establish the foundation of a relationship and build slowly. There is no need to rush into a discussion of business; the topic will come up naturally in time. Start out with icebreakers such as general observations or questions. The Chinese are apt to bring up the weather ("You have brought good weather with you, Mr. Smith") or the minutiae of your trip to China (e.g., whether your plane arrived on time, what sights of interest you have already seen in the city, whether you have eaten a particular local delicacy) before any issue of substance is broached. For your part, feel free to ask if the host has ever visited your country, how long he or she has held the present position, etc. From there you can move on to more substantive, but still safe, territory, such as what the host's area of responsibility is within his ministry or corporation. Usually the matter at hand will find its way into the conversation this way.

Chinese cadres seldom hold meetings with foreigners by themselves; there is usually a retinue of lesser-ranking officials and staff members on hand as well. Even in very small-scale meetings there is invariably at least one other person present. Occasionally the Chinese do not even bother to introduce all of the participants at the start of the meeting, though this happens less and less frequently. It is usually quite clear why certain individuals are invited; they may have some say in the business at hand, be responsible for liaison with the foreign guest, or be charged with essential tasks such as translating or note-taking for the meeting.

But equally often there are others present who have no apparent reason for being there. It was once thought that true decision makers sometimes went deliberately unidentified, eager to make a firsthand assessment of the foreign guest but happy to leave the task of running the meeting and formally receiving the guests to someone of lower rank, but this in fact is seldom if ever true. Unnamed participants are more often there as observers or apprentices, and so the Chinese do not think it is necessary to introduce them. They may also be there as representatives of the Party, however, and the fact that they are sometimes not introduced may be due to Chinese embarrassment at admitting that the Party has a watchdog role in the issue at hand.

Discussions with Chinese officials are not free-for-all exchanges; they are structured dialogues between principals on both sides that are generally witnessed by others. Participants other than the principal host and guest—and perhaps one or two other very high-ranking members of the group—are present for the entire meeting, but they participate in the conversation only upon explicit invitation.

The principal host will probably begin with a short welcoming speech after the initial formalities are over. If the Chinese have asked for the meeting, the host will also likely state the business at hand as part of his or her opening remarks. If the meeting is being held at the behest of the guest, then after the welcome the host will turn the floor over to the guest to begin the substantive discussion.

In general, the Chinese prefer to be in the position of reacting to others' ideas, and not to bear the onus of setting the scope of the discussion themselves. On one level this can be seen as little more than a courtesy—letting the guest speak first is basic good manners. But I have long suspected that more is at work here than just regard for etiquette. In matters relating to international business, many Chinese tend to feel a certain amount of insecurity, due to the fact that the PRC was cut off from the rest of the world during a vitally important period in the development and maturation of international commerce. Some Chinese, especially those from the hinterlands, do not fully understand all of the intricacies of foreign trade, and they are smart enough to know it. So allowing the guest to frame the conversation and put forth the proposal permits them to avert the possibility of saying something foolish or naïve. It also provides precious time to consider the suggestions of the guest and to react to them.

Chinese listeners will often punctuate the remarks of other speakers with nods or affirmative grunts. They may come as often as every sentence. What they mean is, "I have heard you," or "I have understood what you are saying." These interjections do *not* mean "I agree with you" or "I give my assent," and should *never* be taken as such. Many serious misunderstandings have resulted from a foreign guest mistaking this signal for some sort of accord or permission.

During a meeting, it is always important to keep in mind who holds the floor at any given time. Remember that these meetings are not free exchanges but rather structured conversations; there is a rhythm at work here. Typically, if you are the person who states the business you have two alternatives: you can put the entire question on the table in all of its complexity, or you can break the subject down into parts.

In the first instance, you may begin by speaking for a full five or ten minutes without interruption as you lay out the intricacies of the issue at hand and catalog your organization's positions on all of the components that need to be discussed. In the context of a discussion of the impediments to a joint venture, for example, you might bring up foreign exchange, exporting, and quality control as the major areas of concern. Once you have finished this, it is your counterpart's turn to speak to all of these issues. The Chinese are very diligent about following the flow of such expositions and their responses will generally meticulously touch on all of the points raised.

Alternatively, you may define the issue and then raise the component points individually. You may actually enumerate the points to be discussed, saying at the outset, for example, that you intend to cover six important considerations.

In this case your counterpart is free to speak to each point as it is brought up, with you reclaiming the floor each time a point is fully discussed to raise the next one. There need be no mystery about which approach a speaker chooses to take; it is good form, in fact, to make clear up front whether you intend to talk about the whole subject or deal with it piece by piece. Flagging it in this way helps everyone to know whose turn it is to speak at any given time.

It is important to know who holds the floor because it is considered rude to interrupt a speaker while he or she is talking. An occasional short intervention is acceptable—it is fine, for example, to fill in a relevant piece of information that may not be known to the speaker. But you must not break in and speak so long as effectively to reclaim the floor. Since ownership is not always a major concern in Western-style meetings, it is important that you monitor your own behavior in this regard when dealing with the Chinese.

Another cardinal rule of conduct during meetings is never to put anyone on the spot, at least not in person. This means never to put someone in the position of having to divulge information that he or she seems unwilling to talk about, or to challenge someone who has already told you that to do something you have requested is "inconvenient" or "under study." You should always offer a way out so that your counterpart can preserve face. On the other hand, there are few limits to frankness in written form; sometimes a well-crafted follow-up letter can make important points that would have been too awkward to make in a face-to-face discussion.

Count on the Chinese to take detailed notes of proceedings

and circulate them to all interested parties; don't be surprised if someone else you encounter later who was not at the initial meeting appears fully informed about the proceedings. You can also count on the Chinese to retrieve these notes and quote them back to you chapter and verse if subsequent events cast any doubt on what was said—provided that consulting the record advances the Chinese position in the matter at hand.

USING INTERPRETERS

It is still unusual to run into Chinese managers or high-level bureaucrats who speak foreign languages fluently enough to conduct business; in the vast majority of cases business is transacted through interpreters. Even managers who do speak foreign languages frequently prefer to use interpreters anyway, in order to save face, buy time, or simply speak more fluently. Any Chinese organization that has dealings abroad can be relied on to have access to interpreters who speak English, Japanese, Russian, and even German and French.

It often makes sense to bring your own interpreter to China, but it is not essential to do so for protocol purposes. For complicated negotiations your own interpreter can be worth his or her weight in gold in communicating sophisticated legal and business concepts and intricate details, as well as in reporting back on discussions that take place in Chinese among the negotiators themselves. Some business representatives favor bringing along their own translators to ensure that they are not hoodwinked by one who is partial to the Chinese position. In fact, while clarity is a sound reason to hire your own interpreter, self-defense is probably not. It is the job of any translator to communicate clearly in both languages, and you are far more likely to bump into an incompetent interpreter in China than one who is actively trying to deceive you.

Sometimes a good interpreter can even save you from yourself. Foreigners sometimes thoughtlessly say things that would offend Chinese hosts if they were directly translated—such as calling the host by the wrong name or title or referring to China by an outdated name (see "Drinking and Toasting" in Chapter 7). In such situations, a crackerjack interpreter will correct the remark as it is translated, thus saving face for all concerned.

Don't expect a member of your team to do double duty as a substantive contributor to the discussion *and* an interpreter. To use someone as a translator is for all practical purposes to lose that person's services as a negotiator, since interpreting is hard work and it takes a good deal of quick thought and concentration. Be sensitive, too, to the fact that a team member who is of Chinese extraction may not wish to be seen by the Chinese as an interpreter, especially if he or she is on the team because of a different area of expertise. The person's face may be at stake here.

When you bring your own interpreter, the custom is that he or she will translate your remarks, and the other interpreter will translate the remarks of your Chinese counterpart. When there is only one interpreter, no matter from which side, the person serves as the voice of both principal host and principal guest.

There are ways of assessing how good a job the interpreter is doing. A sure sign of a pro is lack of hesitation on his or her part and obvious ease in expressing thoughts in both languages. A good interpreter will also occasionally query you if you use an expression he or she doesn't understand. This often happens when you use slang. On the other hand, if the questions you receive back from the Chinese don't seem to track with your remarks, if the technical terms create delays and seem to pose insurmountable problems, or if other bilingual members of the Chinese group are constantly offering corrections or filling in blanks, chances are that the interpreter is in over his or her head.

Getting the Chinese to find a substitute for an inept interpreter is dicey business. You can't very well transmit this message through the interpreter in question; it must be done out of the person's hearing through some other liaison person. Since this is an assault on the interpreter's competence and hence his or her face, it is a serious matter. If a replacement is made, chances are good that the foreign delegation will never see the first interpreter again. On the other hand, raising the issue is preferable to conducting a series of inconclusive meetings characterized by miscommunication. By all means try to work with an interpreter who shows some competence and promise, but if the situation is beyond repair, don't hesitate to ask for a change.

There is an art to talking through interpreters. The cardinal rule is to pause frequently, breaking your remarks up into bite-sized pieces. The longer you speak without stopping, the greater the likelihood that something you say will be mistranslated, or not translated at all. One thought—one or two sentences—at a time is a good standard. This pace also allows you time in between remarks to think through what you wish to say next. Avoid slang and excessively colloquial expressions, which are often not understood at all. English, for example, boasts a number of expressive metaphors from the world of sports, but woe unto the English speaker who asks a Chinese for a "ballpark figure," or expresses a fear of "striking out," not "getting to first base," or "being out in left field." It's a rare interpreter who has enough experience with the game of baseball to figure such terms out.

Many colloquialisms will simply be misunderstood, a worse fate than those that are not understood at all, since they stand an excellent chance of being translated literally. I remember, for example, one instance when a foreign businessman accused his Chinese partners of using a particular obstacle as a "red herring" for another problem. The translator's faithful and literal rendering of this remark succeeded only in bewildering the Chinese audience.

Another cardinal rule concerning the use of interpreters: don't make the mistake of addressing your remarks directly to the translator. It's easy to fall into this trap, since speakers tend to be very aware of the fact that it is the interpreter and not their counterpart who is actually understanding what is being said. It is natural to study the face of the translator to be certain that he or she, at least, understands the nuances of your remarks. But you should fight the impulse. Focusing on the interpreter is impolite in the extreme because it fails to accord proper respect to the Chinese host or guest.

Similarly, fight the all-too-common urge to deal with a situation in which you are not being understood by repeating

your remarks at double volume. Ninety-nine percent of the
time the problem is comprehension, not hearing. Don't shout;
a far more effective solution is to come up with simpler words
that convey the same idea.

CONCLUDING A MEETING

Before a meeting is finished, it is an excellent idea to restate
your understanding of exactly what was accomplished. This is
an obvious but very worthwhile strategy for making sure that
both sides agree on what happened and on what the next steps
will be. If it is a first meeting, you can also ask the Chinese
host—who, if he or she is a high-ranking official, will likely be
difficult to reach in person in the future—to designate a
contact person for future dealings. The Chinese are generally
quite willing to do this and it offers the practical advantage of
continuity; you don't have to reinvent the wheel and bring a
new contact person up to speed on the matter at hand each
time you approach the unit about it.

It also serves an additional purpose. If a high-ranking cadre
assigns to a staff member a responsibility such as future liaison
with a foreign concern, it is a way of putting his or her
imprimatur on the matters that have been discussed. It means
that the relationship with you is a matter of personal concern,
and it increases the likelihood that you will receive cooperation from the unit in the future.

It's usually fairly obvious when the business has been
transacted and the meeting is over. As far as protocol goes,
either side can end a meeting. The host may observe that the
guests must be tired, or hungry, or must have important things
to do with the rest of their day during their all-too-short visit to
the city. Or the principal guest may point out that the group
has already taken up a great deal of the host's time, and that
they are grateful to him or her for spending the time with
them. In either case, the host generally sends someone to
escort the guests to their car; occasionally he or she will do the
honors in person.

RECAP: A DOZEN
NOTES ON BUSINESS MEETINGS

1. Chinese organizations typically request background information before they agree to formal discussions. Provide as much information as possible about the topic that you wish to discuss, and give the Chinese side some time to study the request.
2. The Chinese dislike surprises, preferring to hammer out their own positions in advance of a meeting. Knowing what will be discussed beforehand also permits them to select the proper participants for a meeting.
3. In China, meetings are generally held in conference rooms rather than offices. Chairs may line the perimeter of the room or be a arranged around an oblong table in the center.
4. Punctuality is considered a virtue in the PRC, so it is important to arrive at a meeting on time—not late and not early. Guests are greeted upon arrival by a representative and escorted to the room.
5. Chinese generally expect foreign delegation leaders to enter the room first, and to do so avoids confusion. Important guests are escorted to seats, with the principal guest placed next to the principal host in a seat of honor. Others may sit where they like.
6. Chinese meetings begin with small talk. Avoid the temptation to lay all your cards on the table at first; start out with icebreakers such as general observations or questions.
7. Chinese seldom hold meetings with foreigners alone; staff members are invariably present. Not all of the participants are necessarily introduced; those who are not are usually observers or apprentices, however, not active participants.
8. Chinese meetings are structured dialogues between principals on both sides; others participate in the conversation only upon explicit invitation. The Chinese prefer to react to others' ideas, and not to bear the onus of setting the scope of the discussion themselves.
9. Chinese often signal the speaker with nods or interjections that they understand what he or she is saying. These do

not necessarily signal agreement. Remember who holds the floor and don't interrupt a speaker.

10. Never put anyone on the spot during a meeting. Always offer a way out so your counterpart can preserve face.

11. A good interpreter can help you immeasurably in China. When talking through an interpreter, pause frequently and avoid slang and colloquialisms. Always talk to the host, never directly to the translator.

12. Restate what was accomplished at the close of a meeting to guard against misunderstandings. Asks for a contact person for future dealings.

6

Relationships with Foreigners

THE CHINESE
VIEW OF OUTSIDERS

Despite outbreaks of xenophobia that have characterized certain periods in Chinese history, the Chinese are an extremely hospitable people who frequently go far out of their way to make guest feel at home among them. While they may sometimes be rude and impolite to fellow countrymen they do not know well, they are typically quite pleasant to Western visitors, who are obviously guests in their country. Don't be surprised if someone you hardly know—or even someone you meet on the street—offers you some tea or approaches you to practice a little English. This is the Confucian emphasis on hospitality at work.

There is nevertheless a certain schizophrenia involved in the Chinese view of Westerners, feelings of inferiority and superiority that may curiously exist side by side. Lu Xun, a great twentieth-century Chinese writer, once quipped that through the ages the Chinese have either looked down on foreigners as brutes or up to them as saints, but have never

actually been able to call them friends or speak of them as
equals. On the one hand, the Chinese see Occidental society
as highly advanced in many ways. They view its achievements
in the development of science and technology, manufactur-
ing, transportation, and agriculture, not to mention its significant economic accomplishments, as worthy of note and even
some envy.

On the other hand, however, China has a proud 5,000-year
history and a civilization and culture that the Chinese consider
second to none. Western civilization may well be more
advanced materially, but many Chinese see it as clearly
lacking in moral fiber—how else to explain the preponderance
of drugs, illicit sex, and other degenerate conduct that they
read and hear about in the United States and elsewhere? By
this reckoning, Westerners can not possibly be the moral
equals of Chinese. As far as the Chinese are concerned, when
all is said and done, in social customs, Westerners are ultimately not much better than barbarians. They don't understand the finer points of etiquette and can't be counted on to
behave properly in any given situation.

What this underscores is the propensity of the Chinese to
judge Westerners and their behavior according to Chinese
standards. For Chinese, there are relatively few choices as to
what constitutes proper and improper behavior; they grow up
imbued with very clear ideas of what is right and what is
wrong. Lacking another set of standards, they can hardly be
faulted for using this yardstick to judge others, even those not
reared in their culture. How much this tendency is actually
expressed correlates strongly with a Chinese's station in life,
and especially with level of education and geographical location. Rural Chinese, for example, who may lack sophistication
and contact with the world outside of China, are more likely
to view foreigners exclusively through Chinese lenses. Urban-
ized and educated Chinese, on the other hand, are far more
likely to make allowances for cultural differences.

Excuses are frequently made for transgressions by foreign
guests on the grounds that they don't know any better. There
is a real double standard at work. It is the very fact that there
are no expectations that foreigners will ever really measure up

in the area of protocol and manners that is at issue here. It's precisely this condescending attitude that condemns Western-ers to be termed "barbarians"—the same classification used to describe the Mongolian hordes who pillaged northern China for many hundreds of years—especially when the Chinese are angry with them. On the other hand, the fact that expectations are so low also affords a significant opportunity for Westerners. If you display some knowledge of Chinese customs, however small, you can easily earn accolades and admiration.

Foreigners who are themselves very careful to preserve the face of those with whom they deal and to observe the rules and regulations governing *guanxi* may nonetheless sometimes be nonplussed, however, when a Chinese occasionally displays callous disregard for their *own* sense of face, or fails to treat them with the same courtesy that would be accorded to a fellow Chinese. Indeed, it is sometimes true that a Chinese may actually be *less* concerned with exhibiting strictly correct behavior when it is a foreigner who is involved. He or she may maneuver you into an embarrassing situation or put undue pressure on you to deliver a favor.

For example, a colleague of mine once agreed to support a Chinese acquaintance in his application to obtain a U.S. visa for his wife. Although he made it clear that he would call the Chinese as soon as any news was received, the man nagged him *daily* about the matter, something he would have been unlikely to do had it been another Chinese doing the favor. Curiously, this, too, is the double standard at work; as a foreigner you may be seen by some Chinese as exempt from the normal rules that govern interpersonal relationships and thus fair game for behavior that would otherwise be considered unacceptable.

Foreigners should approach China knowing that no matter how long they stay or how well they learn the language and the customs, they will always be considered different. There is basically no such thing as ever really blending in completely. While the Chinese generally respect an outsider who has a knowledge of their culture—labeling him or her a *Zhongguo tong*, an affectionate term meaning "China hand"—there are limits to acceptance. No outsider is ever completely successful in an effort to be more Chinese than the Chinese.

Exactly how much the differences matter to the Chinese depends in part on the prevailing political situation in China. Even those Westerners who lived in the PRC as Chinese citizens for decades following 1949 were ostracized during the Cultural Revolution, their "foreignness" suddenly making them suspect during that unfortunate period of rampant xenophobia.

Many "China hands" have found that the best strategy is to glory in the cultural differences, while minimizing the barriers. That is, they try to learn as much as they can about how the Chinese do things and use this knowledge in their interactions with them. But they never lose sight of the fact that they are indeed different, and that this very distinction confers considerable advantages on them when they interact with the Chinese.

BUSINESS RELATIONSHIPS

It is the business and professional relationships between Chinese and foreigners with which the PRC government feels most comfortable. After all, the principal justification for China's opening to the West has always been to acquire the technology and know-how that the West can offer China in its drive to modernize. The PRC's opening has never been driven by a strong sense that China can realize much benefit from the culture or social thought of foreigners. Thus it is professional relationships that the government recognizes and supports, not personal liaisons.

Such relationships with the Chinese generally only go so far. The fear of corruption—or the perception of it—on the Chinese side is a real one. No Chinese wants to be accused of compromising a business relationship between his or her unit and a foreign company. Too close a friendship with a foreigner renders someone suspect in the PRC, and in rare instances can lead to an accusation of the heinous crime of leaking state secrets to a foreign party.

Business relationships always begin rather formally. Informality is acceptable only after those involved have spent sufficient time together to know one another well, and even then it has its limits. In such situations, the Chinese don't always say what they mean or what they feel, but try instead to say and do what is proper and correct. They deal with foreign businessmen not as individuals but as representatives of their organizations. This is true even in the relatively informal social settings of banquets. While the Chinese work hard trying to establish common ground and interests—even personal interests—they never lose sight of the fact that the reason they are spending time with you is a professional one rather than a personal one.

Rank is extremely important in business relationships with the Chinese. Even though it is often hard to determine the rank of someone who comes from an entirely different system, still less to relate it to your own organizational standards, the Chinese can be counted on to try their best to do so. It's unusual to talk business with someone who ranks far higher or far lower than you do, and if you find yourself in such a position, it's a safe bet that something is wrong somewhere.

On the other hand, you will frequently find yourself dealing with someone a step or two higher or lower. If it is an initial meeting, it may just be an accident that that person is present. Maybe the Chinese misjudged your rank and couldn't figure out how important you really are, and sent an important official because they didn't want to take the chance of offending you. It may also be a deliberate signal by the Chinese that they attach great importance to your company. If someone of somewhat lower stature is sent, it may again be a misunderstanding, or it may be a signal that little importance is placed on you and your business.

When you have a great deal of contact with individuals in a Chinese organization—in joint-venture situations, for example—it's natural for some of the formality to break down as individuals get to know one another better. For many democratic-minded Westerners this is an invitation to abandon artificial distinctions and establish "buddy" relationships with the Chinese. While this approach can work—and work well—with Chinese of equal rank, it can spell disaster with those of higher or lower stature.

Whether you like it or not, it's important in business situations to keep rank distinctions squarely in mind. This is probably as true among Chinese in Taiwan, Hong Kong, and elsewhere as it is among mainlanders, though the pecking orders may be a bit different when they are not set down by the government, as they are in the PRC. You should behave politely in any case, but with Chinese who rank higher, you must be extra careful to be correct in behavior without appearing in any way presumptuous. Bear in mind that they do not see themselves as your equals, at least as far as their positions go. Although it is a hallmark of Chinese etiquette that someone of higher rank never appear to be condescending in behavior toward someone of lower rank, that's really just form—not substance. Don't use the chance opportunity of a meeting with the head man to try to establish *guanxi*; the attempt will probably backfire and you will appear ill-bred and gauche for trying.

When dealing with those who rank lower, the same principles apply. Never do anything to give the impression that you think yourself more important than the other person—that would be immodest and would earn you only contempt. The Chinese admire people who don't put on airs, but neither should you be overly friendly or too informal. It is often the case that lower-ranking Chinese, especially less-educated, less-sophisticated, and more old-fashioned ones, *want* to be deferential to you. Knowing exactly where you fit in makes them comfortable. It's when you attempt to bridge the gap and deal as a peer or a friend that they become uneasy and uncertain how to behave.

Remember also that if you are a foreigner, for better or worse you are automatically considered to be someone worthy of some deference among many Chinese. There is a certain amount of rank—and privilege—that just goes with the territory. A Chinese factory manager may drop everything and give you a personal guided tour of his or her plant, or a Chinese store clerk may wait on you before a whole line of Chinese shoppers who arrived before you did. However undeserving you may be of this extra bit of attention and solicitousness, it's better to accept it with grace and style—not as your due, but rather as the unselfish show of hospitality that it is—than to refuse it in protest. It's just one of the ways the Chinese have of showing you that you are welcome.

A former colleague of mine reports a memorable experience that illustrates both how much regard the Chinese may hold for foreigners and how unaware we sometimes are of the turmoil we can cause when we are doing no more than being ourselves. She had been invited to give a talk to a Chinese unit about a business matter in which they were very interested. This was apparently one of the very few meetings where someone forgot to serve the obligatory tea, and as she talked on her throat became more and more parched, until she finally asked for a drink of water. Time passed, but no water ever came. A few days later, my friend happened to run into the woman responsible for setting up the meeting. The hostess thanked her profusely for an excellent presentation and added that she was sure my friend would be interested to know that a meeting had been held and the worker who had been responsible for providing liquid refreshments that day had been soundly criticized for dereliction of duty.

FOREIGN WOMEN AND BUSINESS

The Chinese are generally fairly accepting of business relationships with foreign women, a major difference between them and their Japanese and Korean counterparts. Women are nominally equal in China, the communist Chinese maintaining that they were "liberated" along with men in 1949 when the PRC was founded. In actual fact, females in important government or business decision-making positions in China are really quite few, and proportionately not too much larger than the number one sees in the more developed societies of the West.

For Chinese on the mainland and elsewhere, the operative word in the term "foreign female" is more often "foreign" than "female." Foreign businesswomen receive the respect due their positions, and no less of it than would a male with the same status. Since informality is not a necessary ingredient to drive a successful business relationship in China, a foreign woman's sex does not place her at any particular disadvantage when dealing with the Chinese. The same dynamics would apply to a foreign businessman dealing with a Chinese businesswoman. The best course is to keep things cordial, but always somewhat formal.

It would be exceptionally rare for a Chinese male to engage in behavior toward a foreign female business acquaintance that could possibly be construed as untoward—unless he was indeed pursuing a sexual relationship with her. Such situations, while not unknown, are nonetheless rare in the extreme.

Wives of foreign businessmen are welcomed by the Chinese to accompany their husbands on business trips to China. Traditionally, they are not present during business meetings and negotiations, but are enthusiastically hosted at social occasions such as receptions and banquets. A wife is considered to share the rank of her husband, as is evidenced by the fact that she may even be called by her husband's title—not his name—with the addition of the term *furen*, meaning "Madam." Wives thus generally receive comparable treatment in terms of protocol. Although foreign spouses are commonly seen as banquet guests, Chinese spouses seldom show up at social occasions in the PRC, unless they have a business reason to be present. This often tends to be true in Taiwan and Hong Kong as well.

The Chinese are comfortable with this double standard and no foreign guest should ever have second thoughts about bringing a spouse along on a social occasion, provided the spouse has been explicitly invited to participate. When extending an invitation to a Chinese business associate, it is acceptable to invite the person's spouse along, especially if your own will be present. But don't ever press the issue. And when you are a guest, it's a good idea not to inquire why your host has not brought along a husband or wife.

PERSONAL RELATIONSHIPS

Left to their own devices, Chinese people will often go out of their way to befriend foreign guests in their midst. It is one of their most endearing qualities, probably motivated as much by genuine altruism and hospitality as by curiosity about people who are different from them. It does take a certain amount of boldness to approach someone of another culture, however, and not everyone is comfortable being so forward. While it's not uncommon to run into people who are apparently indifferent to foreigners, it's rare to bump into someone who is actively hostile. Sometimes in rural and far-flung areas in particular the hospitality foreigners receive is exceptionally warm and genuine.

Among Chinese in Hong Kong, Taiwan, and Singapore, where there are no restrictions on these types of associations, it is common to find people who deal every day with Occidentals, and who even number some Westerners among their close friends. Many an American or European student of the Chinese language has made great progress living with a Chinese family or in a dormitory with a Chinese roommate.

In the PRC, however, because of the risks—real or perceived—associated with deepening relationships with foreigners, many Chinese are pointedly circumspect about keeping them at arm's length. The government's schizophrenia on this issue came out clearly with the launching and rapid suspension of the "anti-spiritual pollution campaign" in 1983–84. During this period one faction of government officials railed against corrupting influences stemming from China's opening to the West and urged a return to conservative socialist values. Western music, dress, and values in general came under shrill attack. And individuals who cultivated close relationships with foreigners were considered suspect, subject to being hauled in for questioning on the most tenuous of pretexts. A few months after the campaigns began, however, cooler heads prevailed and it was summarily abandoned by the government.

Even in less politically charged periods, foreign journalists and diplomats continue to be most carefully scrutinized. They are viewed in more paranoid Chinese circles as differing little from spies. But as the number of foreigners resident in China grows, Chinese authorities become less fearful of even these relationships. Many Chinese citizens are now forthcoming with foreigners of all stripes and they seem far less concerned about potential hazards than was the case a few years ago.

If you are interested in developing a personal relationship with a Chinese, it's best to follow his or her lead. By all means show your interest, but if you encounter any apprehension at all, it's best to back off and not apply any pressure. Your Chinese friend is the best judge of whether any serious threat exists. If he or she seems unconcerned, there is probably little reason for excess caution.

A Chinese friend will view the requirements of friendship through his or her own lenses, and so in entering into a friendship, you must expect to be judged according to Chinese standards. Casual acquaintance does not demand any significant commitment among Chinese, but friendship implies obligation—obligation to drop everything and help out a friend in need, obligation to use *guanxi* on behalf of a friend. Not to deliver puts you at risk of being labeled as insincere—a cardinal sin.

Even healthy personal relationships with the Chinese may sometimes strike Westerners as a bit too formal or "correct" for their taste. This behavior should not be misinterpreted as coldness; it is precisely because the Chinese values the friendship that he or she will want to make sure that nothing goes wrong with it. Chinese sometimes say that Westerners are frequently overly polite to strangers and rude to their friends; they themselves tend to err in the opposite direction. A Chinese doesn't feel it incumbent upon him or herself to be at all solicitous of a stranger, but to be discourteous or disrespectful to a friend is a serious offense.

While it is thus a good idea to be circumspect when dealing with Chinese friends, it doesn't by any means imply that you must always be grave or serious. "Kidding" relationships can work well with the Chinese, just so long as the ground rules are made clear. Joking and jesting may not be understood at first, but once Chinese realize that all is in fun and that any barbs that come their way are not to be taken seriously, they can learn to play the game as well as any Westerner.

My own personal relationships with Chinese people have been most successful when they are honest and fairly frank. Because the cultural barriers offer so much opportunity for misreading signals, being less than candid can result in serious misunderstandings. Holding frank discussion of issues sometimes bears the risk of running afoul of the Chinese propensity for correct, cordial relations and surface harmony at all times. It is, however, a fairly effective precaution against any serious threat to the relationship posed by unspoken feelings that are allowed to fester when an action or a statement is read incorrectly.

SEXUAL RELATIONSHIPS

Given the overall conservatism in the area of social customs, it should come as no surprise that sexual relationships between Chinese and foreigners are officially frowned on. The Chinese are somewhat puritanical about sex; the only approved sex is that which takes place within marriage. Sexual experimentation before marriage is taboo, and to make matters worse, in the PRC people are encouraged to marry later—in their late twenties—as a means of controlling population growth.

Foreigners, on the other hand, are perceived to be extremely permissive in the area of sex, and when they become involved with Chinese they are frequently seen as corrupting influences. As a practical matter, you should not take sexual relationships with Chinese citizens lightly—more than one foreigner has gotten into trouble with Chinese authorities for what is regarded as promiscuous behavior. In such cases, the foreign party has generally been expelled from China and the Chinese party sent away for a period of time.

Prostitution, which the communists proudly claimed to have eradicated fully after they liberated China in 1949, has made a decided comeback. Although it is not practiced openly, it undeniably exists in larger cities, and probably elsewhere as well. Since it is illegal, however, it is also dangerous, and foreigners caught in the act can readily be expelled.

Among cross-cultural intimate relationships, it is probably fair to say that the Chinese find it easier to accept those involving foreign women and Chinese men than the opposite. But intimacy with the Chinese is always tricky business, and if you wish to stay out of trouble, it is best reserved for situations in which marriage is both a possibility and a stated intention.

BEING ENTERTAINED
IN A CHINESE HOME

When the PRC first opened up to foreigners in the 1970s, they were virtually never invited to Chinese homes. Foreigners who traveled to China were always there on some sort of business, and business entertainment in China generally takes place in hotels and restaurants. There was never any call to entertain at home, a practice that was usually reserved for hosting very close friends. In the few cases where such invitations were issued, the host had first to secure the approval of his or her work unit.

In this early period there was a real fear of being perceived by neighbors as deliberately trying to cultivate foreign friends for personal benefit—an offense that could lead to investigation by the public security authorities in the area. In China there is nothing like a visit by a foreign guest to draw the neighborhood's attention to the host, and one of the indelible lessons of the Cultural Revolution is that being in the spotlight can often lead to trouble.

Then too, most Chinese live in very modest and Spartan settings, and they are painfully conscious of the fact that they may lack the amenities necessary to make foreign guests comfortable—hot running water, Western-style toilets, carpeted floors, or comfortable furniture, for example. Discharging social obligations through entertaining at restaurants is still the most common course in China.

The use of public places for entertainment—both business and personal—is common practice among Chinese in Hong Kong, Macao, Taiwan, and other Asian countries as well. Foreigners are frequently invited out to restaurants by Chinese people. These can be very pleasant occasions, though there is sometimes an almost obligatory battle at the end over paying the check. Splitting the bill is unheard of among Chinese; one person is expected to take responsibility for the whole check. If it has been made very clear up front who is host and who is guest, then there will be relatively little disagreement when the time comes to settle the bill; the guest may make a gesture toward paying, but the host will generally prevail. If it is unclear, however, there may be a considerable amount of back and forth before agreement is reached.

Unless it has been made clear at the outset that your counterpart is the host for the meal, it is always polite to offer to pay, but sometimes it is not polite to prevail. And it is often hard to know if a Chinese really wishes to treat or is just being polite. If you are unclear on this point, think back to who "owes" whom in the grand scheme of things, that is, who invited whom out last, who did a favor for whom most recently, etc. And think back to who suggested the meal in the first place.

The practice of inviting foreign friends over for a home-cooked dinner is growing in popularity in the PRC. It's often easier for a Chinese with whom you have absolutely *no* business connections to do this than one who may be in a position to negotiate with you at some point. But at any rate, it is no longer unusual for a foreigner resident in China—or even a visitor with a number of Chinese friends—to receive such an invitation.

If you are asked to a Chinese home, the visit will almost always revolve around the taking of a meal. To offer less would be to fail as a host, according to Chinese standards. When the invitation is first extended you may possibly receive a mixed message: although you will be warmly welcomed, and your host really wants you to accept, he or she is also likely to offer endless apologies for the rudimentary nature of the facilities. It's proper in this situation to do what will probably come naturally: reassure the host that wherever he or she lives and whatever has been planned will be fine with you.

If you must decline the invitation for some reason, by all means explain what the conflict is. If you don't take the trouble to do this, the Chinese will read your response as a rebuff, and will assume that your real reason for declining is that you do not wish to pursue the relationship with him or her. Since this constitutes something of a loss of face, you will likely never be asked again, and it's possible that you may notice an unpleasant change in your relationship with the person. It's best not only to give a concrete excuse, but also to make it clear that you would be pleased to accept an invitation for another time.

If you accept the invitation, it's probably best to inform the host if you have any relevant dietary restrictions, either for health or religious reasons. You might do this in any country; it makes good sense and it heads off misunderstandings later. When you arrive, do bring a gift with you. A carton of foreign cigarettes, a bottle of imported liquor, instant coffee, or a box of foreign-made chocolates are gifts that are generally very much appreciated. Avoid cut flowers, as the Chinese associate these with funerals, but fresh fruit is always appreciated. If the gift is wrapped, the host may not open it in front of you unless you specifically request it (see Chapter 8). If you have selected the gift carefully and wish to be present when it is opened, explain to the host that you hope he or she will follow the Western custom of opening the gift in front of the giver. But don't insist if you encounter any resistance.

The preliminaries—tea and conversation in a sitting area— will probably resemble those of a formal banquet held at a restaurant (See Chapter 7). Never ask for food or drink; it's polite to wait until it is offered. Don't be put off by the fact that the hospitality may seem excessively formal to you—again, the correctness probably only reflects the value placed on the relationship with you. As the meal proceeds, you will probably notice that the emphasis on protocol will wane, until it feels more and more like an informal gathering of friends.

In most Chinese households, it is the mother who is responsible for cooking. She is very likely to appear to greet you when you first arrive and then disappear into the kitchen to cook the dinner. Since Chinese meals are generally served a course at a time, and since most Chinese live in one-wok homes, the mother may not reappear until she has churned out all of the dishes. She will then eat what is left. In such situations it is not necessary to wait until the cook is finished before eating; indeed, to do so will only make the host nervous and uncomfortable. It's fine to ask after the mother and to wonder aloud if she will be joining in the feast, but by all means follow the host's lead and eat when the food is first served. Eat a lot to show that you are enjoying the food. But if you know that the cook will eventually join the rest of the group, don't eat the last bit of any dish; leave a taste for mother.

Be sure to find nice things to say about the surroundings and the food. Relentlessly counter every apology you hear (e.g., "The food is really not so tasty," or "My wife is not such a good cook") with a protest and a compliment. After the meal is over, wait a respectable period of time before leaving. If you rise to leave too abruptly, your host may conclude that you have been offended in some way. Since Chinese by and large are early diners, dinner may be over as early as eight-thirty in the evening, or even earlier on weekends. On the other hand, don't stay late into the night; leaving between a half-hour and an hour after the meal is finished is a good rule of thumb.

It's good manners to repay the invitation if this is possible, though this courtesy is not strictly required. If, for example, you are just passing through and will not have enough time in the city to host a return meal, you are relieved of the obligation. Even if you do reciprocate, it need not be in kind; you may invite the host's family on an outing, a picnic, or a meal in a restaurant.

DRESS

It used to be a faux pas to present a tie clasp as a business gift to someone in the PRC—an absurdity in the land of the Mao jacket, where ties were nowhere to be seen. Yet some of the most obvious changes in China during the 1980s have occurred in the notion of acceptable forms of dress. Western clothing is becoming commonplace and to give the occasional tie tack or pair of cufflinks isn't such a bad idea anymore.

Dress in the People's Republic was until recently a fairly dreary affair. There was little choice; men were expected to wear Mao jackets—loose-fitting jackets actually called *Zhongshan zhuang* after the Mandarin pronunciation of the name of Sun Yat-sen, the father of modern China and the man who first made them popular. They were available in blue, brown, green, and gray—period. Loose-fitting white shirts were the rule, worn tucked at the waist under sweaters in cold weather, or hanging out over the belt in the summer.

For women, a pants suit variation on *Zhongshan zhuang* with an open-collared tunic and a pair of slacks was standard. There were no skirts or dresses, and even the traditional Chinese dress, the *qipao*, a tight-fitting garment with a high collar and a long slit up the leg, was forbidden as too revealing. The few colors that were available were dark and conservative in the extreme. Only children were permitted to dress in bold, festive colors. The bright reds, blues, and oranges visible in any kindergarten class gave one the distinct impression that people were enjoying these forbidden colors and styles in the only way they could—vicariously through their children.

This was the era in which communist China was derided abroad as a "nation of blue ants." And indeed, some customs regarding dress were fairly regimented—such as the official switching over to the summer uniform that occurs nearly universally on May 1 regardless of whether the weather has changed or not. This practice continues to this day, in fact.

Standardization of dress probably got its start as the dictum of a government committed to stamping out individualism, but in latter years it became more a function of social pressure than anything else. The Chinese take much comfort in conformity. It's when you are obviously different from others that you turn yourself into a lightning rod for criticism and shame. An old Chinese expression says it all: *chutou chuanzi xian lan.* It means that exposed rafters are the first to rot; that is, he who sticks his neck out bears the brunt.

For many years Western dress has been the rule rather than the exception among Chinese everywhere in the world save the China mainland. More recently it has become common in the PRC as well, and in fact it has received de facto government blessing as members of the party's Central Committee themselves sport Western suits in public situations and permit themselves to be photographed in them. Even Chinese work units sometimes underwrite the cost of Western suits for their employees. Though the suit has by no means supplanted the Mao jacket, both are now considered acceptable forms of dress for Chinese men. Skirts and dresses are now worn by women as frequently as the Chinese-style pants suits described above. Bright colors are being worn increasingly by adults. And even makeup, once roundly criticized as an unacceptable remnant of capitalism, is becoming more and more widespread.

You should infer no particular political significance from a Chinese person's choice of costume. The Mao jacket does not imply that the wearer is a zealous communist, nor does a sleek, European-cut suit necessarily signal a sophisticated democrat. And the old saw that you can tell how important a Chinese cadre is by counting the number of pockets on his tunic may once have been true within the military, but is not a useful distinction today. The only feature that seems to correlate consistently with status is quality of material—not unlike the situation in the West.

Because many offices and meeting rooms in the PRC are unheated, it's important to dress warmly during the winter months. To cope with this problem, Chinese in north China generally dress in layers—long underwear, a shirt, a sweater, a bulky tunic, and a winter coat. It's a simple matter to peel off a layer or two should the surroundings get too warm, as in foreigners' hotels, which may be overheated in winter.

It is not an overgeneralization to say that as a rule, Chinese in the PRC couldn't care less how foreigners dress, unless of course they wear clothing that offends the Chinese sense of propriety. As long as you stay with reasonably conservative garments, this should not be much of a problem. Women should avoid clothing that is too revealing, however, such as sleeveless tank tops, halter tops, see-through blouses, and short skirts. Bikini bathing suits are also unacceptable. It's a good idea as well to wear only a small amount of jewelry when in the PRC and to forego expensive-looking fur coats. This is not so much for propriety's sake as it is to avoid appearing ostentatious in what is and remains a poor country.

Short pants on foreigners have traditionally evoked stares, though this is changing somewhat as they grow in popularity among the Chinese themselves. Still, if you have exceptionally hairy legs, count on raising an eyebrow or two on the streets of most Chinese cities if you opt to wear shorts. And stay away from all-white outfits, especially during festive occasions: white is the color of mourning in China.

There is little understanding in China of the concept of matching the formality of an occasion with appropriate dress.

Since most Chinese in the PRC own only a few changes of clothes, it is not uncommon for them to wear the same suit frequently over a period of a few days, regardless of the setting. You won't see this in Taiwan or Hong Kong, where fashion is considered quite important and wardrobes are extensive.

In the PRC, however, most men don't really understand the difference between a suit jacket and a sports jacket, demonstrated by the fact that they will often wear a suit jacket with a nonmatching pair of slacks. Look out also for untucked shirts, ties that dangle outside of pullover sweaters, and iridescent socks.

Don't bother asking the Chinese what the appropriate dress is for a particular event; they will probably only suggest that you wear what makes you comfortable. A sweater and skirt will generally do as well as a dress, and a jacket and tie can generally fill in for a suit. For important occasions like a banquet in Beijing's Great Hall of the People, you will certainly want to dress well, if only because the other foreign guests who attend will probably be decked out. But a dark suit is as formal as China gets for men; by all means leave the tuxedo at home.

RECAP: TEN TIPS
FOR FOREIGNERS IN CHINA

1. The Chinese are generally extremely hospitable and quite pleasant to Western visitors. Their view of the West is often schizophrenic, however. The West, they believe, is highly advanced in many ways, but somewhat immoral at the same time.

2. Lacking another set of standards, many Chinese judge Westerners and their behavior according to their own norms. But expectations are low. Displaying some knowledge of Chinese customs earns you admiration.

3. Business relationships begin formally. Rank distinctions are important; with those of higher station you must be careful to be correct in behavior and not to appear presumptuous.

4. When dealing with lower-ranking people, never give the impression that you think yourself more important than others, but don't be too informal, either.

5. The Chinese accord foreign businesswomen all the respect due their positions. Spouses of foreign businessmen
are welcomed by the Chinese at social occasions. A wife
is considered to share the rank of her husband. Chinese
spouses seldom show up at business receptions in the
PRC, however.
6. Chinese are often circumspect about keeping foreigners at
arm's length, though this is changing. Casual acquaintance does not demand any significant commitment, but
friendship implies obligation to the Chinese.
7. The Chinese are puritanical about sex; sex outside of marriage is taboo. Foreigners are perceived to be extremely
permissive in this area. You should not take sexual relationships with Chinese citizens lightly.
8. If you are asked to a Chinese home, the visit generally
includes a meal. If you must decline, explain what the
conflict is; if you don't, the Chinese will read your
response as a rebuff.
9. If you accept, bring a gift with you. Eat a lot to show that
you are enjoying the food. Counter every apology you
hear with a compliment. After the meal, wait a respectable period of time before leaving. And reciprocate the
invitation if possible.
10. Western dress is growing in popularity in the PRC, but the
Chinese remain uncomfortable with clothing that is very
revealing. The Chinese are not otherwise particularly
sensitive to what foreigners wear, so wear what makes you
comfortable. Formal dress is never necessary in the PRC.

7

The Chinese Banquet

A colleague of mine who was walking down a street in Beijing once happened to run into a Chinese government staff member whom he had escorted around the United States on a delegation trip earlier that year. The Chinese was delighted to see him and asserted immediately that Vice Minister Guo—who had headed that delegation—would be happy to learn that my coworker was in town and would insist on inviting him out to a banquet.

The Chinese being magnanimous hosts, they invited me to go along as well. But when we arrived at the restaurant at the appointed time, it was apparent in short order that Vice Minister Guo, who was at that point on the verge of retirement, didn't really remember my colleague at all, and in fact only had a dim recollection of his trip to the United States. But that didn't really make much difference. Though the conversation was somewhat labored, the food was excellent, and everyone had a good time.

I learned two lessons from this experience. First, that foreigners are not necessarily invited to Chinese banquets because of any strong personal bonds. The feasts are principally used by the Chinese as vehicles to deliver on social or business obligations—in this case, a way to say thanks for the hospitality the Chinese group had received some months before in the United States. The second lesson was that banquets aren't necessarily held for the guest. Equally often, the guest simply provides a convenient excuse for Chinese workers to partake of a good meal at the State's expense, or to deliver on obligations to fellow Chinese who can be invited to the same banquet.

This isn't to say that there aren't often very warm feelings between hosts and guests at banquets, especially when they have shared experiences together—whether that be a trip down the Yangzi River or days of protracted contract negotiations. It is simply to point out that among the Chinese, banquets serve many purposes in addition to sampling good food and drink.

ENTERTAINING OUT

As discussed in the previous chapter, the Chinese seldom entertain foreigners in their homes; they may be embarrassed about their modest living conditions, or they may simply not have enough room to accommodate a full complement of dinner guests. Playing host to a guest at a meal in a nice restaurant has always been a practical solution; it is common practice in the PRC as well as elsewhere in Asia.

Among the Chinese, there are a thousand excuses for holding a banquet: to welcome or say farewell to a visiting delegation from a foreign country; to mark the signing of a business agreement; to reciprocate a banquet held in your honor the night before; to celebrate a birth, a wedding, or a relative's sixtieth birthday; to observe the Spring Festival, mid-Autumn Festival, or some other holiday; to show appreciation for a kindness or a favor; to send a friend off on a long trip or to welcome one back. Banquets vary in formality depending on the nature and importance of the occasion, the number of people, the individual personalities involved, and their relationships with one another.

Banquets have become so commonplace, in fact, that from time to time the government cracks down on some of the excesses associated with them. Specific units have been criticized for spending too much money on them. Municipal governments have ordered units under their aegis to keep the number of formal meals to a minimum and to keep expenditures on such entertainment to reasonable levels.

THE FORMAL BANQUET

For more formal banquets, guests receive invitation cards that officially request their attendance prior to the occasion. The cards are generally mere formalities, issued only after the host knows the guest has agreed to attend. An intermediary has usually made contact and determined whether the time is convenient. The cards specify date, time, place, and the name of the host, often using fairly honorific language (e.g., "Please grace us with your honorable presence").

Invitations are generally written in Chinese or in both Chinese and English. They may request an RSVP, which can be delivered in person or by telephone. They are often hand-delivered, and may arrive as late as a few hours before the meal is scheduled to begin, though only after a verbal invitation has been proffered and accepted. Only at large gatherings in locations such as Beijing's Great Hall of the People must invitations actually be produced in order to gain entry to the banquet hall.

If the banquet is being held in honor of a delegation, the members of the group are expected to arrive together. This avoids any awkwardness that could ensue if an important guest were late but others arrived on time. Promptness is considered a virtue among the Chinese, and it is never polite to keep a host waiting—still less a guest. It is proper for the hosts to arrive at the restaurant early and be in the banquet room waiting when the guests appear. As with business meetings, the host typically stations a representative outside the door to the restaurant to escort the visitors to the banquet room upon arrival.

RECEPTION OF GUESTS

Chinese banquet rooms generally include large or small groupings of comfortable, overstuffed chairs immediately adjacent to the dining tables. As a guest, you will be received in these seating areas when you arrive, unless the gathering is too large; in such cases only the principal guests will be so received. As in business meetings, if you are the principal guest you will be seated to the right of the principal host, with an interpreter stationed nearby to facilitate conversation. The second-ranking person in your party should be placed to the left of the host or somewhere else nearby and within earshot.

Tea is served, either by restaurant attendants or by someone in the host's party, and cigarettes are offered. Washcloths are often provided as well for all to clean their hands and wipe their faces; they are provided piping hot in winter and cold in summer, and are very refreshing. They are useful for cleaning up, because many restaurants in China do not provide napkins during the meal. They may be left on a table or returned to a service person after use.

Conversation during this initial reception period, which generally lasts only about five minutes, is normally kept light and nonsubstantive. Your Chinese host may inquire about the details of your day, ask how you are enjoying your visit to China, or comment that you have managed to bring good weather. After a signal from the restaurant staff that all is in readiness, the host will suggest that the group adjourn to the tables to begin the meal. He or she may say something like *bian chi, bian shuo*, which means "let's continue the conversation as we eat."

SEATING

When the host announces that it is time to sit down, all members of his or her party will help the guests find their seats, a polite gesture. Name cards at each place setting announce who is to sit where. They are often written in the native language of the diner, a practice that helps you to find your own place but does not give much help in figuring out the name of the person seated at either side. When prepared properly, the name cards are written in both languages.

Seating at formal banquets is determined before guests arrive and is arranged according to fairly rigid protocol. It is not uncommon for the Chinese to change the seating plan a number of times before the event as RSVPs are received. High-ranking guests must be accorded all of the respect and honor that their ranks dictate, and everyone moves up a notch when someone of higher station does not appear.

Knowing who outranks whom is key to making proper seating arrangements. An ostensibly egalitarian society, the PRC is in fact exceptionally protocol-conscious. As a result, if the Chinese are not properly informed they will make assumptions that are not always accurate. When Chinese travel abroad, any delegation list they produce can be relied on to be an accurate indication of the relative rank of each of the members—people are listed in strict protocol order, from the top down. This protocol is important to them, and it helps everyone to understand each person's proper place in the scheme of things.

An early foreign visitor to China I know can recall a situation in which seemingly random seating arrangements at a banquet was later traced to a simple alphabetical list of delegation members that had found its way into the hands of the Chinese hosts. Even today, anomalies still occur when the Chinese are not adequately informed. They find it as difficult to divine whether a senior vice president outranks an executive vice president in a given company as a foreigner might if he or she were trying to figure out whether a bureau chief is above a division director in a Chinese ministry.

The Chinese, as discussed in the previous chapter, encourage foreign friends to bring their spouses to banquets, and invitations are usually extended explicitly to spouses. They seldom bring their own wives or husbands along, however, unless the relationships between host and guest are particularly close. When you host a banquet, it is polite to ask Chinese counterparts to bring their husbands or wives, but you should never push the matter if you are rebuffed—which you probably will be.

Banquets typically take place around round tables that seat between ten and twelve people each. As many tables will be set up in the room as are necessary to seat all of the guests. The group should be distributed relatively evenly across all available tables so that a thirty-person banquet, for example, would most likely break down to ten people at each table rather than twelve, twelve, and six. If possible, the number of Chinese and foreigners should be in approximate balance at each table.

The table furthest from the door to the room is usually designated as the head table. The principal guest is seated there in a place of honor at the immediate right of the principal host, facing the door. An interpreter sits in the immediate vicinity, usually to the right of the guest, as shown in Figure 4.

The second-ranking Chinese may sit directly across the head table from the principal host, with the second-ranking person in your party at his or her immediate right, just across from the principal guest. An interpreter is also placed in the immediate vicinity, as shown in Figure 5.

If this arrangement is used, the third- and fourth-ranking Chinese hosts and foreign guests are seated at the second table, fifth- and sixth-ranking at the third table, and so on, in a fashion similar to the head table, taking care that the main hosts at each table can maintain eye contact with the principal host.

Alternatively, the second-ranking Chinese may be seated at the second table, with the second-ranking foreigner at his or her immediate right, mirroring the arrangement at the head table. The angle is shifted somewhat, however, again allowing the hosts to maintain eye contact, as shown in Figure 6.

Following this scheme, a third-ranking host and guest would be seated at table three, and so on until all available tables were filled. Then the next host in the hierarchy would fill in the second position at table one, then table two, etc. In either scenario, lower ranking guests are placed in empty seats until all tables are complete.

In China, round tables are the rule, but seating can be adapted to rectangular tables fairly easily. The same rules apply, except that the host is placed in the middle of one of the long sides of the rectangle, with the guest at his or her right. The interpreter may be seated across the table from them or to their left or right.

Banquets often involve guests from organizations other than those of the hosts and the guests. A Chinese business executive

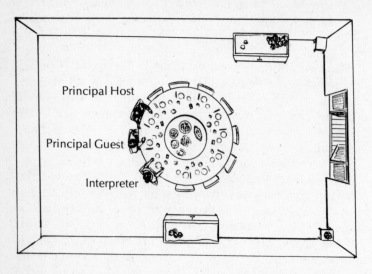

Principal Host

Principal Guest

Interpreter

FIGURE 4. The principal guest at a Chinese banquet sits facing the door to the room, to the immediate right of the principal host. An interpreter is stationed nearby to facilitate conversation.

may invite a representative of another Chinese organization to a banquet for a foreign visitor, or perhaps more than one foreign company has sent delegates to China for a particular purpose, and the Chinese host is entertaining all of them together. In such cases, the rule is that the highest-ranking individual from every organization represented at the banquet should be accorded a place of honor, and this generally means being seated at the head table. The place to the immediate left of the principal host is often used for such guests. Spouses of invited guests are accommodated at the same table as their partners unless this is not feasible (e.g., there are too many VIPs present, and including spouses at the head table would force some of them to table two). It is considered a special honor to place a spouse in the seat immediately to the left of the host.

Common sense dictates that there be exceptions to any rigid seating protocol, and there are. The Chinese find it as awkward as anyone else when people seated at the same table

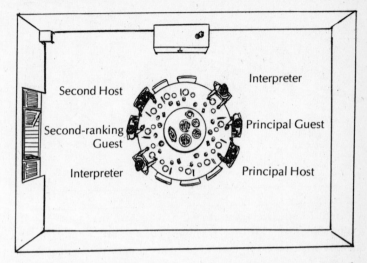

FIGURE 5. The second-ranking host is seated directly opposite the principal host, with the second-ranking guest immediately to his or her right.

cannot communicate with one another because they have no common language. Thus interpreters are seated where they are needed, without regard to their rank or status. And other bilingual people, even if not officially designated as interpreters, are also dispersed as necessary.

THE PLACE SETTING

The place setting at a formal Chinese banquet consists of a bowl for rice or soup, a shallow dish for main courses, a smaller dish for condiments and sauces, a dessert dish, a porcelain spoon, a pair of chopsticks, and a metal or porcelain chopstick rest. There may be as many as three drinking glasses: a medium-sized glass for beer or soda, a smaller wine glass, and a piece of stemware reserved for hard liquor that is smaller still.

Not all of the utensils are present at all times; some are changed frequently, after a course or two has been served. A

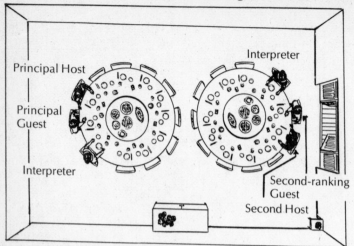

FIGURE 6. Alternatively, the second-ranking host may be seated at a second table, with the second-ranking guest to his or her right. The angle is rotated a bit so that hosts may maintain eye contact during the meal.

lazy Susan sits in the middle of the table; entrees are placed on it and individuals may rotate it at will in order to reach a dish. In China, everyone shares the entrees; you don't appropriate a dish for yourself, but rather you are served, family-style, from a common plate.

Visitors to China should endeavor to learn to use chopsticks if at all possible, if only because they may run into situations where no forks are available. The Chinese are not offended by those who have not mastered the art of using chopsticks, but they do appreciate the effort. It isn't as hard as it may appear. When all else fails, the porcelain spoon present at every place setting may be used to scoop up food. It's a bit inelegant, but no serious breach of etiquette.

You'll seldom see knives at a Chinese table. They are occasionally provided at the end of the meal for the purpose of peeling an apple or a pear, but they are not part of the standard table setting unless the meal is intended to be some kind of blend of East and West. The Chinese don't use knives while dining because they consider the knife a weapon, and it is of course impolite to brandish a weapon at a table where friends are sharing a meal. Also, since cutting and chopping are both part of the Chinese chef's craft, they are typically done in the kitchen before Chinese food is cooked.

THE MEAL

A plate of cold—or rather, room-temperature—appetizers is generally on the table when the party first sits down, or else it is served very shortly thereafter. There are usually at least four different types of delicacies on the cold platter, and there may be many more. To the Chinese the presentation of food is as important as its taste, and nowhere is this more evident than in the cold platter, which begins the meal. The appetizers may be artfully arranged in the shape of a flower, a dragon, a goldfish, a peacock, a phoenix, a Chinese lantern, or a butterfly, to name just a few examples. And they may be made out of barbecued pork, duck, chicken, ham, pickled vegetables, bean curd, jellyfish, cuttlefish, seaweed, or any of a couple of dozen other ingredients.

When the table is laid, the place settings of the principal and second hosts at each table are augmented with an additional set of chopsticks, and perhaps a serving spoon. These implements are not used to eat; only to serve. This is as much a sanitary measure as it is a point of etiquette.

No one samples a dish until the principal host has broken into it first. He or she will serve the principal guest first and then any other guests within reach. Following this—or, sometimes, simultaneously—the second host does the same.

Frequently the restaurant's serving staff takes over from there, dividing the remaining food among all the guests. This is not traditional, but the practice is becoming more common in China today, since hepatitis, a growing danger, can be readily spread when individuals dip their personal chopsticks into a common dish of food.

Only after a dish has been broken into and the guests served may individuals—Chinese or foreign—freely help themselves to more. The banquet begins without fanfare when the host breaks into the cold platter; no grace is said, nor are any other rituals observed. The host may say something like *qing yong*—literally, "please use"—or may simply signal by example that it is time to start.

A cardinal rule of Chinese banqueting is that it is the responsibility of the host and his or her party to make sure that all guests are served. This obligation continues throughout the meal and will find its expression in constant monitoring of the guest's plate. When the plate is empty, someone from the Chinese side will reach over to fill it—and without necessarily checking to see if the chosen morsel meets with approval. If you continue to clean your plate, someone nearby will continue to serve you food. Thus it is vitally important to leave a small amount of food in your dish when you have finished eating; this is the only clear signal you can give that you are not hungry for more.

Although the host is theoretically responsible for feeding the guests, there is nothing that says a polite guest can't try to turn the tables. In point of fact, the Chinese will attempt to serve foreign guests at Chinese-style banquets whether they are technically the guests or the hosts, and whether the meals take place in China or abroad. If you as a guest attempt to return the compliment by reaching to fill the plate of a Chinese host, you may get a good-natured protest—in the form of *buyao keqi* or "You needn't be so polite"—but regardless, it is seen as a very well-mannered and even somewhat flattering gesture. If you don't have access to the special pair of serving chopsticks laid out for the hosts, you should take your own chopsticks and reverse them, serving others with the larger ends, opposite those that have gone into your mouth.

A banquet may feature a dozen courses or more. Glance at the menu that is often placed next to the principal host; even if it is written in Chinese, counting the number of lines will give you a rough idea of what is in store and will help you pace yourself accordingly. A common mistake is to eat heartily of the first few dishes and have no appetite left for what follows. This not only prevents you from enjoying some of the best entrees; it also may sometimes be misinterpreted by your hosts. If, in the middle of a banquet, you suddenly appear to lose interest in eating, they may mistakenly conclude that they have done something to offend you.

After the cold platter come two to four stir-fried dishes,

followed by a soup, and then three or four larger hot dishes that are considered to be the main courses. Look for considerable variety in ingredients, methods of preparation, and tastes in these courses. Likely as not there will be some red meat, some poultry, some fish, and some vegetables; something steamed, something roasted, something stewed, and something deep-fried; and something sweet, salty, sour, and spicy. Sweets may occasionally be served in between courses to cleanse the palate.

The signal that the meal is coming to an end is usually the presentation of a whole fish, the last of the main courses. This is sometimes followed by a starch, either rice—a symbolic gesture, since people are seldom hungry for it at this point—or noodles or buns. Finally there is a sweet soup and a dessert, usually fresh fruit of some kind.

The ingredients in most of the dishes are self-evident, but it's fine to ask what you are eating if you don't know. The Chinese love talking about food, and given half a chance they will be happy to give you a discourse on regional variation in Chinese cuisine. A word of warning, though: some fancy banquet dishes have poetic names that give no information about their actual ingredients, such as "stuffed fairy feet with shrimp" (duck feet filled with ham, peas, and shrimp paste), "eight treasures rice pudding" (glutinous rice with lotus seeds, dates, peanuts, lychees, walnuts, raisins, candied orange peel, and red bean paste), and "ants climbing up a tree" (ground pork with rice vermicelli).

You should endeavor if at all possible to try at least a taste of each dish that is served. While it will never cause an international incident if you decline some food, to do so can be seen as somewhat ungracious. If you absolutely cannot steel yourself to down a rubbery piece of sea slug or a translucent green thousand-year-old egg, declining is certainly a better alternative than gagging at the table. Learn to push the food around in your plate a bit so it looks as if you have sampled it, and smile politely when you decline additional servings. And remember this feeling when a Chinese visiting you in your own country politely abstains from the raw cauliflower in bleu cheese dip you have so carefully prepared (see Chapter 11).

CONVERSATION

There are no set rules concerning what may or may not be discussed in a banquet situation except to let good common sense govern. Even if a delegation is in China for lengthy and complicated negotiations, the Chinese will not necessarily choose to continue those discussions over a meal. They may try to use the time to get to know their counterparts a little better and engage in some lighthearted conversation and fun.

There is no reason, however, that substantive conversation can't take place during a meal, provided that the exchange remains cordial and face is preserved at all times. Sometimes the principal host at a banquet is not a member of the negotiating team, but rather an official of very high rank with an interest in the particular project under discussion. The banquet may provide the only opportunity the foreign delegation gets to meet with this official, and to limit the conversation to simple pleasantries would be a waste of everyone's time. One caveat, though: under no circumstances should the principal host be put in a position of having to refuse a request made by a member of the delegation. This constitutes a serious breach of etiquette.

When both sides already know each other reasonably well, conversation generally flows freely, since there are shared experiences to discuss. When this is not true there can be some awkward moments. While it is not necessary to fill every moment with witty conversation, prolonged silences are to be avoided if only because they make so many people uncomfortable.

Fail-safe topics of conversation that can come to the rescue include weather; Chinese food, geography, or language; your own history of travel in China or elsewhere in the world; your Chinese counterpart's travels abroad; or your business reasons for visiting China. Even international politics can be discussed, as long as the discussion does not get heated. Chinese seldom stray from the official government position on geopolitical issues, and are even less likely to do so in a public situation. So as long as you don't expect to change anyone's way of thinking, and so long as you don't mind a mini-lecture on China's point of view, it's perfectly all right to touch on Sino-Soviet relations, the Cultural Revolution, or even—and this may surprise you—the future of Taiwan or Hong Kong. Just be sensitive enough to steer the conversation elsewhere if you sense the mood stiffening at all.

Though the ostensible purpose of the banquet is for everyone to have a good meal and a good time, these situations—like any social situations—carry with them some obligations. For example, you are expected to keep a running conversation going with your counterpart on the other side. When Westerners find it difficult to identify common ground with their Chinese hosts or guests, they sometimes try to ameliorate the awkwardness by chatting in their native language with their own colleagues. Though it is perfectly acceptable to involve your teammate in a discussion, it is a real faux pas to give up trying to bridge the gap with the Chinese. Most often it isn't much of an effort at all, but if it is, keep trying anyway. It's worth the effort.

TABLE MANNERS

There are certain differences between the Chinese and Western conceptions of appropriate table manners of which you should be aware. Most important, it isn't generally polite in China to touch your food—still less anyone else's food—with your hands. Chinese food is deliberately cut up into bite-sized pieces in the kitchen before it is served, so that chopsticks will be the only equipment necessary at the table. Only rarely do Chinese use their fingers: when consuming large steamed buns, animal joints, and wings or shellfish, for example. Just keep an eye on what your hosts are doing and follow suit and you won't ever go far wrong.

Though the morsels of food are of manageable size, they may still contain bones or shells. The Chinese are fond of hacking through bone when cutting meat or poultry, or of leaving the shells on shrimp or other shellfish to preserve the flavor. You may see Chinese discard bones or shells on the table next to their place settings or even on the floor; this is not the finest of manners, but it is often done, especially at less formal occasions. At banquets you should remove bits of bone from your mouth (with chopsticks if possible) and place them in a small dish that is part of your place setting and is frequently removed by service personnel. Occasionally a bowl will be passed around for the express purpose of discarding these pieces.

Some of the finer points of Western table etiquette are unknown in China. It is not impolite to place your elbows on the table, for example. Nor do you need to wait until everyone has been served before you begin eating any particular dish. Dishes are not, as a rule, passed around the table; they are placed in the center and you reach across the table to get at them, even if you need to stand up to do so. You needn't worry about keeping your napkin in your lap, since frequently no napkins are provided at all. Service personnel are as likely to serve from the left as the right; there is no rule in China.

There is also no taboo against being a noisy eater. Don't be shocked if your host continues to talk through a mouthful of food, slurps soup, or coughs, hiccups, or sneezes rather loudly during the meal.

When you are helping yourself at a Chinese banquet, use your eyes before you move your hand. That is, select the food you wish to retrieve in advance and then reach directly for it with chopsticks. What is to be avoided here is picking and poking through a common dish to find a chosen morsel. Also, try not to use the chopsticks to spear your food. This is no sin, but the Chinese don't do it. Try if at all possible to capture your food between the tips of two chopsticks.

If you should happen to drop a piece of food on the floor, don't pick it up; just leave it there. If you drop a chopstick, pick it up and give it to a service person, who will replace it. If you pause during the meal, rest the tips of the chopsticks on the chopstick rests provided as part of the place setting. If these are not present, rest them on the rim of a dish; if only for sanitary reasons, they should not touch the table. Nor should they ever be stuck straight up into a bowl of rice when not in use; this reminds the Chinese of sticks of incense burned to commemorate the dead. And you should never point at something with chopsticks. Toothpicks are generally provided at the end of the meal. Feel free to use them, but cover your mouth with your free hand while you do, so that your teeth are not visible to other guests. Finally, it is not particularly polite to belch, though to do so is no cardinal sin in China.

DRINKING AND TOASTING

Drinking figures prominently in the art of Chinese banqueting, just as it does in Chinese literature and mythology. Banquet guests most often are served wine and spirits as well as a choice of beer or soda. You can tell what's coming by a glance at the sideboard as you enter the banquet room. Service personnel have usually lined up bottles of the beverages of choice before the meal begins.

Drinking begins officially when the principal host offers a toast to the entire group. No one should really be drinking spirits before then. If it is a large group the host will stand and address all of the tables; a microphone may even be used. The toast will be relatively short—three to five minutes is about par for the course—and may be anything from a series of platitudes to a well-crafted discourse pregnant with meaning and symbolism. In matters of high-level statecraft it's often the case that there is more to a dinner toast than meets the eye. China watchers in foreign governments often pore over the remarks Chinese leaders deliver to visiting heads of state in order to divine that obscure nugget of meaning lurking in the ambiguity. But a toast may also be no more than a hearty welcome or a statement of principles.

A few courses after the principal host offers the toast, it is the principal guest's turn to do the same. Your remarks should be no longer than those of your host, and generally speaking words that seem to come from the heart evoke the best results. Sharing hopes for the successful conclusion of some business or warm feelings about your counterparts is a tried and true path. Also well-trodden—but safe—are toasts to friendship between the people gathered in the room and their respective countrymen, pledges of cooperation, testaments to the principles of "equality and mutual benefit," and offers of reciprocal hospitality when your counterparts visit your own country.

The toasting ritual is pretty much the same on both sides of
the Taiwan strait, though it is adhered to much less strictly in
Hong Kong. A word of warning is in order, however. If you
offer the toast on behalf of the visiting delegation, you should
take extra care to avoid an all-too-common pitfall of calling the
PRC by the wrong name. The official name of the country is
"The People's Republic of China." It is also acceptable to refer
simply to "China" in a toast.

What is not tolerable, and is in fact particularly offensive to
PRC Chinese, is any reference to "The Republic of China,"
the name still claimed by the Nationalist government on
Taiwan. As far as the communists are concerned, the Republic
ceased to exist in 1949 when they gained control of the
mainland; Taiwan has no national status of its own and is
simply a province of the PRC. It is also not considered correct
in the PRC to use terms such as "mainland China" or "communist China," as both of these imply that there is more than
one China, and any hint of a "two-Chinas policy" is thoroughly anathema to just about any Chinese.

Needless to say, the situation is different if you are offering
a toast to an audience in Taiwan. There any mention of "The
Republic of China" will be extremely welcome, as it confers
legitimacy on the government's decades-old claim of sover-
eignty not only over the island of Taiwan, but over the whole
of the China mainland. In Taiwan any mention of the PRC is
considered anathema. And any reference to "Chicoms" or
"Chinats"—wartime nicknames for the Chinese communists
and the Chinese nationalists—is considered to be in as bad
taste in Taiwan as it is on the mainland. Similarly you should
avoid at all costs the use of the word "Chinaman," which is
also offensive.

In large and convivial banquets, the principal host and guest
will sometimes leave the head table and walk around to all the
other tables in the room, offering toasts to each. This is a very
polite gesture, and those sitting at the other tables are expected
to rise and acknowledge the toast.

Following the toast, you typically say *ganbei*, a Chinese
phrase that literally means "dry glass," and has the same effect
as "bottoms up" in English, though an overzealous interpreter

once was heard to translate it as "bottoms together," to the amusement of the English-speaking guests. All stand up and join in at this point, and proceed to empty their glasses of spirits or wine. After drinking, the cups are turned upside down to demonstrate that they contain no more liquid. Emptying them is a bit easier than it may sound, since the glasses provided for these beverages are really quite small, and hold less fluid than, say, a shot glass.

On the other hand, consider for a minute the contents of the glass. More often than not the beverage of choice for toasting is *maotai*, a fiery, 106-proof wheat- and sorghum-based liquor that can quite literally catch fire or take the paint off of the ceiling. Downing a glass of it is considered somewhat macho by the Chinese, but it is not required. You may also toast with wine, beer, or a soft drink, even if the person offering the toast is drinking something harder. You should not, however, begin the meal by drinking spirits and switch halfway through to something softer; this could be misconstrued as a means of demonstrating that you have taken offense at something that was said or done during the meal.

There is an alternative to *ganbei* if you don't feel up to emptying the glass. You can say *suiyi*, which means "at will" or "as you please." This frees you to drink as much or as little as you wish. If you do not wish to drink alcohol at all, you must simply make this clear at the start of the meal. One effective way is to tell your hosts that you are allergic to alcohol. If you use another excuse, be prepared for some good-natured ribbing on the part of the Chinese, who may attempt to goad you into drinking. But rest assured that if you don't choose to drink, they can be counted on to forbear; many Chinese don't drink liquor, either.

Strictly speaking, it is not polite to pour a drink for yourself; someone else at the table should notice that your glass is empty and take the initiative. This is especially true when drinking tea. If no one seems to notice that your glass is dry, pick up the decanter and fill someone else's glass; this generally results in the same being done for you. Among the Cantonese, natives of China's southeasternmost province who also constitute most of the population of Hong Kong, there is a custom of rapping your knuckles on the table to say thanks to someone who is filling your tea cup; when you stop tapping, the person knows to stop pouring. This practice may or may not be understood by Chinese elsewhere, however.

Traditionally, it is not considered polite to drink alone at a Chinese banquet. You really should not drink at all before the initial toast and return toast are offered, except for beer or a soft drink. After that, however, it's pretty much a free-for-all. Anyone may offer a toast, either to the entire table, or to one or two individuals present. If you're really thirsty but don't have any meaningful remarks on the tip of your tongue, simply catch the eye of someone else at the table and raise your glass in his direction. He or she will then join you in a drink. Or, if you wish, steal a sip of beer or a soft drink on your own. Just be sure you are toasting someone else when you imbibe harder spirits.

CONCLUDING THE BANQUET

Chinese banquets tend to last no more than one and a half to two hours. Dinners usually begin rather early—generally at about six-thirty—and so by around half past eight the meal is essentially over. Unlike the West, China has no tradition of lingering after the meal; after the fruit is served, the banquet is over. A final glass of tea may be offered, and a second washcloth may be presented. The Chinese host may then observe that you are probably tired after your long day, or you may seize the initiative and remark that it has been a delightful meal and thank the host on behalf of your group. It is good manners to indicate to the host during the last course that you have eaten to satiation. The Chinese expression *chi bao le*, which means "eaten to the point of satiation," is useful here.

The guests rise to leave and are escorted to the door of the room by the principal host; it is not necessary for him or her to see them to their cars, though a member of the host's party will probably accompany them that far. The host remains behind. The bill is settled with the restaurant only after the guests have departed; it is considered rude to handle money in their presence.

RECIPROCATING

No formal thank-you notes for banquets are written in China. The way to show appreciation—unless the banquet was offered to reciprocate some other favor in the first place—is by returning the favor in kind. It is not uncommon for a delegation with only two nights to spend in a particular city to be hosted at a banquet the first night and to treat the Chinese to a reciprocal feast on the next.

If you are in the position of playing host, there are some details of which you should be aware. First, you need to make a reservation as early as possible at a restaurant or a hotel that has private banquet rooms. Many restaurants in the PRC will not accept large groups without one or two days' notice. In making arrangements, you specify the price per head—the *biaozhun*—that you are willing to pay. The restaurant will often give a range of fees from which to choose. Some negotiation can occur here, but in the PRC you are generally successful in shaving no more than about 10 percent off of the figure quoted by the restaurant. Any of the prices quoted will result in enough food for the party; after a point, adding to the *biaozhun* only means that more exotic ingredients will be used—the sign of a quality banquet—not that more food will be served.

The fee does not include liquid refreshments, which are charged according to the amount consumed. You will be asked what beverages you wish to offer, however. It's a safe bet to include *maotai*, a wine, beer, and a soft drink. You might consider ordering *maotai* even if you don't plan to drink any yourself, since it is another sign of a quality banquet. But substitutes are available. You will also be asked if you wish cigarettes to be provided in the banquet room; this is traditionally done.

It's generally safe to leave the specifics of the menu to the discretion of the restaurateur; you'll seldom be disappointed with what you are served. If you have a particular dish in mind, however, don't hesitate to suggest it. And you may review the menu in advance and suggest changes if you so desire. Resist the desire to scratch the sea slug or the fish maw from the menu; as unappetizing as these entrees may be to foreigners, the Chinese relish them as delicacies. They are also tangible evidence that you haven't skimped on the price.

The restaurant's manager may also want to know who your Chinese guests will be. This is not necessarily idle curiosity; the manager may want to know how important your guests are in order to determine how hard the staff needs to work on the meal to preserve the face of the restaurant. He or she also may know the principal guest and want to be on hand personally to express a greeting when the cadre arrives at the restaurant.

You should also know that it is a Chinese custom to provide for the chauffeurs who bring attendees to the banquet. This does not mean that drivers take part in the meal itself; it simply means that a fee—considerably less than the per-head charge for your banquet—is often paid to the restaurant to feed them in a separate room. It is customary to provide for your own group's drivers as well as those of the guests. Recently, however, the custom has evolved into a direct cash payment to drivers, who may either eat at the restaurant—which is probably excessively expensive by their standards—or go elsewhere and pocket the difference.

When planning the banquet, draw up your guest list and check with your Chinese liaison to see if you are asking the right people. The principal guest should be of approximately equivalent rank to the head of your group or else there may be some discomfort on the Chinese part. Use an intermediary if possible to sound out the guests; it isn't polite to put someone in the position of having to decline an invitation to your face. If someone cites a concrete conflict when declining, he or she is probably sincere. If a vague excuse is given, however, chances are the person just doesn't want to accept your hospitality.

When you are offering the banquet, the host's tasks detailed above, e.g., arranging name cards, seating the guests, making sure that plates are kept full, and toasting, are all your responsibility. Remember that even if you forget some of the finer points of Chinese etiquette, a good-faith effort to do things according to Hoyle will not be wasted on the Chinese. They will happily pitch in and make the banquet a pleasant experience.

RECAP: THE TEN COMMANDMENTS OF BANQUETING

When You are the Host:
1. Make sure your guests are met at the door and escorted to the room. Be present in the room before they arrive so that you can welcome them.
2. Pay close attention to protocol and don't slight anyone by seating him or her inappropriately. If you are not sure exactly how high someone's rank is, be sure to ask. Following standard seating arrangements is always a good idea.
3. Lead your guests to the table and help them find their seats. Use place cards to signal assigned seats; these should be in English and Chinese if possible.
4. Keep a sharp eye on your guests' plates and make sure they are kept full of food. Keep serving them even if they protest.

When You are the Guest:
5. Always leave something over in your plate at the end of the meal. Not to do so implies that you are still hungry.
6. Try to sample every dish if you possibly can. It is not a cardinal sin to eschew a particular dish, however. If you simply can't stomach something, just push it around on your plate a bit and pretend you have sampled it.
7. Pace yourself; there are more dishes coming than you think. Count on about a dozen of them in a formal banquet.
8. Don't suddenly stop eating or drinking in the middle of a meal, lest you make your Chinese counterparts think they have offended you.

9. Decide in advance whether you will drink alcohol or not, and stick to it. Don't start out with *maotai* and suddenly switch to Coca-Cola.

10. Never drink the toasting beverage alone; always find someone to drink with you. Whenever you are thirsty, however, it is all right to drink some beer or a soft drink.

8

Gift-Giving

The Chinese—indeed nearly all Asians—are inveterate gift-givers. Gifts may be given as tokens of esteem or gratitude, as souvenirs, as gratuities, or as payoffs. They may also serve to discharge obligations or mark occasions, or they may accompany overt requests for favors or some other type of patronage. It's especially important for business travelers to be aware of when gifts are and are not expected, and what types of gifts are most appropriate. But even casual travelers should be prepared to offer gifts when the situation requires it.

BUSINESS GIFTS

Delegations visiting China are generally expected to offer to those who host them some sort of token of their visit. Conversely, Chinese traveling to other countries are nearly always prepared with gifts for those who receive them. In the PRC, the modus operandi is to present one large gift to the host organization as a whole rather than a number of small gifts to its individual members. This approach sidesteps an issue peculiar to a socialist system, i.e., whether the delegates should be permitted to keep individual gift items themselves, or whether the items should more correctly be turned in to the organization's leadership and allocated to those workers in the unit who are most deserving or who will find them most useful. A gift to the unit as a whole is thus a very fair way to proceed, since all workers ostensibly benefit equally from such gestures.

Not surprisingly, this is not the way things always work. It is not true in Hong Kong or Taiwan, and it is not even consistently the case in the PRC anymore, especially where foreigners are involved. The practice of giving individual mementos to members of a host group is becoming very common, even among the Chinese themselves. And it is perfectly acceptable in China today, provided that it is done in moderation.

In the early 1970s, when communist China first opened its doors to the West, it was official policy to decline individual gifts from foreigners, and a worker could get into a great deal of trouble if he or she were found to have accepted any sort of present. The reason was fear of corruption: rich foreigners, so the argument went, could afford to offer substantial bribes and entice otherwise model Chinese workers into revealing state secrets or granting concessions in business.

For a number of years, Chinese policy has been guided by a somewhat more moderate approach. Recognizing that more and more contact with foreigners ensures that Chinese officials are frequently offered individual gifts and that policing a very restrictive policy is difficult if not impossible, the Chinese leadership has decreed that small gifts of nominal value may be retained by the recipients, and only more valuable items must be surrendered to the unit. The rule of thumb remains about ten dollars; gifts worth more must technically be turned over to the *danwei* or work unit, where they may be allocated to those who need them most, given as a reward to model workers, or presented to the winners of a drawing.

That's the rule. It's not always the way things happen, however. One constantly hears stories of larger gifts presented to powerful Chinese decision makers by business representatives eager to make a sale or close a deal, similar to practices employed elsewhere in the world. There are also persistent rumors about Chinese officials who actively solicit such gifts. There is unquestionably an increased willingness on the part of many Chinese to play fast and loose with the rules, and more and more instances of corruption are being exposed. Every once in a while the Chinese government will publicize the bringing to justice of a corrupt official in the hope that he or she will serve as a negative example to would-be offenders.

Because gift-giving is an area in which common practice departs somewhat from the published rules, it's hard to be categorical in giving advice on how best to proceed. It really depends on how comfortable you are with taking chances. The most conservative approach is the traditional one: a single large gift for the whole group, presented to the leader either during a meeting or a banquet. Next would be individual gifts to all participants, or even personal tokens presented together with a major unit gift; the personal gifts may be put at the place settings before a banquet begins, and the overall gift presented at the appropriate moment. This approach is not really risky if the dollar limit mentioned above is respected. On the more reckless end of the spectrum would be a very valuable gift presented in private to a powerful individual; the chances of this being misunderstood if discovered are great.

TIPPING

In Hong Kong, and to a lesser extent in Taiwan, you can offer a cash gratuity to waiters, bellhops, and doormen. Except in the deluxe hotels and restaurants, where service charges are often added into your bill anyway, tipping in Hong Kong generally means leaving behind some loose change; there is not really a set percentage as there is in many other parts of the world. In Taiwan you are not traditionally expected to leave a tip at all; though again, with Westernization the custom is gaining a certain amount of popularity in the big cities.

In the PRC tipping is officially forbidden. The Chinese see it as an unpalatable vestige of the more exploitative aspects of capitalism. In the early days when foreigners were first permitted to visit the PRC, it was not unusual for a service person at a restaurant to chase a foreign guest for half a block simply to return a stray coin left on a table after a meal; it often did not even cross the person's mind that the money was meant for him or her.

The government's position has always been that motivation for providing good service to visitors should be the desire to serve the socialist motherland rather than cold cash. But since the motherland doesn't buy you cigarettes and cash does, service in China is notoriously indifferent, and sometimes downright surly. You'll still occasionally run into a selfless waiter or a solicitous room attendant, but personnel at hotels, guesthouses, Friendship stores—hard currency outlets with primarily foreign clientele—and other installations in the PRC that cater to foreigners are increasingly likely to be openly covetous of gratuities. They may let visitors know that government policy notwithstanding, they wish to be tipped. And implied also may be the unstated message that absent such a tangible expression of appreciation, you can just as well whistle for your dinner or your fresh towels.

Again, since standard practice is at odds with the rules, you have to play this one by ear. At many of the joint-venture hotels tipping has become *de rigeur* in recent years, and service personnel such as waiters and taxi dispatchers accept gratuities willingly and openly.

Whatever official policy dictates, there are often situations in which you wish to reward someone for a kindness, or for service above and beyond the call of duty. In these situations, it is best to take some precautions, because service personnel in some places are still occasionally at risk of being severely chastised for accepting gifts from foreign guests. They can be accused of abusing their positions for personal gain.

To reward someone who has been especially solicitous, first make sure that you do it in private; no one else, especially colleagues of the person in question, should be present. Give a gift that fits easily into a pocket, out of sight; some suggestions are given below. Don't pay attention to the one or two obligatory refusal gestures; place the gift in the person's pocket if necessary. On the other hand, if you sense a genuine reluctance to accept the gift, don't force the issue. Count on the Chinese to know better than you whether he or she is at any risk for receiving it.

WHAT TO GIVE

Chinese delegations visiting foreign countries often arrive laden with suitcases. Each delegate generally brings only one or two changes of clothes, however; the rest of the valises are packed full of gifts. Companies, universities, or other organizations that host members of the group or simply meet with them are rewarded with these gift items. And generally speaking, the more the organization has done for the group, the more valuable will be the gift.

The Chinese are fond of giving objects of art and handicrafts produced in China. These may range from the sublime to the hideous; for every painstakingly crafted cloisonné vase, lacquerware serving piece, or hand-painted scroll there is a garish porcelain Buddha, an iridescent velvet wall-hanging, or a grotesque rendering of a bouquet of flowers in bits of shell. It is, however, the thought that counts, and no one can accuse the Chinese of not being thoughtful when it comes to gifts.

If you are giving a major gift to a Chinese organization, objects of art are thus clearly acceptable. One approach is to try to give something created in your own country, and ideally something representative of local arts and crafts. Steuben glass, Revere silver, Wedgwood or Hummel figurines, for example, would all be acceptable. Keep in mind, however, that many Chinese lack the criteria to evaluate objects of Western art, and probably wouldn't fully appreciate the difference between Steuben glass and a molded glass paperweight purchased at a five-and-dime store. A book featuring beautiful photographs of your native land would also be a good gift; many workers who will probably never travel abroad could thumb through the pages and learn something of the world outside.

Another approach is to give something useful. If you are visiting the local harbor officials in a given city, for example, providing a book on port planning or one covering the latest techniques in movement of container cargo would be a very practical present. In such a situation don't worry if the book is written in English; if its contents are valuable to the unit, someone will be charged with translating it into Chinese. Appliances and consumer electronics such as personal computers also qualify as useful gifts; if clearly presented to the unit and not to any individual, they are also acceptable. Just be sure that the voltage is compatible with the Chinese system.

Still another appropriate memento is one that says something about your company. It might be a book about the history of your firm, or perhaps a model or sample of one of your products. If you are in China on a return visit, an album of photographs of your counterparts taken during their trip to your country is a sure winner. If you give a book, having your company's chairman or president inscribe it is an excellent idea; it's a signal to the Chinese that your visit to China has received attention at the highest levels of your organization.

Individual gifts should be small and of modest value. Many items that companies regularly produce in quantity as giveaways are well-received in China: pen and pencil sets, solar calculators, cigarette lighters, tape measures, pen-sized flashlights, penknives, inexpensive digital watches, leather folders, and tote bags are all examples. By all means, leave the company logo on; a logo changes a gift into a memento. If you give individual mementos, it's important to make sure that everyone receives one—not only your hosts, but also the interpreter, the driver, and anyone else involved in offering you hospitality—so bring extras along just in case.

Gifts given to friends or those presented in nonbusiness situations can be more personal. Audio cassettes are always welcome; choose music representative of the type popular at home. Many Americans find that folk and pop music go over extremely well. Foreign liquor, cigarettes, and coffee are also highly appreciated, as are T-shirts with English words on them—it hardly matters what they say. For women, small makeup kits and pantyhose are great gifts, though Chinese women sometimes express a little harmless embarrassment at receiving such objects from foreign men. I've also had great success giving perfume, cologne, and other personal care products that may be difficult to obtain in China.

WHAT NOT TO GIVE

There are relatively few taboos as far as what constitutes an appropriate gift. One traditional prohibition revolves around clocks. The Chinese expression "to give a clock," which is rendered as *song zhong*, is a homonym for a phrase that means "to attend a dying parent." Though most Chinese don't really care, the very superstitious still balk at clocks as presents for this reason. Since it's easy enough to come up with other ideas, if you don't know your audience well it is probably best to stay away from clocks. Similarly, cut flowers should be avoided as these are reminiscent of Chinese funerals.

You should also avoid giving gifts of excessive value. Because of the reciprocal obligation that surrounds gift-giving (see below), to give an extremely expensive present is often to put someone in the position of being unable to repay it in kind. Rendering someone unable to discharge an obligation can result in a loss of face.

Presents are generally wrapped in bright red, which is a festive color for the Chinese; they may be covered in other colors as well, but never in white. To the Chinese, white connotes death and mourning. This does *not* mean that the color white may never appear in a magazine or a newspaper or on a garment; as a background color it is perfectly acceptable. But when it is the featured color, such as in a white carnation or in all-white wrapping paper, it is to be avoided. If you lack wrapping paper, putting a red ribbon on a gift box is often all that is necessary.

PRESENTING GIFTS

There is a certain amount of ritualistic behavior that goes along with presenting gifts. Most important, there is a custom common to many countries in the Orient that dictates that any gift, even one a person plans to accept, should be refused at least once, and often as many as three times. A Chinese may even push the gift back at the giver, protesting loudly that he or she has been embarrassed by the gesture and can't possibly accept the item.

Since this type of behavior is not common in the West, it's important to take it for what it really is. Don't withdraw the gift at this point. Continue to press it on the recipient through as many as three obligatory refusals. Only if you begin to sense that the protests are in earnest and that the individual genuinely does not want the item (e.g., because he or she might get into trouble for receiving it, or may not want to be obligated to you) should you back off. While being rebuffed in this way is not a pleasant experience, it is not necessarily an embarrassing one. It's best afterwards to continue to relate to the individual as if the incident never took place.

Like any other object, a gift should be given with both hands as a sign of courtesy. Individual gifts presented at banquets may be left at place settings, but delegation gifts must be presented formally, so remember the two-handed method.

If you are giving a delegation gift, the very best time to present it is during the toast at a return banquet hosted by your side in honor of the Chinese hosts. If there is to be only a welcoming banquet and no return meal, then the gift is generally given during the second toast at that banquet. There should be no surprises here; it's always best to let someone on the Chinese side know that a gift is coming. This avoids the embarrassment of receiving a present empty-handed; it allows the other side to prepare a reciprocal gift.

It is not customary for Chinese to open gifts in the presence of the giver. On my first trip to China I made an embarrassing error in this regard. I came laden with gifts for a number of Chinese friends whom I knew from their recent delegation trip to the United States. In my meeting with them I persistently urged them to open the gifts so that I might learn from their faces whether I had chosen properly or not. I wasn't sensitive to the fact that they did not wish to open the items in front of each other, probably because once it was known what each was given they would have to turn the gifts in.

More and more, however, the Chinese are flexible on this point. If your delegation is presenting a major gift to a Chinese host group at a banquet, you might well explain to them that it is a Western custom to open the gift in front of the giver and that you would be pleased if the Chinese host would open the gift at that point. If it's a delegation and not an individual gift, your Chinese host will probably happily comply with your request.

There is something to be said for opening personal gifts at home, however. It does avoid ludicrous scenes of people oohing and aahing over gifts they never really wanted and do not really need. The Chinese are more pragmatic and are less concerned with selecting individual gifts with the recipient's interests and idiosyncrasies in mind. It's not of vital importance that a gift be just what you wanted, or obviously selected with you and only you in mind. For a Chinese it truly is not the gift that counts, but the thought. As the Chinese say, *li qing; ren yi zhong.* It means that "the gift is trifling, but the feeling is profound."

To the Chinese, opening the gift in public would focus too much attention on the object itself, and not enough on the thought. Among themselves, in fact, the Chinese commonly pass gifts around from person to person. In a small group of friends they may even occasionally arrive back in the hands of the giver.

THE PRICE OF RECEIVING

The Chinese attach a price to the receipt of gifts and this is as true outside the PRC as it is in China. Chinese often offer gifts when they are about to ask favors. This can be extremely unsubtle: an acquaintance with whom you have been out of touch for years may suddenly show up bearing a gift—a sure sign that you are about to be asked for a favor of some sort. A Chinese college professor I barely knew once showed up at my door with a neatly wrapped present. Once invited in, he wasted little time in getting to the point: would I be willing to escort his daughter to the U.S. Embassy and negotiate for a visa for her?

Sometimes it is the favor that comes first, not the gift. If someone gets your brother a job, or helps your son get a visa to study abroad, or even helps you get a hard-to-get ticket for a train trip or a cultural performance, a token is often expected. The value of the gift should correlate roughly with the magnitude of the favor, except in hardship situations where the recipient can't afford much.

While it would be unfair to describe such offerings as bribes, especially when they are presented before a request is actually made, the line is in fact often a fine one. And although the situation can be awkward all around, if you have never done a favor for the person and don't intend to, the best way to proceed is to decline the gift. In such cases, life remains much less complicated if you stay away from the economy of obligations created by giving and receiving gifts.

RECAP: TEN CAVEATS ON GIVING GIFTS

1. Gifts are given to show esteem or gratitude, as souvenirs, as gratuities, or as payoffs in China. They discharge obligations, mark occasions, or accompany requests for favors.
2. Delegations are expected to give presents to their hosts. The conservative tack is to present one large gift to the host organization as a whole rather than a number of small gifts to its individual members.
3. Giving individual mementos is becoming very common, however. Despite the fear of corruption, the Chinese leadership permits individuals to keep small gifts of nominal value.
4. More and more Chinese are willing to play fast and loose with the rules, but to give a very valuable gift to a powerful individual is still a highly risky proposition.
5. Tipping is officially forbidden in the PRC and service is notoriously indifferent as a result. Service personnel in many places are making it increasingly clear to foreign visitors that they desire gratuities anyway. Standard practice is at odds with the rules here, so you should use your own discretion.
6. One way to reward someone is to give a small gift rather than cash. Wait for a private moment and give something that fits easily into a pocket.
7. Chinese often make as many as three obligatory refusal gestures when offered gifts; only if you sense genuine reluctance should you stop offering.
8. Objects of art are acceptable business gifts for Chinese units, though many Chinese lack the criteria to evaluate their true worth, artistic or otherwise. Useful gifts and company mementos are also acceptable. Individual gifts

should be small and of modest value, such as pens, calculators, lighters, tape measures, and tote bags. Gifts to friends may be more personal.

9. Don't give clocks (for superstitious reasons) and avoid gifts of excessive value. Wrap presents in bright red, never in white. Give gifts with both hands as a sign of courtesy. Don't expect your gift to be opened in your presence unless you specifically request it.

10. Gifts often carry unspoken obligations, such as granting favors. If you have never done a favor for a person and don't intend to, decline his or her gift politely. Gifts given in return for favors should correlate roughly with the magnitude of the favor.

9

Negotiating with the Chinese

The reputation the Chinese enjoy for being tough, canny negotiators is, on balance, well-deserved. They can be counted on to do their homework and to pursue their own agendas relentlessly. They use a variety of tactics to get the other side to come around to their way of doing things, and are known to press hard and patiently for further concessions even after agreements have been signed.

The strategies and maneuvers employed by the Chinese in negotiations are in large measure predictable, however, and it goes without saying that a knowledge of them will be helpful to those who sit on the other side of the table. Forewarned is, after all, forearmed.

HOW THE CHINESE VIEW NEGOTIATIONS

Doing business, like nearly everything else in China, depends in great measure on personal relationships. Legalism, though on the rise, has never been the be-all and end-all for the

Chinese, because traditionally the law has been susceptible to manipulation by the authorities and has hence provided relatively little protection or stability. Words, too, hold little value in and of themselves; it is strong personal relationships that provide some assurance that an agreement can come to fruition in China.

A crucial strategy for negotiating a successful venture with the Chinese is to identify common interests, not just a common outcome. The Chinese saying *tong chuang yi meng*, which means "two in the same bed dreaming different dreams," is an accurate description of the dynamics of too many failed negotiations. Chinese motives often differ from those of foreigners in important ways. In many technology-transfer agreements, for example, the foreign company covets access to the domestic market, while the Chinese counterpart wishes to earn foreign exchange through exporting. In such cases, problems inevitably arise when Chinese exports to third-country markets threaten the market share already held by the foreign partner.

The Chinese are thus looking more for a commitment to work together to solve problems that may arise than for a neat package with no loose ends. They know there will *always* be problems to overcome in any endeavor in China; these can never be fully anticipated, still less provided for. So you devise solutions for those problems you can identify in advance and simply rely on a network of relationships to solve those that inevitably come up without warning. A cosignatory to an agreement has established himself as a "friend," and one of the principal responsibilities of this status is to help friends solve problems.

What this implies, of course, is that negotiations with the Chinese are never really over. The Westerner who leaves China for home in ostensible triumph carrying a signed piece of paper is in for a rude awakening if he or she thinks the document represents anything chiseled in stone. For the Chinese, the signed agreement is only a punctuation mark in an essay with many chapters left to be written. There will be more concessions to be wrung and more compromises to be struck. Little is ever really settled; there is *always* room for more negotiation.

The Chinese generally keep their commitments. And though they may use tactics that others deem unfriendly and even ruthless in the pursuit of their objectives, they reject wholesale the characterization of negotiation as in any way an adversarial endeavor. Nor would they accept a portrayal of the process as simply one of haggling and compromising. They are looking for accord and harmony, and for an expression of mutual interests that implies a set of mutual obligations. To them, only strong, solid organizational—and individual—relationships constitute an appropriate basis on which to do business.

THE CHINESE
NEGOTIATING TEAM

Chinese negotiating teams are often quite large, especially when major investment projects are being discussed. In such situations the members generally outnumber their foreign counterparts: there may be eight to ten people in the room on the Chinese side, even though relatively few are likely to play an active role in the discussions.

Among the predictable participants in investment negotiations is, first and foremost, a team leader. This is often a general manager or deputy general manager of a Chinese corporation, and he or she possesses considerable authority in the negotiating process. Leaders or deputy leaders from the relevant bureaus of the corporation will probably also be present, e.g., if the agreement involves exporting a commodity, a responsible official from the export bureau will probably be present. And so will engineers and technicians who know the area being discussed.

There is also quite likely to be a representative of the Communist Party in the room. This person may have nominal responsibility for administration, personnel, or even propaganda in the work unit, but is also there to ensure that any agreements reached do not run counter to the Party line. During the Cultural Revolution—when the Ministry of Foreign Trade was derided as the "Ministry of Selling Out the Country"—negotiators were admonished by the Party to at all costs avoid getting duped by unscrupulous capitalists. Attitudes are far less fanatical today, but the Party representative may still occasionally take a somewhat accusatory tack with foreign negotiators when this is seen as in the Chinese interest, especially in straight buying and selling agreements.

Chinese negotiating teams always include translators who serve as interpreters for both sides if the foreign team does not have any bilingual capability. They may or may not be from the chief negotiator's unit, and they may or may not be competent in the particular technical area being discussed, or in legal terminology. Other team members may include note-takers and apprentices who will seldom contribute anything of substance to the discussion.

Increasingly, Chinese lawyers are also showing up in negotiating sessions. Their presence is a relatively novel occurrence, since lawyers as a class were despised as recently as the Cultural Revolution. The Chinese lawyers who participate in these sessions are typically from units other than the one negotiating, and they may or may not have the respect of the chief negotiator. Theirs are generally conciliatory voices, however, working to defuse otherwise contentious situations.

Then there are the "silent" team members—those who are never present for face-to-face discussions but who must give or withhold approval once the draft agreement is reached. It is the attitudes and potential criticisms of these decision makers that are most squarely on the minds of the Chinese negotiators, since they have the authority to make or break a deal. When negotiators argue over wording, seek to gloss over potentially contentious issues, or haggle over prices, they are usually thinking of how best to make the agreement acceptable to these "silent" higher-ups.

It's worth noting here that in straight buying and selling discussions the teams may be considerably smaller and simpler. There may be no Party representative at all—only a delegation leader, an interpreter (if necessary), and a staff member or two. The decision maker may well be present in the room and clearly identified as such; in such cases talks can often proceed quite swiftly.

Even among the members of the Chinese team there may be important differences of opinion. Indeed, there are nearly always some internal tensions on the Chinese side when more than one unit is represented. The interests of the end users, for example, who want quality above all else, and those of the business managers, who are concerned primarily about price, are often on a collision course.

FORMING YOUR OWN TEAM

Initial discussions that are the forerunners of formal negotiations generally take place between one or two representatives from both the Chinese and the foreign sides. Only after the general parameters of the business arrangements are established should a company go to the expense of dispatching a complete negotiating team.

It is of vital importance that your company send the right people to China both for the initial discussions and later for the substantive negotiations. Protocol is one reason, since the level of the team head will help determine the attitude of the Chinese host organization toward your company. It will also determine the rank of the Chinese chosen to host your group, and since individuals below a certain level have no power to make decisions, it is in your interest to ensure that the discussions are led by someone of sufficient stature.

Since many demands will be made on the negotiating teams, it is important to include people knowledgeable about any technological and financial arrangements to be discussed, and about getting things done in China. And since the team will be subjected to a great deal of pressure, you will also want to look for people with the right personalities.

The initial contact should be made at a level that is neither too low nor too high. If your company sends a low-ranking person to China to do initial reconnaissance, your hosts may be insulted and conclude that their business is not of much importance to you. On the other hand, there's a strong argument that the pioneering trip should not be led by the chairman or CEO, either. The Chinese love to see senior officials from the companies with whom they do business, but these visits can do much more harm than good at the opening stages of discussions. The "visionary" chairman who thinks he or she is paving the way for the company in China with an early trip and a vague letter of agreement to cooperate has done the company no favors. All that has been done is to undermine the negotiating positions of the team that must follow.

This is true for a number of reasons. First of all, because the Chinese know that the team will be under a great deal of pressure to succeed in the talks: the chairman's visit was probably covered in the media, and the board of directors has probably been put on alert that a China venture is in the cards. They know that such pressure can often translate into concessions at the bargaining table. As a direct result of the chairman's visit they may have at their disposal a letter of intent that can prove useful for browbeating the foreign negotiating team if they ever violate the letter or the "spirit"— as defined, of course, by the Chinese side—of the agreement. And if the members of the negotiating team were not present during the chairman's trip, the Chinese can bring up and use to advantage "understandings" that they may—or, in truth, may not—have reached with the top leader.

This is not to say that there is no role for senior officers of the company. They may be very useful later on in the process in getting stalled negotiations back on track, or in securing an audience with an authority higher than the chief negotiator if this is desirable. And chairmen and CEOs are the officers of choice to come to China for signing ceremonies.

While the head of the foreign negotiating team should not be the company president, he or she *should* be someone with sufficient authority in the firm to make important decisions. A chief negotiator without authority soon loses his or her credibility, and the Chinese may ask to work with someone of higher stature. On the other hand, it is sometimes a good idea to send a slightly lower-ranking team when talks are in very preliminary stages. This can help qualify leads and ferret out information that can help you decide whether to pursue the deal.

The team leader should ideally be someone knowledgeable about the substantive area being discussed and familiar with similar ventures the company has established in other countries. Someone who has been with the organization a long time is desirable, though not required, and given the Chinese respect for age and experience, gray hair is a definite plus. The person should be secure in his or her own position in the company, and not be someone whose career advancement will depend on a successful outcome in the China negotiations. In personality, choose someone who is, first and foremost, *patient*. Other desirable traits are affability, tolerance, and ability to control temper. Send someone who is unflappable, not particularly susceptible to flattery, and who is naturally predisposed toward conciliation over confrontation.

Individuals with expertise in the technical area under discussion should also be on the team, as should representatives of the divisions of the company that will eventually be involved in implementation of the contract. The team should also include one or more people familiar with China and how to get things done there. One of them should be a lawyer experienced in working with China. It's best when team members are already company employees, but knowledgeable outside consultants can be useful as well. Such individuals can be extremely helpful in reading signals, and in pointing out ways of exploiting the sometimes divergent interests of the Chinese team members.

Overseas Chinese—people of Chinese extraction who are not Chinese citizens, such as Chinese-Americans, Chinese-Canadians, and even Hong Kong Chinese—can often fill this role admirably, since many of them are seasoned observers of Chinese bureaucratic processes. Some may even have *guanxi* of their own that can be brought to bear in resolving problems. As biculturals they can often relate to both sides of a discussion and can help to promote mutual understanding and bring about harmony among all the players.

On the other hand, such individuals are also frequently subjected to strong pressure from the Chinese team. PRC negotiators assume that "Chinese" is the operative word in the expression "overseas Chinese," and that such people not only are more likely to understand them, but actually have a responsibility to help them out. In some cases they may also receive less respect from the Chinese, who are occasionally prone to treat them as lackeys. This is true whether or not the person speaks Chinese or has ever lived in China. Chinese often appeal to their overseas compatriots to help explain their positions to the foreign team and to help them convince the foreigners that they are right to press for their demands. They are also far more likely to hit them up for personal favors and even for kickbacks.

Having an overseas Chinese on your negotiating team is not an automatic advantage; whether such a person will be a valuable team member depends primarily on the individual's personality. If he or she is someone susceptible to manipulation in the manner described above, who is likely to be maneuvered into pleading your counterpart's case, best to leave the person at home. But if it's someone who can use the status to further *your* position—eliciting the confidence of the Chinese and convincing them of the rightness of your arguments—then he or she is a teammate worth having. Selecting such a person—like selecting any other member of a negotiating team—is ultimately a judgment call; there's really no fail-safe way to predict success or failure.

Serious consideration should also be given to bringing your own interpreter along. Though the Chinese side will provide interpretation, a good translator on your team can do far more for you than simply render your words into Chinese. He or she can help explain your points more clearly, help persuade the opposing side of your viewpoint, and, by taking note of the Chinese side's inevitable asides, provide insight into the Chinese position. An interpreter can also point out any discrepancies between the English and Chinese versions of contact language. You'll need to balance these capabilities against the expense of bringing an additional person, of course.

There is no hard and fast rule governing the number of people on a negotiating team. Some say that the Chinese may view a large delegation—a dozen people, for example—as an invitation to divide and conquer. The size might be construed as evidence that a company's position has not been fully decided, hence the need for all voices to be represented on the team. On the other hand, a company willing to incur the expense of sending a number of people to China may be perceived as highly committed to success, while a very small team—one or two people—could send the opposite message.

It is important to use the same team members throughout

the talks if at all possible. Sometimes, especially when
negotiations are protracted, companies find such continuity to
be a real problem, since employees often do not view China
business—with all of its starts and stops—as a ticket to success,
and actively seek other assignments. The Chinese find constant rotation of personnel to be disruptive and confusing, and
a sign that a company does not have its act together. They are
also likely to use such comings and goings to advantage,
because changing personnel makes their side the de facto
guardian of the institutional memory. It's far easier to quote
back ostensible "understandings" reached during earlier talks if
none of the members of the original team is around to refute
the interpretation.

THE EBB AND
FLOW OF NEGOTIATIONS

There is a definite rhythm to negotiations with Chinese in the
PRC, very effectively chronicled in Dr. Lucian Pye's seminal
work, *Chinese Commercial Negotiating Style*, required reading for anyone contemplating serious negotiations in China.
Strictly speaking, the process actually begins well in advance of
any face-to-face meeting, with a major research effort designed
to identify and qualify potential partners. The Chinese generally require a great deal of basic information before they are
willing to sit down and do any significant bargaining. Their
research involves consulting reference works, company literature, and other Chinese units that may have dealt in the past
with the firm in question.

Pye divides the formal negotiating process into distinct
stages. First there is the initial period of "opening moves,"
during which general principles are expressed and mutual
goals established. This is followed by the "substantive negotiating session," during which positions are explored further and
the sincerity and trustworthiness of the partner are appraised.
It is during this stage that either agreement is reached or else
discussions are suspended. Lastly, Pye reminds us that nothing
is ever really final in dealing with the Chinese. Substantive
negotiations continue well into the implementation stage of
any contract.

Before Discussions Begin

What you do before negotiations can have important implications for the success or failure of the talks. It is vitally
important to get as much information as possible about:

- who the Chinese negotiating partners are, what their
  bureaucratic interests are, whether they have jurisdic-
  tion over the matter at hand, and whether they have the
  authority to negotiate;
- which other Chinese organizations have a say in the
  success or failure of the business, what their positions
  are, and how much clout they are likely to mobilize;
- whether preliminary government approval has been
  secured (e.g., for an investment project or the purchase
  of a controlled commodity);
- whether the transaction or venture is feasible in terms
  of sources of funding, the condition of the factory, the
  availability of raw materials, utilities and transportation, domestic and foreign markets, environmental
  impact, etc.;
- which Chinese laws pertain to the negotiations and
  what similar agreements have already been struck that
  can serve as precedents; and
- what other foreign companies, if any, have held similar
  discussions with this or any other set of Chinese
  officials.

Much of the above information might have been genuinely
unknowable as recently as the early 1980s, when even the
Chinese frequently misjudged the political landscape sur-
rounding negotiations, e.g., what other units might have a say
in the outcome, what laws were relevant (when, indeed, they
existed at all), and how much authority the negotiating unit
actually possessed. Now, increasingly, these are areas that can
be effectively researched in advance of negotiations. Some, in
fact, may be easier for foreigners to explore than for the
Chinese, given the excellent information sources available
abroad as compared to China's rudimentary communications
system.

New laws and myriad regulations codify the approval process and have much to say about acceptable and unacceptable provisions in business agreements. Many model contracts have been published and opinions rendered, giving ample precedents and guidelines for certain types of agreements. And there is a growing body of hands-on knowledge concerning what will and won't work in transactions and joint ventures with the Chinese.

It should also be pointed out that there is no one inviolable rule for how deals must work in China. Some business arrangements that pose problems for negotiators in Beijing may be implemented easily in Tianjin or Shanghai; different localities possess a great deal of autonomy and may approach problems differently. For example, companies interested in setting up wholly owned subsidiaries in China have traditionally had a difficult time convincing local officials that such ventures are in the interests of their city or province; now, given the track record of such ventures in certain areas, some pragmatic local officials feel much more positively about them.

For their part, the Chinese can be relied on to do *their* homework. They will make it their business to find out all they can about your company—how big and reliable you are, what your lines of business are, what other projects you may be involved in in the PRC, and what kind of a partner your firm has proven itself to be in such ventures. If they sense lack of sincerity or commitment at this stage, they are quite likely never to proceed to face-to-face discussions.

Glossing over feasibility issues and going directly into negotiations with the expectation that they can be resolved through discussions can be an expensive mistake. If due caution is exercised at this stage, you can avoid the expense and prolonged time investment involved in entering into negotiations that are predestined to be fruitless. Just as the Chinese qualify partners, so should foreign companies. China doesn't lack for governmental or quasi-governmental agencies willing to try their luck with international business. Identifying the right projects and the right partners is thus a very important consideration.

Indeed, it is very important to realize at the start that China does not behave as a monolith in its approach to foreign business, or, for that matter, in much of anything else. Despite the fact that most corporations are owned by the government, you should never assume that a particular venture or proposal has "government support" in the PRC. There is really no such thing. The government is merely a collection of agencies with their own ideas of what is needed and what is best; for every agency that supports an idea there is generally another that is staunch in its opposition to it.

Then, too, clarity is often lacking about which organization has authority over any given transaction or issue. So the desires of your counterpart organization for support in the form of materials, utilities, or approvals from elsewhere in the bureaucracy may not count for much when push comes to shove. Powerful organizations have the most resources to bring to bear to solve problems, but even they cannot necessarily guarantee success.

Opening Salvos

Traditionally it was technical seminars, detailed presentations given by foreign companies concerning the products or services they wished to sell, that served as starting points for negotiations with the Chinese. The Chinese used these meetings as a means for engineers, end users, negotiators, purchasers, and government officials to learn about the products and processes that were available internationally, and to get information about how they might be applied to solve problems in the PRC.

Technical seminars were part of a screening process used by the Chinese. Indeed, more than one company was sometimes asked to conduct such seminars before formal negotiating sessions began. In recent years, however, as the Chinese have become increasingly familiar with foreign companies and their technology, the sessions have increasingly been skipped entirely, the parties launching immediately into negotiations.

Generally speaking, formal negotiating periods consist of two sessions per day: a morning meeting and an afternoon meeting, with a two-hour lunch break in between. There is no set time limit, and discussions can go on until one or both sides are tired, or someone suggests adjournment. Occasionally, if there is time pressure, talks can go on well into the night. They may continue for many days straight without a break—even through Saturdays, which are half workdays for the Chinese, and Sundays, which are generally days off. Occasionally a holiday is declared during which the Chinese caucus and foreign guests are on their own.

When formal discussions begin, the Chinese tend to focus first on articulating general principles and securing agreement on mutual goals. They prefer to start with major areas of accord and work only eventually toward discussing specifics and details that may be bones of contention. If they are successful in securing agreement on basic principles, they can later berate the other party for any perceived transgressions against such principles that may be construed as violations of the spirit of the agreement.

To Westerners—especially impatient ones—these drills sometimes appear to be little more than formalities and, as such, a waste of time. Occidentals, interested in using time efficiently, tend to give short shrift to areas of agreement and focus immediately on outstanding issues. But the Chinese use this stage for a number of types of reconnaissance.

They are looking above all to size up your negotiating position, your sincerity and trustworthiness, your vulnerabilities, and anything else that may help them later in the process. They are trying to determine if you and your company are going to be appropriate and reliable business partners. At this stage they are not really negotiating at all; they are just continuing to gather information. They wish to understand all they can about the product or the technology being discussed so that they can pass this information up the chain of authority to the "silent others" who will render all final decisions.

If you attempt to use this initial period to get a better sense of Chinese priorities and their level of interest you may sometimes find the process a difficult one. Chinese participants are frequently less than candid about their actual needs at this stage; this is the time for pumping you, not tipping their own hands. They themselves may be uncertain about how the foreign product or technology will fit into their plans, and they may hope that the information gleaned from you will help them clarify their own priorities. They may also be trying to avoid giving you information that you could use as ammunition in the bargaining process, such as the depth of their interest or magnitude of their need for the product under discussion. If your company is well-known to the Chinese negotiators—a true "old friend"—you may have an easier time of extracting information, since in such cases the Chinese are often less fearful of giving away this type of information.

Typically they ask a lot of questions at this stage, encouraging you to "tip your hand." Not infrequently the questions go right to the heart of matters that your company deems proprietary. It is thus important to decide in advance how far you are prepared to go, and stick to that limit religiously. The Chinese may try a number of different approaches to get at the answers they seek, but if it is made clear that such information is not forthcoming, they will eventually get the message. One American automotive executive reports that he defused just such a situation with an audience of nearly a hundred people by telling them with a big smile that getting the answer to a question they had posed in three or four different ways would cost them a sum of money. The audience chuckled and went on to other questions.

Substantive Negotiating

This period accounts for the bulk of the time spent, and is perhaps best understood as a prolonged test period. Substantive issues are discussed at this stage, though at first they may well not be the ones that you feel are most critical. What is really going on is that the Chinese are trying to find the "give" in your position. Having heard your initial proposals, they continue to draw out your position, applying pressure and testing reactions. Occasionally a meaningless concession may be offered at this stage to see what it can fetch in the way of reciprocal compromise.

This strategy may continue for days or even weeks. It is generally only when Chinese negotiators are satisfied that they have probed your position from all angles that they become more willing to discuss their own. This is seldom accomplished as an explicit step; most often you must divine Chinese

assumptions and problems indirectly from the increasingly
pointed questions that they ask.

Similarly, if the Chinese have chosen *not* to pursue further
negotiations with your company, they may communicate this
only indirectly, though their signals may be none too subtle. If
a Chinese team consistently presses for outrageous terms and
won't budge from them for an extended period, it's likely that
they are no longer seriously interested in doing business. This
behavior is calculated to make *you* the one who breaks off the
talks; it saves them the dicey task of having to explain their
change of heart.

The Chinese have a veritable arsenal of negotiating strategies and tactics that they put to work during negotiations.
Some are more appropriate to trade discussions, while others
tend to be more useful in joint-venture talks; many are equally
applicable. A number of them are described in the section
below. Keep in mind that these tactics are available for your
use as well, though many cagey negotiators have been bested
by the Chinese when they attempt to beat them at their own
game. Remember also that the Chinese do not take the use of
such tactics personally—they are all simply a part of the
negotiating process—and so neither should you, if you can
avoid it.

When negotiating in earnest, the Chinese become extremely interested in the contract language that may eventually bind them to certain courses of action. This is a good sign
that things are moving along and that the Chinese side hopes
to strike an agreement. Sometimes it leads to what attorney
Ellen Eliasoph has called "the battle of the drafts." In *Law and
Business Practice in Shanghai*, Eliasoph quotes a Shanghai
regulation in which negotiators are enjoined to "strive to use
our side's proposed texts as the basis for negotiation."

Once substantive negotiations are in full swing there may
indeed be many battles over language. Spirited discussions
often occur on how exactly to phrase contract provisions.
Again, what motivates the Chinese is the desire to come up
with language that will please—or at very least, not offend—
the higher-ups who will eventually decide whether the draft
agreement is acceptable. You may thus frequently encounter
situations in which the Chinese press you for concrete

commitments while resisting your efforts to get them to make any promises on paper themselves. In a joint-venture negotiation, for example, a Chinese negotiating team might push hard to get you to guarantee to export a fixed percentage of product produced, but for its own part may only commit to making its "best effort" to have a gas or sewer line installed at the same factory.

You may never get any overt indication from the Chinese when you have moved from the discussion stage into the final rounds of negotiations; there is often no clear demarcation point between negotiating and closing a deal. There are, however, some good indications. The Chinese generally focus on very concrete issues at this stage, such as contract language and price. It is also then that issues previously postponed will be raised for discussion. Despite what they say about the goals of negotiations, some horse trading does indeed go on, and this is the stage when it happens. Issues previously discussed that appeared insurmountable may suddenly prove to pose less of a problem than had originally seemed to be the case, especially when the Chinese sense that a concession on one of them can fetch a price break.

PREDICTABLE CHINESE NEGOTIATING TACTICS

Though the Chinese may be masterful negotiators, there are ways of dealing with them successfully. The first step is to be prepared for some of the ploys they are likely to use. Pye and others have described some of the strategies and tactics the Chinese often employ during negotiations. I have discussed a number of them below, together with a bit of advice on countering them:

Controlling the location and schedule. Most negotiations take place on Chinese soil, because, for several reasons, the Chinese prefer to play host. Saving money is an obvious motive, but there are more subtle ones as well. The Chinese have traditionally enjoyed the opportunity to make foreigners appear as supplicants, visiting the Middle Kingdom in the hopes of being granted some favor or concession. Holding talks in China also has the practical effect of making consultation between Chinese negotiators and their superiors convenient and easy. In that respect meeting in China may indeed hurry the negotiation process along somewhat.

There are, however, distinct disadvantages to playing on the Chinese home court. Chief among the drawbacks is that every day you spend in China costs time and money—and a good deal of the latter. If the Chinese know when you intend to leave—which they generally do, since your host unit typically handles reconfirmation of your ongoing tickets—they can manipulate the schedule to squeeze you somewhat. Time is on their side; they can use it to wait you out. They can test whether your position is as firm as it appears at first and determine where your bottom line really is. Concentrating the haggling over the most important issues into the last day or two may make you more willing to make concessions just to get your agreement signed and get out on time.

Controlling the schedule also helps the Chinese in other ways. When the negotiations take unexpected turns and they need time to sort out their own position, they can summarily declare a day of rest and send a foreign delegation off sightseeing. Or worse, they can tell you that they'll call you when they are ready to resume negotiations and in so doing make you a virtual prisoner in your hotel room. And the Chinese can also use this advantage to manipulate attitudes. If they can alarm you into thinking that the reason for a hiatus in negotiations is that you have done something to offend them, they can often accelerate the pace of ferreting out your true fallback position.

One countermeasure you can sometimes use is to insist that the talks—or some of them, at least—be held on your own home turf. Another is to discourage the war of attrition by announcing up front how long you are willing to participate in talks and stick to your guns. This can work in your favor provided you are not feeling any acute pressure to reach agreement during that visit.

Exploiting vulnerabilities. One strategy often employed is to identify areas of vulnerability, either in your position or in your personality, and use them to their own advantage. Any of your traits is fair game for manipulation. For example, if, after sizing you up, they sense that you have a strong personal need to return home with a signed agreement—to "plant the corporate flag" in China—you are quite likely to find yourself hostage to demands that may be very difficult to accept. Your fear of failure is often put to excellent use: "If you can't give us better terms, you will be responsible for the failure of our discussions." And even your friendship can be useful: "You are a good friend of China, and so you can understand our need for high-quality training. We need your help in convincing your colleagues to expand the training element in this technology transfer."

A good Chinese negotiator will not only use your side's vulnerabilities to advantage, but also his or her own. If a Chinese senses that you can be swayed by such arguments, he or she may point out that China is a very poor country and can't afford to pay the price you ask; or that accepting a particular provision would put the Chinese unit at a distinct disadvantage. Trying to get you to understand their problems and help them solve them is a common tack. Count on appeals to your generosity: "Your company is rich and can afford to give us a concession on this point." And expect flattery: "You have a deep understanding of China. You know why we need help on this point."

The best defense against this tactic is awareness of it. Expect flattery and don't take it particularly seriously. And if you really are under pressure to strike an agreement, try as hard as you can not to let that fact be known.

Guilt tripping. The use of guilt—national, ethnic, institutional, or personal—is also a very common ploy. The Chinese will not hesitate to bring up historical or political issues if they sense that these may be effective. Japanese business executives are reminded of the atrocities committed on Chinese soil by their country's troops during World War II. Attempts are also sometimes made to hold Americans responsible for alleged wrongdoings by the U.S. government with respect to Taiwan and even occasionally Korea or Vietnam. If you rise to the bait, the Chinese will keep hammering on these points. But if you indicate that you feel no responsibility for actions taken by your government or your fellow countrymen and wish to deal only with the matter at hand, your Chinese counterpart will probably switch tactics.

The Chinese are diabolical note-takers, and you can be certain that anything you say in or out of the negotiating room will be recorded. They consider it fair game to throw your words back in your face whenever it serves their purposes. If they can remind you of something you once said that is in conflict with your current position, rely on them to keep your feet to the fire. And as ready as the Chinese are to bring up the record if it suits them, they are equally prone conveniently to forget anything ever said or agreed to in the past if it does not.

Instilling shame. Closely related to the use of guilt is the use of shame. If you can be accused of violating some sacred principle—ideally one established early on in the process during the general discussions—the Chinese will attempt to use that ostensible transgression to embarrass you into doing things their way. If you make a remark that they can call "unfriendly," for example, or do something that violates the canon of "equality and mutual benefit," then you are a candidate for this type of treatment.

The use of both guilt and shame are effective only if you allow them to be. Keeping in mind that these are negotiating ploys rather than deeply felt allegations can often help you keep your perspective. And keeping your own detailed notes of proceedings can help you counter later allegations that you have been disingenuous in your dealings with the Chinese.

Playing off competitors. Another favorite ploy is to pit competitors off against one another. Sometimes this is done blatantly—the Chinese have been known to invite competing companies to China at the same time for negotiations, often in the very same building. Chinese negotiators will frequently hint that competitors have offered certain types of information that you have refused to provide or made certain concessions that you have so far resisted. They may even allow that your technology is better and assert that they believe your company would make a better partner, but point out at the same time that another company is offering better terms, making it very difficult for them to choose you unless you offer a similar deal.

All these are gambits to try to get you to come around. Evoking the image of dozens of competitors all vying for the gold serves Chinese purposes handily, and they are quite happy to project it to anyone gullible enough to be swayed by it.

One American multinational company held talks for over two years with a Chinese hand tool factory that took an opposite tack—it assured the firm that all previous discussions with one of its competitors had broken down. Only much later did the corporation discover through a third party that the factory's talks with their competition had in fact continued all through the period of their own discussions. Worse, the company learned that its own confidential proposal had been leaked to the other company as a device for extracting concessions.

In this case, the American company concluded that the only appropriate course was to walk away from the negotiations since the insincere behavior of their Chinese counterpart was proof that it was not an organization worth doing business with. But the tactic of playing competitors off against one another can be very hard to resist, especially when it is your own company that is offered "confidential" information about another's proposal.

Using intermediaries. Just as intermediaries are useful to the Chinese in the initial stages of getting acquainted with foreigners, they may also play a role during negotiations. For reasons of face, Chinese sometimes prefer to communicate unpleasant information or offer trial balloons through others not directly involved in the negotiations, or even through members of the team outside of formal negotiating sessions. If a proposal offered in this way is unacceptable to their counterparts, no face has been lost and the Chinese can even deny that the idea ever had official approval. Two can play at this game, however; if you see an opportunity to use a go-between in this way it is appropriate to do so.

Feigning anger. Although public expressions of anger, as clear violations of the Confucian ethic (see Chapter 4), are frowned on by the Chinese, even solecisms such as these are acceptable in negotiations as a means to an end. Chinese negotiators

sometimes use displays of temper to try to get what they want.
A Chinese might pack up his or her papers with a flourish and
storm out of the room, or suddenly turn bellicose and lecture
the foreign counterpart about ostensible slights or high crimes.
Chinese are seldom truly angry when they behave this way;
such outbursts are generally best viewed as theater.

The Chinese sometimes use this tactic when they are really
trying to scuttle a deal, but more often than not an explosion
is calculated to alarm the opposing team into making concessions to mollify the supposedly injured Chinese party. When
foreigners do not respond in kind, such breaches generally
prove to be fairly easily repaired—if they are not summarily
dropped as issues by the Chinese.

The best defense against this tactic is knowledge. Precisely
because of the strong taboo in China against showing temper,
you can safely assume most of the time that the anger is for
show. As with most other tactics, if the Chinese find out that
you are not susceptible, they will move on.

You may be able to use this same ploy to your own
advantage. Westerners, far more accustomed to dealing openly
with temper, can generally project anger far more convinc-
ingly and effectively than the Chinese. Communicating un-
happiness can fetch concessions, but it's probably fair to say
that it isn't a tack you can use repeatedly. So reserve it until it
will be most effective, and try not to use it when true anger can
cloud your judgment.

Revisiting old issues. Foreign negotiators commonly report
instances in which problems that have ostensibly been resolved
are revisited by the Chinese later on in the process. When a
Chinese team raises an issue anew, the first reaction of the
foreign team members is often to conclude that they had been
in error in their initial belief that the issue had in fact been
settled. Most of the time this is the wrong conclusion.

The Chinese are always ready to exhume issues in which
they did not get all they wanted the first time around. As
discussed earlier, this extends to the period after which
negotiations are officially over, and can occur at any time,
even on the way to the airport or immediately after the foreign

team has left China. Like many of the other tactics discussed here, this one is simply a tool that is sometimes useful for extracting additional concessions.

Consider the case of an American firm that finally saw the light at the end of the tunnel in protracted negotiations over the purchase of some equipment. Getting agreement on specifications and delivery had taken so long that the Chinese insisted at the eleventh hour on renegotiating the price to which they had agreed earlier in light of changes in market conditions.

The best defense against this stratagem is, again, to take excellent notes. If your records show that something was agreed to on a particular date, you are within your rights to use these grounds as a basis to refuse to discuss the issue again. Or at the very least you can attempt to make reopening the discussion contingent on revisiting an issue of your own choice previously decided in favor of the Chinese.

Invoking the law. Sometimes the Chinese will try to get their way by falling back on the law. They are technically at advantage in this area since some regulations germane to foreign business are considered *neibu*, that is, for internal consumption only, and are never published in a form available to foreigners. The law can conveniently be cited to prohibit anything the Chinese team doesn't particularly want to do. Here again, forewarned is forearmed: most Chinese laws relevant to international commerce are published, and many foreign attorneys actually know Chinese law better than some PRC negotiators. Often it is they who can cite appropriate precedents for arrangements being discussed.

A related ploy is badgering foreigners with model contracts. Many such documents exist in China, and they are, not surprisingly, written in ways extremely favorable to the Chinese. Take the inevitable warnings against any deviations from these models with the proverbial grain of salt. The predictable admonition, "it's the only contract our leaders will approve, so if you want this deal, you must accept it" is generally rubbish. Just about everything is negotiable. If all else fails, tell them that as a matter of policy *your* leaders never accept certain types of contract terms.

Raising and lowering expectations. Flirtations may go on for months or even years, but when the Chinese finally decide to go ahead with a project they often convey a strong sense of urgency. This tack frequently proves helpful to them, because it raises expectations and generates excitement, both powerful motivating factors in a foreign delegation eager to make a deal. At other points in negotiations, however, they are equally capable of trying to lower others' expectations. This strategy can be useful when the Chinese know that they will not be able to deliver as much as the other side desires. Keeping expectations low makes foreign counterparts grateful for whatever outcome they are able to achieve.

As a general rule, take Chinese promises to provide information by a certain date with a grain of salt. Obtaining any information requiring the input of another work unit is likely to take the Chinese more time than anticipated, and so it will be longer in getting to you.

SOME ADVICE

Finally, here is a checklist of twenty dos and don'ts that you would be well-advised to keep in mind as you contemplate negotiating with the Chinese:

The Dos

1. Do your homework. As noted above in the section entitled "Before Discussions Begin," there is a lot you should find out before you even sit down at the table. One point worth reiterating: make sure you are negotiating with the ultimate authority. Many state agencies will ask for proposals and negotiate them, but if they don't have authority to conclude an agreement, they will eventually turn you over to some other unit that does. You are back to square one in that case, and actually even worse off: the new unit can be counted on to treat the agreement as nothing more than a starting point for further discussion and negotiation.

2. Do take detailed notes. Be sure your records are thorough, and if necessary assign someone on the team the respon-

sibility of note-taking. Pay close attention to how things are left at the end of sessions. In the best of situations there are occasionally misunderstandings as to what was left pending and what was nailed down. And since the Chinese are apt to construe any issue in the light most favorable to their own position, good notes are crucial.

3. Do always be able to walk away from the table. Never put yourself in a position where you *need* to have an agreement. If the Chinese sense this, they will definitely play on it.

    Sometimes pushing you to the brink of terminating the negotiations is exactly what the Chinese are trying to do. This is one very effective way of determining your *true* bottom line. It's a tack they sometimes take with negotiating partners about whom they are not particularly serious; they are less interested in concluding a deal than in gleaning information they can put to use in parallel negotiations they are having with the competition.

4. Do remember that final decisions will be made by people absent from the negotiating room and that even agreements forged during negotiations are subject to their review. Helping your Chinese counterparts devise language that will be acceptable to these decision makers is a key consideration in negotiating successful agreements.

5. Do display a high level of commitment to doing business in China. The Chinese will pick up very quickly on any doubts you may have concerning the ultimate feasibility of a project, and may interpret any wait-and-see attitude as insincerity. You can actually use your own enthusiasm to motivate the Chinese to come to terms: "We really want to do this deal—but we know our leaders won't accept these terms."

6. Do pad your price. Not so much that you will be way out of line with those quoted by your competitors, but enough so that you have something to shave off when pressed. The Chinese will assume that any price you quote has some give in it, and won't rest until they have gotten some concessions in this very important area. Play the game. If you go in with an extra 15 percent and you give away 10 percent of it, you're still ahead of the game and your

Chinese counterpart will have some good news to report to his or her boss.

7. Do check your ego at the door. The Chinese are naturally free with their compliments, and they are likely to be quite a bit more so in negotiating situations when flattery has additional uses. Compliments—such as your deep understanding of China or your proven track record of friendship—really mean very little. And too often they are setups for the inevitable "responsibilities" that these honors carry with them. Those who understand China, so this line of reasoning goes, also understand why our unit doesn't have as much money to spend as your team is asking for; those who are friends should naturally help out other friends who are weaker or less advanced.

8. Do go through every single detail of the contract. Leave no stone unturned and make absolutely certain that you discuss *all* the issues. Resist any urge to hurry this stage along. Indeed, the Chinese themselves may not have thought through some of the ramifications of the contract language, or if they have they may not tell you about areas where the ambiguity is likely to help them later. It is inevitably the one minor point that you fail to examine carefully that proves to be your undoing at a later stage.

9. Do be careful what you say to the media. The Chinese don't usually publicize agreements until they are completely buttoned down, as they abhor surprises and hate to risk public embarrassment. One firm that went public about a very controversial contract provision actually got its Chinese partner into some trouble, since, strictly speaking, the unit did not have authority to deliver on the promise. When the relationship began to sour, the Chinese side cited the company's bad faith in going to the press and badgered the firm for more concessions.

10. Do be prepared for a lot of backtracking, repetition, ambiguity, and inevitable misunderstandings. These things are bound to happen, and it is best to take them in stride when they do. Avoid finger-pointing and approach your partners with an attitude of understanding and conciliation. And remember that the person you rebuke

today just might turn out to be your joint-venture partner tomorrow.

The Don'ts

1. Don't be quick to resolve individual problems as they are brought up by the Chinese side. Do as they do: listen to all of the problem areas first and only then decide what concessions you are prepared to give. Being eager to please earns you very little, and may very likely come back to haunt you later. Once you have conceded something it is next to impossible to backtrack. Telling the Chinese that a concession on one point will require revisiting one made on a point already covered is dicey business and often doesn't work; this despite the fact that they may try to do the very same thing to you. Always keep a concession or two up your sleeve; you may have to offer it up in order to close the deal.

2. Don't concede anything easily, even something that is not very important to you. You may be offering a concession for nothing. To do so will merely convince the Chinese that you don't value it, and it will also make it useless as a bargaining chip to fetch something that you do value. The Chinese lead is a good one to follow in this case: they seldom give up anything without a fight, even if it is unimportant to them. It can always be used to extract something from you.

3. Don't reject a Chinese position out of hand. Even if the Chinese side comes up with a preposterous proposition, resist the temptation to reject it outright. It is better to counter it by drawing your counterpart into a discussion of the issue, and steer the discussion into a more constructive vein. You can communicate the fact that the suggestion is a "nonstarter" in ways more subtle than an overt rebuff; parry is usually far more effective than thrust.

4. Don't assume that there is any such thing as "China, Incorporated." As discussed elsewhere, the Chinese bureaucracy is little more than a loose conglomeration of fiefdoms; cooperation among units is the exception rather than the rule. Don't overestimate your counterpart's

abilities to resolve intramural rivalries and objections—
he or she may not even have anticipated all of them.
And don't underestimate the ability—and willingness—of
other units to scuttle your deal. Never assume that China
speaks with one voice on any given matter.

Also, beware of being placed squarely in the middle of
intramural rivalries. Sometimes Chinese units despairing
of getting any concessions out of an unfriendly *danwei*
will try to maneuver foreign counterparts into the role of
approaching the third unit on the assumption that a
foreign voice can be more persuasive. You should only
consent to running interference if you really know what
you are doing; otherwise you risk damaging relationships
all around.

5. Don't project a sense of "victory" at a successful agreement. The Chinese believe that where there is a winner
there is also a loser, and they are positively paranoid about
being taken advantage of. Nothing will earn a Chinese
negotiator more criticism from his or her superiors as
much as an "unfair" agreement in which China gets the
muddy end of the stick. This doesn't mean that you can't
show happiness when a deal is struck; just be sure that
happy isn't mistaken for triumphant.

6. Don't hesitate to cut your losses. An executive from a
large American company tells the story of being led on for
more than a year by the son of a very high-ranking cadre
in a southern Chinese province who assured her that he
could match her company up with a factory that could
supply them with a particular light industrial product.
After visits to numerous inappropriate facilities, she and
her colleagues finally concluded that the man, although
well-connected and well-meaning, simply wasn't going to
be able to deliver on his promise. Though much money
had already changed hands, the company correctly concluded that enough was enough. Like that firm, you
should know the point at which it's time to cut bait.

7. Don't assume that your counterpart's decisions are necessarily made for economic reasons alone. It's tempting to
assume that joint-venture partners are both equally committed to the common goal of maximizing profits, but the

profit motive is a relatively new influence in People's China, where things have traditionally been done more for political than for economic reasons. Even in straight purchasing agreements, politics very often plays a role. Remember that even if a venture loses money for the Chinese in the short run, after a period of years the foreign partner will be history anyway; it's the technology that will remain in China.

A good example of a provision that found its way into a contract for other than economic reasons is a "hold back" clause ultimately agreed to by an American dealer in chemical processing equipment. The company offered its Chinese counterparts the option to pay for a $1 million set of equipment up front, with a standby letter of credit for 5 percent of the purchase price issued at the same time, redeemable for a full year if the Chinese side could certify that the equipment failed to work properly. The Chinese unit refused in principle to pay in full prior to installation, however, and ended up agreeing to a 95 percent up-front payment, with the balance to be paid either after both parties agreed that the equipment was up and running, or after six months—whichever came first. The chosen option was actually far less favorable to China's interests, since it provided for payment in full at six months, whether the equipment worked or not.

8. Don't ever speak "off the record." As in dealing with the news media, there is really no such thing. Anything you say or put on paper can come back to haunt you, whether you are chatting at a banquet, sightseeing at a Buddhist temple, or speaking formally in a negotiating room. The Chinese are notorious for taking people to task for chance, off-the-cuff remarks.

9. Don't show your temper. There are generally plenty of reasons to lose your temper when bargaining with the Chinese, but try to keep your cool at all costs. Blowing up puts you at risk of losing the respect of the other side, since it displays a lack of self-control that the Chinese find contemptible. As noted above, the Chinese may sometimes affect pique in order to win a point, but this is not the same thing as a true loss of temper. You may of course

adopt a similar strategy and fake anger yourself when it is helpful, but try hard not to let any truly felt hostility show through.

10. Don't lose patience. Doing *anything* in China takes time, and any type of arrangement that requires the Chinese to spend money takes even more time. Actually, now that there is a body of laws and regulations and an ample supply of precedents, striking agreement often takes a lot less time than was ever the case in the past. A protracted negotiation lasting many years is now much less common than it used to be, except in the case of a very large project.

RECAP:
SEVEN POINTS ON NEGOTIATING

1. To the Chinese, negotiations are not adversarial. They are looking more for a commitment to work together than for an airtight contract with no loose ends. Negotiations are thus never really over for them; a signed agreement is only a milepost on a long journey.

2. A Chinese negotiating team may have eight to ten people and generally includes a team leader, engineers, technicians, an interpreter, possibly a Communist Party representative, and an attorney. There may be important differences of opinion among them. Their work is subject to review by higher-ups who may never be seen.

3. For your own team, select people knowledgeable about the issues to be discussed. The leader should be secure in his or her position, patient and tolerant. Include a lawyer experienced in China and perhaps an Overseas Chinese liaison and consider bringing your own interpreter. Avoid constant changes in the cast of characters if possible.

4. Chinese begin negotiations by gathering information and assessing trustworthiness. General principles are usually discussed first; only when your position is clear are the Chinese more amenable to discussing their own. Not until the final rounds do the Chinese focus on concrete issues such as contract language and price.

5. Predictable Chinese negotiating tactics include asserting control over the location and schedule of the talks, exploiting vulnerabilities, instilling guilt and shame, playing competitors off against one another, using intermediaries to float ideas and possible positions, feigning anger, revisiting old issues, invoking legal precedents, and raising or lowering expectations to suit their purposes.

6. Always do your homework in advance of talks, take detailed notes during negotiations, and go through all the details of a contract before signing. Show commitment to the talks, but be prepared to walk away and cut your losses if necessary. Resist their efforts to flatter you into concessions. Be sure to pad your price so that you can satisfy them by lowering it later on. Watch what you say to the media; best not to say anything at all during negotiations.

7. Avoid resolving problems as they are raised; wait until you hear all the issues. Don't concede anything too easily; reserve some easy concessions for later. Never assume the Chinese bureaucracy is all in agreement on any project, or that decisions are necessarily made for purely economic reasons. Never speak off the record; anything you say in any situation or context could come back to haunt you. Avoid showing your temper, and never, never lose patience!

10

Getting Things Done in China

Learning how to get things accomplished in the PRC is no easy task for a foreigner. The workings of the Chinese system often seem patently irrational to Westerners, though they do possess an internal logic all their own. An appreciation of how things work and why they happen as they do is the key to manipulating the system to serve your own ends.

This understanding requires the grasp of a few basic points about the Chinese system. First of all, China's bureaucracy is vast, omnipotent, and exceptionally resistant to change. Second, China is an economy of scarcity, with simply not enough of the most desirable products or services to go around. Though these resources are allocated in ways that are not necessarily fair or equitable, there is a certain rationality in the process (see the section on "Going Through the Back Door" below). And third, the Chinese abhor open conflict among people, so disputes and animosities are expected to be resolved in peaceful ways if they are not permitted to fester, quietly unresolved, for years. Preserving decorum and harmony is always very important.

THE HOST ORGANIZATION

Generally speaking, foreigners in China, whether there for a quick business trip or a prolonged residence, are invited under the auspices of a *jiedai danwei* or "host organization." The host is responsible for the guest during the latter's entire time in China. This means working on behalf of the guest to accommodate requests for meetings, site visits, travel, etc., and running interference with the rest of the Chinese bureaucracy in order to fulfill these requests.

The "host organization" system is so powerful and so universal that for a time many Chinese units refused to recognize foreigners, or even foreign organizations with operations in China, as entities with which they were empowered to deal. If a hotel was approached by a foreigner for a room or a travel service asked to make travel arrangements, for example, either would be quite likely to insist that before anything was done, an official request for assistance had to come not from the foreigner, who had no status, but from the host organization.

With the advent of foreign representative offices and joint ventures this practice has diminished considerably; foreign organizations may now attain legal standing in China and in general may deal on their own. The point here, however, is that if you are trying to get something accomplished in China, your host organization is a very good place to start; it is the one Chinese organization whose job it is to help you out.

Among the types of requests that your host unit may be able to handle for you are travel arrangements, hotel bookings, limousine or luggage service, site visits, business meetings, theater tickets, high-level audiences, VIP tours, etc. This does not mean that many of these services cannot be obtained directly; it does mean, however, that the host can sometimes help out if you encounter difficulty in making the arrangements yourself.

Occasionally, your interests may diverge from those of your host unit, and in such cases the host cannot be counted on to render much assistance. For example, a company being hosted in Beijing by the China National Minerals and Metals Import and Export Corporation, which reports to the Ministry of Foreign Economic Relations and Trade, once asked its host to arrange a courtesy call on the foreign trading arm of the Ministry of Metallurgical Industry, a rival corporation. The host came back a day or two later and said that the meeting would be impossible to arrange, since the Metallurgical Ministry had no wish to receive the guests. This sounded unlikely, so when the company approached me for help I made a quick phone call to a friend at that Ministry and discovered that there had been no truth to the report at all; the Metallurgical Ministry was delighted to meet with the company. The conference was set up for later that afternoon. What had in fact happened was that the host organization, fearing that direct negotiations between the company and the Ministry might eventually cut them out of a deal, attempted to sabotage the meeting.

THE BUREAUCRACY: MANY CHECKS, FEW BALANCES

Because the PRC is a socialist country, many tasks that would be accomplished in the private sector in a Western nation—such as the manufacture of consumer goods, the provision of housing, or the operation of transportation systems—are under the aegis of some unit of the government or other. The government is all-pervasive, and, as indicated earlier, has traditionally controlled many aspects of the personal lives of the people in addition to the country's industry and commerce (see Chapter 4).

Traditionally, central planning dictated that power be concentrated in Beijing, where dozens of commissions, ministries, general bureaus, and agencies planned and coordinated the work of the country. A typical ministry or commission would break out into many bureaus and divisions. Provincial and municipal governments mirrored the structure of the central government. And the 1980s heralded the proliferation of government-run corporations, which are responsible to government agencies but have increasingly been granted authority to make most of their own day-to-day business decisions.

The chain of command among government units has always been a rather Byzantine system of dual reporting. For example, a drug factory located in Shanghai might report jointly to the Shanghai Pharmaceuticals Bureau—a unit of the local government—and also to the State Pharmaceutical Administration, part of the central government in Beijing. And various other agencies—the local labor bureau, the local environmental bureau, the local supplies bureau, to name just a few—would also have a say in certain activities of the factory.

Innovation in such a huge bureaucracy is bound to be a painful process even when everything runs smoothly—and there is never a time when everything runs smoothly. There are countless ways to derail a new idea and nearly always someone or some organization with a vested interest in the status quo who has both a say in the decision about it and a motive to scuttle it. And conversely, there are relatively few ways short of consensus—notoriously difficult to obtain—to accomplish something novel.

To make matters even worse, decisions are made as frequently for political reasons as they are for economic ones. The Cultural Revolution slogan, "Let Politics Take Command," which has been officially repudiated, nonetheless often remains the modus operandi. When politics takes precedence over economics, the laws of supply and demand do not always apply.

Take for example the case of a row of billboards that used to decorate the corner of Chang'an and Wangfujing Avenues in Beijing. These were among the first outside advertisements taken out by foreign companies when the PRC first permitted ads in 1979. The billboards were the source of substantial revenue for the Beijing branch of the State Administration for Industry and Commerce that owned them, and many Japanese consumer products were touted on them.

Then, without warning one day in 1986, the government announced that the billboards would be removed. Many Japanese commercial representatives speculated that this gesture was really a slap at Japan, since most of the billboards displayed Japanese products, and China had expressed annoyance at an action of the Japanese government only days before the announcement. The government denied this, insisting that the decision did not concern Japan; displaying commercial messages so close to Tiananmen Square—China's equivalent of Red Square in Moscow—was simply no longer considered appropriate. Regardless of which was actually true, the point is that a decision with important economic consequences was clearly made for anything but economic reasons.

BUREAUCRATIC DECISION MAKING

The areas controlled by the bureaucracy are vast, and the number of people involved is phenomenal. Yet it would be hard to imagine a more conservative, change-resistant institution. Decisions are made by consensus, and they come strictly from the top down. Since authority is not explicitly delegated to those at lower levels in China, subordinates tend to be insecure about deciding anything. You never go wrong or get criticized for doing nothing; you are only blamed when you demonstrate initiative. The result is that even the most minor matters are referred up the chain of command, and that the highest-ranking cadres are inundated with minutiae.

Decision making can occasionally be fairly expedient, but is more often painfully inefficient and complex. An order by a high-level official is easily executed, for no one would presume to argue with high-level approval. But if a decision requires cooperation among more than one unit in the bureaucracy, look out! Lack of coordination is the mildest way to describe what happens.

You can *always* assume that different units have different interests; you can safely assume *most* of the time that they do not talk to each other. You can *frequently* assume that the units dislike one another and that cooperation among them would be more of an exception than a rule. The only way to get out of a deadlock in which one organization in the bureaucracy is at odds with another is to appeal to an authority superior to both of them; it is often only at this level that a binding decision can be made.

The amount of red tape necessary to accomplish even something very minor can be staggering, and reasons can always be found to foil any request. Precedent is a common one: "We've never had such a request before" often means we are not interested in entertaining such a request now. Equity is another: "If we make an exception and let you do this, we would have to let everyone do it." And then there are the old standbys, "It is inconvenient to do as you wish" and "Your request is under consideration."

Because innovation is frowned on, you stick your neck out only with great caution. The key motivating factor for a Chinese worker in such situations is to avoid accepting responsibility, lest the decision be construed as the wrong one and he or she be made to suffer for it later. So the worker is likely to take a very conservative tack when approached with an out-of-the-ordinary request, especially when this request comes from a foreigner—which by definition makes something unusual.

Then too, sometimes you encounter resistance from Chinese people not so much for bureaucratic reasons as for personal ones. The individual may not like you, or may harbor resentment against foreigners in general. Or something in your manner—often the brazen assertiveness that characterizes many Occidentals—may have put the person off. The Chinese may not be particularly adept at venting anger, but they do a masterful job at passive resistance.

And finally, people may be less than enthusiastic about helping you get something accomplished due to nothing other than a lack of incentive to do otherwise. Why exert yourself when there is nothing to be gained? The socialist system in China has unfortunately gone a long way toward suppressing the normally industrious nature of the Chinese. The reward system in People's China has for decades had little or nothing to do with the amount of effort expended; salaries remained constant whether work was good or bad, productivity high or low. The Chinese call it the *tie fanwan*—"iron rice bowl"— system, an image that makes sense when you understand that one's rice bowl is a traditional symbol for one's livelihood, and that to break someone's rice bowl is to deprive that person of his or her means of support. An iron rice bowl is unbreakable, a metaphor for lifetime tenure in a job, regardless of performance. The system is gradually being replaced by one that includes bonuses and cash incentives, but old attitudes die hard.

TACTICS FOR "GETTING TO YES"

In China as elsewhere, there are some things that truly cannot be accomplished, and efforts to make them happen amount to little more than whistling in the wind. But many tasks that appear impossible can in fact be achieved if you take the proper approach. Just about anything can be negotiated in the PRC, and there are a great many things that *have* to be.

One effective method to get your way when you encounter resistance is to appeal to someone higher up in the chain of command, assuming you can gain access to such a person. If you are in a store or at a ticket counter, you can ask to speak with the manager; you may or may not be successful. The trick is to find someone willing to make a decision and take responsibility for it. While such an action might easily earn you the enmity of the underling in the West, in China it may actually be appreciated. If a higher-up is willing to overrule an employee and be accountable for an action, the employee becomes *empowered* to assist you. The weight of the decision has been taken out of the subordinate's hands and he or she is free to help you out.

Another stratagem that is sometimes successful is firm insistence. If you are convinced that what you are asking for is feasible and ought not to pose any major problems, you can try pressing your point quietly and calmly, but relentlessly. If you refuse to go away, you may be causing the person more of a problem by making a pest of yourself than satisfying your request would cause. You increase your chance of successful resolution by making it in his or her interest to do what you wish.

This tactic is often successful at Chinese hotels that are "completely filled." As mentioned earlier, despite what many desk clerks will tell you, there are *always* vacant rooms in Chinese hotels. If you are without a room, it is just a question of making it to the clerk's advantage to let you use one of the vacant rooms. Hanging around the service desk and refusing to be mollified with a pat answer has been known to make many a clerk come up with a room key—helping you out becomes the path of least resistance.

I once used this device during departure formalities at Capital Airport in Beijing. Members of a delegation of which I was in charge were being assessed a fine by a Chinese customs officer because they lacked a necessary stamp on their customs forms. The charge was patently unfair, since the only reason the stamp was missing was that the customs agent in charge when they entered China had forgotten this formality. Digging in my heels and politely refusing to pay or to leave the counter until the matter was adjudicated to my satisfaction eventually worked; the officer called his superior over to the desk and, after hearing my story, the supervisor gave clearance to waive the fine.

Sometimes getting something accomplished may only be a matter of learning how to push the right button. A Chinese may not fully understand a point you are making, but for reasons of face may be unwilling to admit that this is the case. Or a Chinese may not fully appreciate why you are making a request, and may inadvertently withhold a key piece of information because he or she doesn't see it as relevant. I once spent a full hour at a Chinese post office trying to make arrangements to send a package to the United States. Only after the clerk—who in fact was very accommodating and eager to help—had gone through two different mailing boxes (one was too large for international mail; a second was too heavy and added too much to the postage) and I inquired specifically if there wasn't another way of mailing the item did it dawn on her that using a burlap sack—which was available for sale right at her counter in the post office and which was cheaper than either of the boxes we had tried—would solve the problem and save me money in the process.

Speaking in soft tones generally gets you a great deal further with the Chinese than shrill complaining. In fact, it's often a good idea to speak less directly than you might otherwise prefer, and to imply things rather than state them outright.

The Chinese themselves frequently give only subtle signals as to their desires. This lack of directness can sometimes be infuriating, but learning to hear in between their words is a skill worth developing. For example, if, during a discussion about a trip to the airport to meet a relative, a Chinese asks you whether you have a car, chances are good that he or she would appreciate it if you would offer a ride.

The beauty of such unstated requests is that no face is ever lost as a result of them. Since no request has actually been made, no rebuff has taken place when someone else fails to rise to the bait and make an offer of assistance. No real harm is done if you don't offer to take the trip to the airport. The only problem here arises when these discreet signals are missed entirely by literal-minded Westerners.

"GOING THROUGH THE BACK DOOR"

One of the most important methods of "getting to yes" in China is the use of *guanxi* (see Chapter 4). Knowing people in high—or simply strategic—places, and motivating them to help you out are important tools. Chinese frequently cultivate such people against the future possibility that a favor will be needed. Often the "favor" is something supposedly available to anyone who qualifies, but in actual fact difficult if not impossible to come by.

For example, one spring, while I was in Beijing, I attempted to purchase air tickets—a notoriously scarce commodity—for a business trip to Xi'an. I knew that tickets might be hard to get, so I deliberately arrived at the airline ticket office a full month and a half before I wanted to travel. After fighting my way to the ticket counter (there were no orderly lines, just a lot of people trying to push in front of each other), I was told that I had come too early. Tickets for that particular flight would not be available until the 18th of the month. Taking this advice at face value, I dutifully returned on the appointed date. This time, however, I was told that I was too late; all of the tickets had been sold and there were no more available seats.

Clearly it was not people who came in off the street like me who got the tickets, whether foreigners or Chinese. I'd wager that the seats went to people with *guanxi*: friends and relatives of those who worked for the airline; high-ranking cadres from work units with good institutional relations with the airline; and people who work for units being cultivated by the airline.

Furthermore, it's extremely doubtful that *all* of the tickets had been sold. It's unlikely that any Chinese unit would be so shortsighted as not to keep tickets in reserve to preserve flexibility in case someone with *guanxi* surfaced at the last minute needing tickets. Not only could these tickets not have been sold to me, but the airline would probably have been satisfied even if they were never sold. The chronic underbooking in the PRC is a far cry from the overbooking that is sometimes a problem in the West. In China, it's best to let a plane depart half-empty; preserving flexibility in order to be able to deliver on *guanxi* is vitally important.

Using *guanxi* to obtain personal favors is one thing; using it to obtain services or goods that you might otherwise not qualify for has a special name in China: to do so is to *zou houmen*, or "go through the back door." When someone uses the powers of his or her office, or even those of a network of friends, to deliver personal favors—a job for the daughter of a friend, a place on a delegation to Europe, an apartment for someone's sister, a hard-to-get consumer good, or the use of the unit's car for a personal errand—this constitutes a use of the "back door." Its use is ubiquitous in the PRC, precisely because many things cannot be accomplished in any other way. Witness my futile attempt to obtain tickets by the "front door," which, in this case, was simply a painted image on a blind wall.

Naturally, access to the "back door" is not without its costs. People can be motivated in many ways: there are always reciprocal obligations, and there may also be gratuities involved. Someone might be delighted to pull a string to help you get an apartment in a new high-rise building, for example, if you can scare up a Japanese refrigerator in return. Or the price might be a *hongbao*, literally a "red envelope," which is expected to contain a certain amount of cash. In China's "back door" economy, money, power, and access can all fetch a great deal in return.

GRAFT

One way that many things get accomplished in China—as they do in Taiwan and Hong Kong—is through bribery. There are Chinese, just as there are people in any other culture, who will accept gratuities for providing hard-to-get and often improper or illegal services.

This is not really in the same category as the innocent gift that someone may give you before asking you to do a favor. In that case you receive the gift before you agree to do anything, and, strictly speaking, the present is not contingent on your willingness to help out. Also, the purpose of such a present may be less to gain your cooperation and more to preserve the face of the giver. It's always bad form to owe someone so much that payback is impossible; a person is not quite as beholden to another if a present has changed hands first.

One hears many stories about a Chinese negotiating team choosing one supplier over another because the deal was "sweetened" by an overeager foreign company. It might be the inclusion in the deal of an unnecessary but all-expense-paid "fact-finding trip" abroad for the Chinese partner. Or it might be a more brazen act such as the delivery of a spanking new Japanese television set to the home of the chief negotiator. I think that many of the stories are exaggerated, but there is no question that this type of activity does go on, especially among the Chinese themselves, and especially in southern China where ties to Hong Kong and Southeast Asia are closer. The scrupulous honesty that invariably characterized PRC business people in the early days of the China trade has, alas, gone the way of Chairman Mao's little red book.

This doesn't in any way imply that you won't run into plenty of principled Chinese business people for whom accepting bribes is unthinkable. I believe that the vast majority of PRC officials—most of whom are Communist Party members—probably keep their noses very clean. What it does mean is that graft is one of the many "currencies" that get wheels turning in China.

Interestingly, many of the ostensibly corrupt acts committed in China are actually done for the benefit of the unit rather than the individual. Though there are unarguably cases where the goal is strictly personal enrichment, equally often the object is to get around a vexing bureaucratic restriction that prevents the unit from doing its work efficiently. One company that was initially quite put off at a Chinese request to include delivery of two trucks as part of a technology-transfer deal eventually yielded when it was made to understand that the Chinese unit was not looking for something for nothing. Indeed, the unit was perfectly willing to pay for the trucks; it was simply trying to find a way to circumvent a cumbersome approval process that would never have granted it the authority to import the vehicles directly.

If a Chinese is interested in some sort of payoff, he or she will undoubtedly find some way to let you know. The signal may be a subtle one, but if you are alert for it you can usually pick it up. You need feel no compunction about turning down such a request, however. Simply explaining that such acts are strictly illegal in your country and that to engage in them would subject you to severe punishment at home can often do the trick. Few foreign companies have ever reported being seriously disadvantaged in their business in China due to inability or unwillingness to come through with a bribe.

MANAGING CONFLICT

If you spend any amount of time in China, you are bound to wind up in some contentious situations. The Chinese system is not set up to provide the amount of individual freedom to which most Westerners are accustomed; therefore, if you wish to live a "normal" lifestyle in China—doing what you wish to do when you wish to do it—you are embarking on a collision course with the system. In China, there are always a million reasons why you can't do something, why you must wait your turn, why you must pay a premium, etc.

Given the nature of the beast, you are bound to bump into situations in China that will make you angry. In such circumstances you should do all you can to stifle the natural inclination to lash out. Blowing your cool is generally not an

effective way of accomplishing things. Expressing rage at
someone is likely only to make him or her *more* resolute than
before in denying your request, and may make the person look
down on you for your lack of decorum in the balance. The
Chinese, as a rule, don't like to be pushed; you'll get far more
cooperation from them if they like you than if they resent you.
In the latter case, passive resistance is a far more probable
outcome than accommodation.

You should conduct yourself with propriety. If you must
communicate anger, try to keep from losing your temper.
Simply report dispassionately the fact that you are annoyed
and the reasons. At the very least you'll be respected for being
able to keep your emotions under control.

When you bump heads with a Chinese, one of the most
important things to keep in mind is always to offer the person
a way out. If you maneuver a person into a corner, you can
absolutely count on strong resistance. If, for example, a store
clerk tells you that something you wish to buy has been sold
out for a week and you confront the person with evidence that
he or she has lied to you—such as the fact that someone you
know bought the item there that very morning—don't expect
the reaction to be embarrassment and subsequent cooperation.
You may invoke the former, but in putting the person's
honor—that is, his or her face—at stake, you'll get anything
but the latter. Far better to suggest that perhaps if the person
looks in the storage room a second time he or she may discover
another box of the items in question that no one had realized
was in there.

One way of offering a "way out" is to use an intermediary,
especially if you are in the position of having to deliver bad
news to a Chinese. If, for example, you must fire someone, it's
often best to break the news through a third party. Relaying the
message in this way spares the face of the injured party, who
may be shocked, furious, hurt, or otherwise distressed. It's
important to realize that using an intermediary is not considered to be a coward's way out in China; among the Chinese
there is no premium on confrontation. Conveying bad news
through a go-between is generally a desirable method that is
easier on everyone.

RECAP: TEN TIPS
ON GETTING THINGS DONE

1. Your host organization or *jiedai danwei* is responsible for you in China; it is the one organization whose job it is to help you out. Host units can help arrange travel, site visits, business meetings, etc. Maintaining good relations with the host is very important.

2. The Chinese government is all-pervasive, controlling people's personal lives as well as the country's industry and commerce. The chain of command is complex and innovation is a painful process. There are many ways to derail a new idea and relatively few ways to accomplish something novel.

3. Decisions are made as frequently for political reasons as economic ones. They are generally made by consensus and are strictly from the top down. Even minor matters are referred up the chain of command.

4. Different units always have different interests and strong rivalries and don't communicate with one another efficiently. There is much red tape and reasons can always be found to foil a request.

5. Innovation is frowned on. Chinese workers try to avoid accepting responsibility. If they are not motivated to help you, they can do a masterful job of passive resistance.

6. When you encounter resistance, try to appeal to someone higher up in the chain of command, or refuse to go away, pressing your point quietly and calmly, but relentlessly. Speaking in soft tones gets you further with the Chinese than shrill complaining.

7. To use connections to obtain scarce services or goods is to *zou houmen* or "go through the back door." Its use is ubiquitous in the PRC, precisely because many things cannot be accomplished in any other way. Going through the back door implies reciprocal obligations, however.

8. As in other cultures, in China some people seek gratuities for providing hard-to-get and often illegal services. If a Chinese is interested in dealing in this manner, he or she

will let you know, though the signal may be subtle. You need not comply.

9. Stifle your natural inclination to lash out when you encounter obstacles in China. Blowing your cool is generally ineffective and may be counterproductive. The Chinese don't like to be pushed, and are far more cooperative if they like you than if they resent you.

10. Always offer a Chinese person a way out. If you maneuver a person into a corner, you can absolutely count on strong resistance. Face is at stake. Use an intermediary to deliver bad news; among the Chinese there is no premium on confrontation.

11

Hosting the Chinese

In nearly any business relationship with a Chinese organization, a company can expect sooner or later to find itself in the position of playing host to a delegation. Delegation trips to other countries are Chinese units' favorite methods for assessing foreign technology—and they are real plums for deserving cadres as well.

Companies should select carefully and host only those delegations likely to be important to their business interests in China. Hosting carries many responsibilities and can be costly in both time and money. Once the decision is made to host, there are a number of points to which companies should pay attention. The goal is to make the visit a substantive success and to make sure that the relationships are handled properly and, ideally, deepened as a result of the trip.

Much of the protocol discussed in the previous chapters is equally applicable to dealing with Chinese people in China and abroad. You'll never go far wrong if you choose to cater to Chinese sensibilities in such areas as meeting and greeting, dining, and conducting business meetings. On the other hand, the Chinese expect things to be different when they travel abroad. You should never be in the position of feeling compelled to discard your own ways simply to make them comfortable; there's a difference between taking Chinese customs into account to make their stay more enjoyable and slavishly following their rule book and abandoning your own cultural values entirely. If you do the latter, your unease with the situation will be immediately clear, and the entire visit will probably be not only less comfortable, but also less effective all around.

SHOULD YOU HOST A DELEGATION?

Chinese groups travel abroad for many different reasons. A delegation might be a high-level mission headed by a vice premier or minister looking to sign a protocol with the host government or visit certain facilities of a large company. It might also be a survey group, looking around to see what type of equipment or technology is available but not empowered to sign contracts. Such groups frequently travel abroad to attend conventions or exhibitions, and often attempt to schedule company visits on the side.

On the other hand, the trip could be little more than a ceremonial visit—a reward to some high-ranking cadre about to retire for his or her years of service to the ministry. Or it might be a planning group, eager to assess—or copy— available technology so as to incorporate its acquisition into the country's or the province's five-year plan. It could also be a buying or selling group, empowered to negotiate contracts and commit foreign exchange.

It is vitally important to know something of a group's composition, its goals and its authority before you decide whether or not to play host, since hosting carries with it a set of responsibilities (see below). Many companies are approached by far more Chinese delegations than they could ever possibly receive; some say that if they agreed to meet with every group that requests a visit they would do nothing other than host delegations from China.

It's usually fairly clear from a glance at the name list and the answers to a few basic questions whether a given group has a legitimate business interest in asking for a meeting, or whether it is simply trying to fill time to justify staying abroad for an extra day or two. In fact, a Los Angeles-based company, to its dismay, once came to the conclusion that a Chinese delegation seeking a meeting was interested less in the firm's technology than in whether the company would underwrite a day's excursion for the group to Disneyland.

On the other hand, not every group worth hosting travels with checkbook in hand. Certain survey and planning delegations may not be empowered to contract for purchases, but may have a great deal to say about what technology China chooses when it *is* time to buy.

THE DELEGATES

A delegation, even if it is composed of individuals from many different Chinese units, functions in essence as if it were a unit unto itself. It has a mandate—perhaps more than one—and a definite structure and hierarchy. Delegations are organized according to a clear rank order and the individuals in them may hold many specialized functions.

Hosts can generally count on receiving a delegation name list some time in advance of the visit. Every Chinese delegation used to travel with a complete printed name list which they presented to each host along the way; this custom has gone out of style as individual name cards have become more popular in the PRC, but you still occasionally see such lists. They enumerate the delegates in order of protocol, giving their titles and the rank in the delegation of the top few members. If you are asked to host a group and you do not automatically receive a name list before the visit, by all means ask for one; it can be very helpful in deciding whether it's a delegation worth receiving or not.

Every delegation has a leader called a *tuanzhang*. He or she makes major decisions and speaks for the group in all matters. The leader may be supported by a deputy leader called a *futuanzhang*. If the delegation ever splits up into two groups in order to attend separate functions, this person becomes the head of the splinter group. Senior cadres who may be along on the trip for specific purposes may be designated as advisors or *guwen*. They hold high rank in the delegation, but generally have no administrative responsibility; for many the delegation trip is little more than a well-earned boondoggle in advance of retirement.

Beyond these officers, delegations may have secretaries (responsible for taking notes), treasurers (keeping accounts and handling money for the group), interpreters, and liaison officers, who often hold one of the other titles. There are almost always one or two very low-ranking individuals who tend to administrative tasks such as making sure that the luggage is counted and collected at each stop or keeping charge of the group's air tickets. Very high-ranking groups may also be escorted by a functionary from a Chinese embassy or consulate who is posted in the host country. This person's rank in the delegation can be gauged from his or her position in the delegation name list.

The delegation leader is usually a responsible official from a Chinese government work unit or corporation; the delegates themselves may be technicians or engineers. They can usually be counted on to have done their homework and to understand a good deal of the basic technology underlying any given area of interest. At the very least they will be up on contemporary literature in the field, and will be familiar with your company's products. So it's generally a mistake to underestimate their level of expertise.

DUTIES OF THE HOST

In China, there is a whole set of responsibilities associated with hosting a delegation from abroad. In the past, no foreigners were ever permitted in the PRC unless a government work unit was willing to take responsibility for them during the visit. The routine tasks shouldered by the *jiedai danwei*—the "host unit"—included authorizing the visa, booking hotel rooms, and arranging site visits and any travel within China.

But hosting also carried with it the burden of running interference for the foreign guest with any other units in China—everything from setting up meetings to mediating disputes, especially if the foreigner should get into any trouble in China, such as have an accident, or do something wrong. Though China has changed to the point that one can get a visa based on only a loose relationship with a Chinese host, such an organization is still a very good ally to have in your corner when you are trying to get something accomplished.

The Chinese, as usual, extrapolate from their own system. Since making travel and other logistical arrangements in the PRC has always been such a cumbersome process for foreigners (and, for that matter, for locals), the Chinese assume that it will be equally difficult for them to get around in other countries. For this reason, and in order to fulfill certain official requirements—such as those of foreign embassies that insist on sponsors before they will grant visas, or of Chinese government agencies that demand them before they will authorize passports—they generally seek out hosts in the countries they visit. The hosts are expected to coordinate the trips and generally help things go smoothly for the Chinese delegations.

In China, there is often such a thing as multiple hosts for foreigners, especially when the trip involves visits to more than one city. This frequently happens when the Chinese travel abroad as well. A Chinese delegation may ask one company or one government agency to act as its national sponsor, or it might appeal to different organizations to make arrangements for it as it travels to different cities. Sometimes, however, it will confuse the picture and ask several companies to arrange the same visit. Naturally, with any given trip it's important to know how arrangements are being handled. The cardinal rule of hosting: *always* clarify exactly what is expected of you if you agree to serve as host.

The casual reader might be surprised at how frequently this rule is ignored. Often companies don't focus on the specific demands of their guests until a week or so before the delegation is due to arrive. They may assume that their responsibilities begin with receiving the delegation at their facilities and end with seeing them back to the hotel, whereas the Chinese might have something very different in mind. Their expectations might include helping them apply for visas, applying pressure to your own country's embassy or consulate in China to expedite issuance of visas, scheduling audiences with government agencies, setting up meetings with other companies, arranging for the group to be met at each airport and escorted to the hotel in each city, paying for meals, and handling local transportation to each site visited.

You may not feel comfortable raising with the Chinese specific issues relating to the extent of the hospitality you are prepared to provide for fear of appearing less than gracious should you decline to go to the trouble or expense of fulfilling all the delegation's desires. But it is very important to do so; only if responsibilities are clearly defined can you be certain that there will be no misunderstandings. Far better to have a moment of unease during the negotiating stage than a major snafu when a delegation gets stranded at an airport or caught without sufficient funds to pay a hotel bill.

Companies that host Chinese technical delegations for months at a time often run into a whole additional set of problems. In such situations the Chinese groups need to have their housing, transportation, eating, and entertainment needs addressed. Since delegates frequently do not speak English and do not hold driver's licenses, hospitality sometimes requires assigning a company staff member—ideally one who can speak some Chinese—to see to their comfort.

ACCOMMODATIONS

Sometimes Chinese and foreign counterparts reach reciprocal hospitality agreements whereby the visitor picks up the tab for international travel, but the host bears responsibility for local expenses in the country being visited. Such agreements are good deals for the Chinese, since basic services are cheaper in China—when Chinese units pay for them. If a Chinese unit picks up the tab for a foreign guest's stay in a Chinese hotel, the price is often far cheaper than if the guest paid the hotel directly.

More typically, each side pays its own expenses when it visits the other's country. If you are charged with making hotel arrangements for a visiting Chinese group that will foot its own local expenses, be sensitive to costs. It's a rare Chinese delegation that wants to spend the amount of money necessary for first-class treatment on every leg of the journey. Though high-ranking groups may wish to stay at the best hotels—for reasons of face, if nothing else—most delegations are looking for clean, comfortable accommodations at bargain rates. If in doubt, be sure that you let the Chinese know in advance how much the hotel charges per room.

It's also important to find out whether the norm for the delegation will be single or double rooms, and whether any of the higher-ranking delegates will need suites. It's not important to assign roommates in advance of arrival; the Chinese will do that themselves. Chinese groups often request one suite, which is occupied by the delegation leader and is also used for group meetings that they hold on their own time. If it is an important group and you are picking up the tab, you may want to consider booking a suite for the delegation head; if the Chinese will bear responsibility for local costs, check with them first to see what their wishes are in this regard.

Ask the hotel to endeavor to accommodate the entire group on one floor, or in one wing, if at all possible. Proximity to an interpreter is important to a hotel guest who cannot communicate in the local language and who may need to deal with the hotel staff for such matters as laundry, room service, or long-distance telephone calls.

If it is a first trip abroad for many of the delegates, you might consider offering them an informal briefing on safety and security. First-time visitors may not be well-equipped to deal with the dangers present in many Western cities, and may need to be reminded of a few basic precautions: to avoid flashing large sums of cash and leaving valuables in hotel rooms, to use traveler's checks, and to safeguard items such as air tickets.

Certain amenities are de rigeur, such as meeting a visiting group at the airport (see Chapter 3), hosting them for a meal, or seeing them off when they leave. Other gestures may be offered but are not necessarily required. Transportation for the delegation, for example, may be provided free of charge, or at the delegation's own expense.

One odious practice in the PRC now fortunately on the decline is that of foisting VIP services on foreign visitors first and asking for money later. Many delegations visiting China

in the early 1980s received first-class treatment—luggage
whisked off to the hotel in a special van, limousine service
provided for the delegation—only to be surprised and annoyed
when the often hefty bill for these amenities was presented just
before the end of the stay. The Chinese have gotten much
better about making clear up front what costs money and what
is being provided free of charge. Foreign hosts are well advised
to offer the same courtesy to them. What is essential is that
there be no surprises; it should always be clear at the outset
what the visitors will be expected to pay for themselves.

FORMALITIES

As discussed in Chapter 3, the Chinese place a great deal of
emphasis on the protocol of meeting visitors at the point of
entry and seeing them off as far as the airport on their
departure. Such formal greetings are considered an official
responsibility of the group's principal host and they are
formalities that are best not overlooked when receiving high-
ranking Chinese guests. Furthermore, guests must be received
by someone of suitably high rank in the host organization.
Nothing gets a visit off to a worse start than omitting this ritual,
or fouling it up by sending the wrong person. While Chinese
with more experience with Westerners may understand that
this ceremony is simply not customary in other countries,
those who are less worldly may not be able to avoid viewing it
as a gratuitous affront.

   Make sure that whoever greets the groups is well-briefed.
Note particularly any members of the delegation whom
officers or staff of your company have met before. It's quite
awkward when a Chinese—or anyone else, for that matter—
expects to be remembered and is not. Conversely, it is
appreciated when a company president recalls, or even pre-
tends to recall, a previous meeting with a delegate.

   If your Chinese visitor is a very high-ranking individual or
if you desire for other reasons to receive a Chinese guest in
grand style, providing transportation is a good way to signal
respect. Often a limousine is furnished for the delegation
leader and one or more very high-ranking delegates, with the

balance of the group traveling together in another car, a bus, or a minivan. In such situations, the principal host travels together with the Chinese delegation leader and an interpreter, if necessary. If there are many high-ranking delegates and all cannot fit comfortably into the limousine, a second car may be employed for them.

One caveat here: some delegations prefer not to be split up, and will happily forgo the special treatment in favor of a minibus that will keep all the delegates in close proximity. If you do arrange a limousine it's a good idea to check in advance and make sure the Chinese wish it; alternatively, remain flexible and be prepared to switch modes of transportation on short notice if asked to do so.

Even if your company president can't make it to the airport, scheduling an audience with him or her—or with some other responsible corporate official—is a gesture that is much appreciated. To do so is to "give face" to the Chinese delegation (see Chapter 4), and to signal the visitors that your company takes them and their business seriously.

PLANNING THE SCHEDULE

One of the first activities you should consider scheduling with a visiting group from China is an itinerary meeting. This can be an informal discussion with the delegation's liaison person or interpreter, or it can be a more official session; it depends on the level of formality of the delegation, how well you know the members and whether or not you anticipate that the group will require any last-minute changes to the agenda.

The purpose of the meeting is to secure Chinese "buy-in" of the arrangements that have been made for them. It is a way of confirming that the itinerary and agenda you have planned are satisfactory. Holding such a meeting decreases the chances of things going awry during the visit, such as an important delegation official opting not to attend a crucial meeting, or the group splitting up so that half of them can participate in some activity entirely unrelated to the visit with your company.

The itinerary meeting is your opportunity to determine

whether the Chinese plan on doing anything else in your city during the time they are visiting with you. By holding the discussion shortly after the delegation's arrival, you have also given yourself time to make adjustments to the schedule if for any reason the arrangements are not acceptable.

Many companies make name badges for Chinese visitors and ask the delegates to wear them so their hosts will know how to address them. Chinese accept these willingly when they are offered. Don't forget, however, that they will need to know what to call their hosts as well, so if you hand out name badges be sure your side wears them, too. The labels should be bilingual if possible.

If the visit to your company is the first stop on the group's U.S. tour, you might want to keep the first day's schedule light to permit the delegates time to overcome jet lag, which is particularly severe when traveling such a long distance from west to east. Generally the first official gathering is some sort of briefing about the company—an introductory presentation giving basic facts about the company's structure, history, products, production and sales statistics. Don't worry about boring your guests or even about repeating something most of the delegates already know; you'll probably find them taking copious notes anyway. Most Chinese don't mind repetition; hearing something again simply reinforces their confidence that they heard it right the first time.

Many companies are also asked by the Chinese to arrange factory tours. Here the technicians and engineers on the delegation can be counted on to ask probing technical questions, and to prepare properly for such visits you should certainly have on hand someone who can answer them. If the answers are proprietary—technological secrets that you wish to sell to the Chinese, are prohibited from revealing, or simply do not wish to divulge—be honest and tell the Chinese why. They can accept such limits when they are clearly explained to them.

Though the demands of a tightly scheduled visit often do not permit it, most Chinese delegations will be very grateful if you can engineer an early afternoon nap break for them. A company to whose headquarters I once escorted a Chinese delegation actually provided the group with the use of a lounge and a dozen blankets for an hour after they finished lunch. Inside of five minutes the snoring of a very appreciative band of weary cadres could be heard at the far end of the long corridor leading to the lounge. Even if an hour and a half at lunch time can't be spared, however, be sure to plan sufficient break time between meetings so that your visitors can assimilate what they have learned and so that the interpreters can have a rest.

Strictly speaking, the most senior corporate officer who receives the group at the airport or at a banquet need not accompany the group all through its visit, though the more time he or she makes available, as a rule, the more *mianzi* or "face" will be conferred on the visitors. It is important, however, that someone of sufficiently high stature stay with the group during its visit—unless of course the delegation will be staying for a period of weeks or months. It's also important to make available someone capable of fielding the technical questions that the Chinese delegates will inevitably have.

You should definitely plan to provide your Chinese guests with some materials relevant to their visit. A schedule or itinerary prepared in Chinese will be most welcome, but at the very least an English version should be provided. A complete name list of the company officers the guests will be meeting should also be offered; for the convenience of the Chinese you should attempt to list the individuals and their titles in rank order.

Technical materials related to the product or technology a Chinese group is interested in buying should also be prepared; again, if you can arrange for these materials to be translated into Chinese, by all means do so. If the group will be resident in your city for a prolonged period of time, literature on how to get around will also be welcome.

CONDUCTING MEETINGS

When your company first agrees to play host to a visiting group from China, you should do all you can to find out the exact purpose of the group's visit to your country, and the specific goals they hope to accomplish by visiting your organization.

Establishing the intentions of the Chinese side and determining your own company's objectives in hosting the group are the most important steps in ensuring a successful visit.

A group may well have many goals, not just one. Various delegates, especially if they work for different units in China, can be expected to have divergent interests and to be looking for distinct things. You can often make an educated guess at the area of interest simply by looking at the person's title.

After the goals are clarified, presentations can be outlined accordingly. A coordinator for the visit can make sure that the appropriate divisions within the company are represented and given some exposure to the delegation, and that the material they present is responsive to the information needs of the visitors. Once a tentative program has been drawn up it's advisable to run a copy of it by the Chinese side for their comments, or by their representative if this is easier. The more advance information the Chinese are given, the better prepared they will be, and the more confident you can be that you are on the right track.

Remember in planning presentations that the need for consecutive interpretation will mean that time allotted must be multiplied by two. If you can prepare a bilingual text outline of what will be discussed, so much the better. Give some thought to interpreters, too. While the Chinese side will bring along its own translator, supplying one from your side is an excellent idea, provided that the person is competent. Someone familiar with the Chinese translations for the technical terms of your trade would be ideal. Whoever does the translating should be given an advance text of each presentation, even if it exists only in outline form. A little preparation can make the difference between a rudimentary understanding and a thorough grasp of the material on the part of the Chinese group.

Throughout the visit, the Chinese will probably pose many questions. Those that cannot be answered as they are asked should be noted, together with any requests made by the delegates for further information. It's an important show of sincerity to follow up on such requests religiously and to make sure that the guests receive answers, unless of course there is a reason to withhold the information. In that case, it's best to tell the guests why.

COCKTAILS AND DINING

Formal entertaining generally plays a part in hosting delegations. If time permits, it is customary to treat a delegation to lunch or dinner while it is visiting your organization. There is no need to do this more than once or twice, even if the group stays with you for a long period of time.

In the West, it is often the custom to precede a dinner with a cocktail hour. Milling around and engaging in polite conversation with friends and strangers alike is common practice in the West, but it doesn't happen that way in China. Chinese delegations who visit Western countries have generally been briefed to expect such affairs, though it's probably fair to say that they generally find them rather awkward.

The problem, in essence, is that Chinese are unused to being approached directly by people they don't know—it's really almost a breach of etiquette as far as they are concerned. And in intercultural situations, the language barrier compounds the problem. If you do plan cocktails, make sure there are enough bilinguals present to ensure that mixing can occur. Even so, don't be surprised or overly concerned if the guests naturally gravitate into two separate camps. It doesn't mean the affair is a failure. Mingling will eventually occur over the meal.

Another tip for cocktails with the Chinese: be sure to tell the bartender to stock two or three times the normal quantity of orange juice. Despite the obsession with imbibing *maotai* (see Chapter 7) that you often encounter in the PRC, the Chinese are unfamiliar with the different types of Western liquor. Some may be daring, but most play it safe with fruit juice.

If you plan a luncheon or dinner where Chinese and hosts will be present together, you'll want to assign seats and mark place settings with name cards. This is advisable if only to avoid the otherwise natural phenomenon of Chinese choosing to sit with other Chinese and Westerners with other Westerners. Since the reason for taking the meal together is presumably the two sides' getting to know each other better, it's important to sprinkle representatives of both sides across all of the tables, and make sure that there are interpreters on hand at each table to facilitate communication.

It's probably best in such situations to follow the rules of Chinese protocol seating (see Chapter 7). You need not do this slavishly, but do try to keep within the spirit if not the letter of protocol order. If you place the principal Chinese guest at table 3, far from your company chairman, you're bound to end up with wounded feelings. Similarly, don't put someone at a table for "emotional" reasons; just because your company president enjoyed Mr. Wang's questions during the business meeting is no reason to bump Mr. Wang up five steps in protocol order and seat him at the head table in a seat that would rightfully belong to Mr. Zhou.

As long as you are operating within approximate protocol order, however, it *is* proper to seat people next to each other for substantive reasons. Placing Chinese and Western engineers next to each other so that they can discuss technical matters relating to the venture being negotiated is a good idea, and it's perfectly acceptable.

Do escort your guests to their seats. If possible, make sure that the name cards are bilingual, so the Chinese guests can find their own places, and so the Westerners seated on either side of them can determine who their dining partners are. If the meal is a buffet, the Chinese will need an explicit invitation before they will line up and help themselves.

If you are hosting a dinner, don't keep your Chinese guests out too late. Remember that Chinese tend to eat early, and are generally finished with their meals no later than 8 P.M., and most often somewhat earlier. Making them wait for an eight o'clock dinner and keeping them out past ten will probably tire them out if they don't perish from hunger first. Remember that the Chinese don't customarily linger after the meal is over; their routine is to leave promptly after the last course is finished.

It's probably better all around if you avoid hosting the Chinese for excessively formal affairs. Chinese men who travel abroad invariably wear Western suits, but few Chinese own tuxedos or tails. Chinese groups generally take a "black tie" invitation as a signal to wear national dress, which of course means *Zhongshan zhuang*, or Mao jackets.

PLANNING MENUS

When Chinese visit other countries, it is not necessary for their hosts to offer Chinese-style banquets in their honor. Just as visitors to the PRC expect the etiquette—not to say the food—to be different, the Chinese are aware that in other countries things are done differently. Still, organizing a banquet at a Chinese restaurant is a popular means of entertaining Chinese visitors, and one that they very much appreciate. In truth, the Chinese believe that their cuisine, with all of its regional variations, is the best in the world. After a week or so of "foreign food," *any* Chinese delegation will be glad for a taste of home.

If you are planning a Western-style meal, here are a few tips on choosing the menu. First of all, refrain from serving large chunks of red meat—beef, pork, or anything else—and especially avoid serving steaks that are blood rare or undercooked. Hamburgers don't play very well with people from the PRC, where they are all but unknown. Salads consisting of raw vegetables are also not high on Chinese wish lists; vegetables are almost always cooked in China. Many Chinese also eschew dairy products such as sour cream and cheese—especially highly aromatic cheeses such as bleu cheese. You should forgo pizza for this reason.

A successful Western-style meal is more likely to include rice or noodles than bread. It's also more likely to be a buffet than a sit-down dinner, since the former offers a measure of choice in entrees. Dishes made up of small pieces such as stews and stir-fried vegetables are very welcome. Make sure all vegetables are cooked, though not to the point that they lose their crispness. And poultry and seafood are always welcome, just so long as they aren't smothered in cream sauces.

You'll find that visitors from Taiwan generally have less trouble with Western food than mainlanders; they have been exposed to it longer and are simply more accustomed to it. And Hong Kong residents will have the least difficulty; many eat Western food often and boast palates that are quite educated. All appreciate good Chinese cuisine, however.

Few PRC delegations leave China without rudimentary training in the basics of Western etiquette—how to tie a tie, hold a knife and fork, etc. But expect some lapses in table etiquette, especially if your Chinese guest is from a rural area or not well-educated. This may include talking with a mouthful of food, forgetting to use a napkin, or buttering a roll with a fork or spoon.

AMENITIES AND BUGABOOS

Listed below are a few special ways in which you can make your Chinese visitors feel very much at home, and a few sensitive areas that you'd be well-advised to watch out for:

Snack food. You can count on the fact that Chinese delegations required to eat Western food for any length of time will be homesick for a taste of China. A good way to provide some sustenance for the delegates who only pick at their steak and potatoes—and a treat even for those more comfortable with Western cuisine—is to supply your guests with instant noodles and some way to boil water—an inexpensive, plug-in hot pot, for example. A delegation of Chinese little leaguers I once escorted around the United States began to get visibly depressed around mealtime, and were very clearly unhappy with hamburgers, pizza, and other fast-food fare. A cup of instant noodles before bedtime really worked wonders.

Another favorite snack is fresh fruit. Providing a visiting Chinese with a basket of fruit in his or her room will be a most welcome gesture. If you were thinking of fresh flowers, think again; an apple or a bunch of bananas is a much better idea. And a container of loose tea with a thermos of hot water will also be most appreciated; Chinese hotels provide these in each room as a matter of course.

Lightening the load. Delegations that stay abroad for lengthy periods and that visit many different companies or countries may amass mountains of printed materials. If companies provide copies for everyone on the delegation, that's a dozen or so copies of each brochure and pamphlet. An offer to mail the brochures back to China on the delegation's behalf is almost always graciously received.

Gift-giving. Most Chinese delegations carry gifts with them to present to each organization that hosts them. You can expect to receive a gift if you entertain a Chinese group. Strictly speaking it is not necessary to reciprocate, since it is you who are offering the hospitality. But a memento of the occasion is always welcome. Giving inexpensive individual gifts—pens, cigarette lighters, briefcases, tape measures, etc.—that show your company's logo is common practice. For more on this, see Chapter 8.

Entertaining at home. It's a real treat for a Chinese to be entertained at the home of a corporate host. Not only is this a personal honor; it's a great way to satisfy curiosity about how the other half lives, and an excellent way to break the ice. If you invite Chinese delegates to your home it's fine to have your spouse and children on hand if you wish.

Welcoming signs. One other amenity that is in no way expected or necessary but is appreciated is a sign at the location to be visited welcoming the group. In order for it to be effective, of course, the sign should be written in Chinese. I once escorted a Chinese delegation to the headquarters of a major paper company where they were greeted by a large banner proclaiming the company's enthusiastic welcome. The only glitch was that the banner had been hung upside down. The Chinese were amused by the mishap, but they appreciated the gesture very much nonetheless.

Flags. Some companies also decide to hang the Chinese flag out front as a sign of welcome. This is fine—and much appreciated—as long as you use the right flag. The sensitivity here is to the flag used by Taiwan, which despite loss of recognition by the United States in 1979 (and, indeed, by many Western countries even before that time) still manages to show up in many places. The PRC flag is red with five yellow stars on it, one larger than the other four. That's the *only* flag to use when hosting mainland groups. The Taiwan "Republic of China" flag also has a red background, but it has a blue field in the upper left hand corner with one large, white sunlike star on it. Use it for Taiwan groups if you wish, but be sure it is well out of sight before a PRC delegation shows up. Mainland groups have been known to turn on their heels in outrage and walk right out of a building that displays the Taiwan flag, so this is nothing to be taken lightly.

Maps. In a related vein, something else to watch out for is the use of maps in your sales or corporate literature. Showing Taiwan on any map is perfectly acceptable; the Chinese know companies do business there and they have no objection to this; it is, after all, a part of China as far as they are concerned. Just be sure that Taiwan is not portrayed in any way as an independent country, or as an entity separate from the mainland. Avoid the "Republic of China" label like the plague, and don't show Taiwan in a color different from that of the rest of China.

Interestingly, people from Taiwan tend to share the same prejudice. They regard Taiwan as a part of China, too; the dispute is only over the identity of the legitimate government. For Taiwan groups, stay away from PRC flags and don't use the "People's Republic of China" title if you can avoid it. For Hong Kong groups, don't worry; they aren't really overly sensitive to these issues at all.

For the record, you should know also that there are certain countries that the Chinese do not recognize—South Korea, Israel, and South Africa are the most prominent of these. People used to be advised to avoid all mention of operations in these countries and to avoid depicting them on maps; this is not really necessary. You need not change your maps to accommodate the Chinese, and you really don't have to worry about mentioning facilities in these countries—or even in Taiwan, for that matter. The Chinese are realists and know most companies do business there; no major taboos are violated if you talk about them.

Photography. By all means invite the company photographer out to take some photos of the Chinese visitors. Not only might these be useful for the company newsletter (see below), but they are excellent follow-up gifts for your next trip to China. The Chinese love photographs, and a picture of you and the delegation standing at your company's factory in front of an important piece of equipment is not only a valuable memento; it is also a way to keep your company's products fresh in your guests' minds for many months.

The Chinese will almost certainly come equipped with cameras. If there is any sensitivity regarding the taking of photos in the facility to be toured, say so; telling the Chinese that it is your company's policy to disallow photographs will end the matter then and there. Don't worry about hurt feelings; rules like this are completely understandable to the Chinese. The same regulations apply to sensitive areas, such as military installations, in the PRC.

MEDIA

Visits by important Chinese delegations are often of great interest to local media. Many companies find that when word gets around in the community that a high-ranking Chinese official will be touring their facilities, the local press is eager to cover the story.

In the late 1970s and early 1980s, when Chinese delegations began visiting Western countries in larger numbers, it was official policy to avoid the domestic media. Chinese groups were extremely camera-shy and regularly refused to participate in press conferences, individual interviews, or any other contact with journalists.

Things have changed to the extent that an occasional Chinese delegation will happily agree to talk to the media, especially if the group is selling products or attempting to attract foreign investment. Most delegations still prefer to keep a lower profile, however. The rule of thumb here, as elsewhere, is to avoid surprises. If the Chinese agree in advance to receive a journalist, you need not hesitate to arrange an interview. But if you value your company's relationship with the Chinese group, the media should never be forced on them when they are your guests. Getting off an airplane to confront a crowd of vocal reporters is no Chinese delegation leader's idea of a day at the beach.

Don't interpret this warning to mean that it isn't acceptable to cover a Chinese delegation's visit in your company's in-house newspaper. It certainly is. Just explain to your guests the purpose of the photo or of the interview, and nine times out of ten you'll get complete cooperation.

RECAP: FOURTEEN WAYS TO BE A GOOD HOST

1. Hosting delegations from China carries many responsibilities and can be costly. Since companies are often approached by far more Chinese delegations than they could ever possibly receive, it's important to choose carefully which ones to host.

2. Delegations have definite structures and hierarchies. The name list enumerates delegates in protocol order, starting with the delegation leader, usually a government official. He or she makes major decisions and speaks for the group in all matters.

3. The Chinese expect hosts to coordinate the trips and generally help things go smoothly. Sometimes more than one host is contacted, confusing things. Always clarify exactly what is expected of you if you agree to serve as host, in order to avoid misunderstandings.

4. The Chinese pay their own expenses unless otherwise stated. Be sensitive to what they can afford and let them know in advance how much things cost. Ask the hotel to accommodate the entire group on one floor if possible; proximity to an interpreter is important. Consider briefing first-time visitors on security precautions.

5. Try to arrange someone of suitably high rank in your company to meet important visitors at the airport and see them off when they leave. Make sure whoever greets the group is well-briefed. Providing transportation is a good way to signal respect. Schedule an audience with a responsible corporate official if possible.

6. Schedule an itinerary meeting after arrival to secure Chinese "buy-in" of the arrangements. Keep the first day's schedule light to allow time to overcome jet lag. Offer a basic briefing about the company. Someone of sufficiently

high rank should stay with the group during its visit—unless it is a prolonged stay.

7. Provide Chinese guests with a schedule or itinerary in Chinese or English, plus a name list of the company officers the guests meet. Also distribute technical materials related to the product or technology discussed.

8. Remember the need for consecutive interpretation; time allotted must be multiplied by two. A bilingual text outline of what will be discussed is appreciated. Note as they are asked questions that can be answered and follow up on such requests.

9. Chinese delegations find cocktail parties awkward, but plan them if you must. Don't be concerned if the guests gravitate into two separate camps. Tell the bartender to stock two or three times the normal quantity of orange juice.

10. If you plan a sit-down meal, mark place settings with name cards. Follow protocol order in seating. Don't keep Chinese guests out too late; their routine is to leave promptly after the last course is finished.

11. If you are planning a Western-style meal, avoid large chunks of red meat, blood rare steaks, and hamburgers. Salads of raw vegetables and dairy products are chancy. Try to serve rice or noodles, stews, or stir-fried vegetables.

12. Supply your guests with instant noodles and some way to boil water as a treat; fresh fruit is also welcome. Offer to lighten their load by mailing your company's brochures back to China. Give inexpensive souvenirs; photos of the delegates visiting your company are excellent mementos.

13. A welcoming sign at the site to be visited is appreciated, as is a display of the Chinese flag, but make sure it is the *right* flag. Watch out also for any maps that show Taiwan as an entity separate from China.

14. Media should never be forced on the Chinese when they are your guests. If they agree in advance to receive a journalist, don't hesitate to arrange an interview. Feel free to cover a Chinese delegation visit in your company's in-house newspaper.

A Guide to
Chinese Romanization
and Phonics

You'll get a lot further in China if you learn to say the names of the people you meet and the places you go properly. The Chinese don't expect foreigners to speak their language, but they are tickled when you try. Still, you may have some difficulty being understood without a little guidance. This section provides a basic introduction to Mandarin Chinese phonics that should help you pronounce not only the Chinese terms used in this book, but also the names and other words you'll encounter when you are in China.

PINYIN ROMANIZATION

The Chinese terms used in this book are expressed in a romanization system called *pinyin*—a Chinese word meaning nothing more than "spelling." It is one of many systems of phonetic rendering of Chinese, developed in the 1950s primarily for teaching the language to Chinese children and to foreigners. *Pinyin* is the official romanization system of the People's Republic of China; to the extent that you encounter any romanized words there, this is the system of spelling that will probably be used. It became popular in the West in the late 1970s. You'll probably recognize *pinyin* as the system that dictated that we start referring to Teng Hsiao-p'ing as Deng Xiaoping and Peking as Beijing.

Pinyin is based on the Mandarin dialect (called *putonghua* on the mainland and *guoyu* in Taiwan). You'll seldom encounter it in Hong Kong because it does not provide an effective way of romanizing the Cantonese dialect spoken there. Nor will you see it used in Taiwan—where Mandarin in fact is widely spoken—because it is a communist invention, and as such considered politically unacceptable. The older Wade-Giles system—which gave us Mao Tse-tung before he was Mao Zedong—is more widespread in Taiwan; other, less common systems are used there as well.

The Chinese themselves actually have little use for romanization, so don't expect a Chinese person to be very familiar with *pinyin* or any other latinized spelling system. Written Chinese makes use of a system of characters or ideographs that stand for words and contain little phonetic information. Even though China is a land of many unintelligible dialects, the written language is consistent throughout the country. Though it takes many years to learn to read Chinese efficiently, China boasts a very high literacy rate. The Chinese use characters exclusively in their day-to-day lives. For the purpose of the occasional traveler to China, however, a working knowledge of *pinyin* is all you're likely to need to get by.

PRONOUNCING CHINESE

All Chinese words are composed of one or more syllables. And any Chinese syllable can be divided into three components: an *initial* sound, a *final* sound, and a *tone* or intonation. It's the *pinyin* rendering of the initials that gives Westerners the most trouble, since a few conventions used are not intuitive to native speakers of English. If you remember a few facts about the four most troublesome letters—that a q at the beginning of a word is pronounced like a *ch*, an x like an *sh*, a c like a *ts*, and a z like a *dz*—you're 85 percent of the way there, since most of the other letters perform as they do in English. Here's the complete table of *pinyin* initials, together with some approximate equivalent pronunciations in English:

Initials

PINYIN INITIAL	ENGLISH EQUIVALENT
b	same as English
c	like the *ts* in "cats"
ch	same as English
d	same as English
f	same as English
g	same as English
h	like an *h*, only more guttural; actually more like the *ch* in the German word "ach"
j	like the *j* in "jeep"
k	same as English
l	same as English
m	same as English
n	same as English
p	same as English
q	like the *ch* in China
r	somewhere between the English *r* and *j*; a bit like the *s* in "leisure"
s	same as English
sh	same as English
t	same as English
w	same as English
x	like the *sh* in "she"
y	same as English
z	like the *ds* in "buds"
zh	like the *j* in "jail"

For the finals, too, your knowledge of English will not generally lead you too far astray, except for a few tricky cases.

Below is a complete table of *pinyin* finals with equivalent sounds in English:

Finals

PINYIN FINAL	ENGLISH EQUIVALENT
a	like the *a* in "pa"
ai	like the *ie* in "pie"
an	like the word "on"
ang	like the *ang* in "angst"
ao	to rhyme with "cow"
ar	like the *ar* in "bar"
e	like the *oo* in "wood"
ei	like the *a* in "say"
en	like the *un* in "bun"
eng	like the *ung* in "sung"
er	like the *ir* in "sir"
i	like the *e* in "me" after the initials b,d,l,m,n,p,q,t, and x; like *z* after c,s, and z; and like *r* after ch,r,sh, and zh
ia	like the word "ya"
ian	like the word "yen"
iang	"yahng," to rhyme with "gong"
iao	like the word "yow"
ie	like the word "yeh"
in	to rhyme with "mean"
ing	like the *ing* in "king"
iong	"yawng," to rhyme with "wrong"
iu	like the word "yo"
o	like the *aw* in "raw"
ong	to rhyme with "wrong"
ou	to rhyme with "hoe"

u	like the German *ü* or the French *eu* after n and l; to rhyme with "coo" after all other letters
uai	like the beginning of the word "wide"
uan	like the word "wen" after j,q,x, and y; like the word "wan" after other letters
uang	like the surname of "Suzie Wong"
ue	like the beginning of the word "wet"
ui	like the word "way"
un	like the word "win" after j,q, and x; to rhyme with "won" after other letters
uo	like the surname of "Evelyn Waugh"

Chinese syllables are basically combinations of initials and finals. Thus the word *xiao*, which means small, is a combination of the initial *x*, pronounced like an "sh," and the ending *iao*, pronounced like "yao." The syllable is thus said "shyao." *Ren*, meaning "benevolence," is a combination of the initial *r* and the final *en*. Some words, like these two examples, are just one syllable long. Other words are combinations of two or more syllables, each the sum of an initial and a final.

TONES

To complete the story, however, you must also understand tones. Chinese is a sound-poor language; that is, combining initials and finals yields a relatively small number of possible pronunciations. To increase the size of this universe, every syllable also has a tone, or intonation, in addition to an initial and a final. This means that each syllable must be pronounced in the proper tone of voice in order for one's meaning to be clear. Spoken Mandarin has four such tones: an even tone, a rising tone, a dipping tone, and a falling tone.

We have intonation patterns in English, too, but not nearly to the extent that Chinese does. For example, if you pronounce the sentence "The book is on the table" first normally and then with a rising intonation, you can see that by varying only the intonation you can change a declarative sentence into an interrogative one.

In Chinese, the syllable *tang* can mean "soup" (when said in an even tone), "sugar" (rising tone), "to lie down" (dipping tone), and "to iron something" (falling tone). And, depending on the actual character, it can mean a lot of other things as well, such as a surname, a hall, a kind of poplar tree, an embankment, a door frame, your chest, to bore, a mantis, the state treasury, to shed, or an incidence. Most Chinese words have many homonyms, and tones help cut down the number of options so people can understand one another without too much difficulty. Context generally does the rest.

Any serious student of the Chinese language should concern him or herself with tones; for the casual visitor, however, they may be omitted without sacrificing too much in the way of meaning. To avoid confusion, tone marks have been omitted throughout this book.

Recommended Reading

ON THE CHINESE LANGUAGE

Newnham, Richard, *About Chinese*. Middlesex, England: Penguin Books, 1971.

Seligman, Scott D. and Chen, I-Chuan, *Chinese at a Glance*. New York: Barron's Educational Series, Inc., 1986.

ON CULTURAL DIFFERENCES

Bloodworth, Dennis, *The Chinese Looking Glass*. New York: Farrar Straus and Giroux, 1980.

Hsu, Francis L.K., *Americans and Chinese: Passage to Differences*. Third edition. Honolulu: The University Press of Hawaii, 1981.

Liu, Zongren, *Two Years in the Melting Pot*. San Francisco: China Books and Periodicals, 1984.

Schell, Orville, *Watch Out for the Foreign Guests! China Encounters the West*. New York: Pantheon Books, 1980.

Wilson, Richard W., *Learning to Be Chinese*. Cambridge, MA: The Massachusetts Institute of Technology, 1970.

ON DOING BUSINESS IN CHINA

Business China. Hong Kong: Business International Asia/Pacific, Ltd. Fortnightly publication.

The China Business Review. Washington, D.C.: The U.S.-China Business Council. Bimonthly publication.

China Market Intelligence. Washington, D.C.: The U.S.-China Business Council. Monthly publication.

de Keijzer, Arne J., *The China Business Handbook*. Weston, CT: Asia Business Communications, Ltd., 1986.

Doing Business with China. Washington, D.C.: Office of PRC and Hong Kong, U.S. Department of Commerce, 1983.

Eliasoph, Ellen, *Law and Business Practice in Shanghai*. Hong Kong: Longman Group (Far East) Ltd., 1987.

Macleod, Roderick, *China Inc.: How to Do Business with the Chinese*. New York: Bantam Books, 1988.

US-China Business Services Directory. Second edition. Washington, D.C.: The U.S.-China Business Council, 1988.

ON LIFE IN THE PRC

Bernstein, Richard, *From the Center of the Earth*. Boston: Little, Brown, 1982.

Bonavia, David, *The Chinese*. New York: Harper & Row, 1980.

Butterfield, Fox, *Alive in the Bitter Sea*. New York: Times Books, 1982.

Shapiro, Judy and Liang, Heng, *Son of the Revolution*. New York: Alfred A. Knopf, 1983.

ON NEGOTIATING WITH THE CHINESE

Hendryx, Steven, "The China Trade: Making the Deal Work" in *The Harvard Business Review*. July–August, 1986.

Pye, Lucian, "The China Trade: Making the Deal" in *The Harvard Business Review*. July–August, 1986.

Pye, Lucian, *Chinese Commercial Negotiating Style*. Cambridge, MA: Oelgesschlager, Gunn & Hain Publishers, Inc., 1982.

Randt, Clark T., Jr., "Negotiating Strategy and Tactics" in *US-China Trade: Problems and Prospects*, edited by Eugene K. Lawson. New York: Praeger, 1988.

Searls, Melvin W., Jr., "Negotiating the Contract: Selected Case Studies" in *US-China Trade: Problems and Prospects*, edited by Eugene K. Lawson. New York: Praeger, 1988.

Solomon, Richard, *Chinese Political Negotiating Behavior: A Briefing Analysis*. Santa Monica: The Rand Corporation, 1985.

ON TRAVELING IN CHINA

Fodor's People's Republic of China. New York: Random House, 1988.

Kaplan, Frederick M., Sobin, Julian, and de Keijzer, Arne J., *The China Guidebook*. Fairlawn, NJ: Eurasia Press, 1988.

Malloy, Ruth Lor and Hsu, Priscilla Liang, *Fielding's People's Republic of China*. New York: William Morrow & Co., 1987.

Nagel's Encyclopedia Guide: China. Geneva: Nagel's Publishers, 1986.

ON WORKING AND LIVING IN CHINA

Greenblatt, Sidney L. and others. *Organizational Behavior in Chinese Society*. New York: Praeger, 1981.

Multinationals in China. New York: Organization Resources Counselors, 1986. Special report.

Turner-Gottschang, Karen with Reed, Linda A., *China Bound: A Guide to Academic Life and Work in the PRC*. Washington, D.C.: National Academy Press, 1987.

Glossary of Chinese Terms Used in this Book

ai 愛, "love." One of the eight Confucian virtues.

airen 愛人, PRC term for "spouse." Also means "lover."

ayi 阿姨, "aunt."

bian chi bian shuo 邊吃邊說, "Let's continue the conversation as we eat."

biaozhun 標准, "standard." Used also to mean the standard price per head that a restaurant charges for a banquet.

bobo 伯伯, "uncle."

bomu 伯母, "aunt."

buyao keqi 不要客氣, a phrase meaning "You shouldn't be so polite," and often used to mean "You're welcome."

buzhang 部長, "minister" (government position).

changzhang 廠長, manager or director of a factory.

Chen 陳, a common Chinese surname.

chi bao le 吃飽了, to have eaten one's fill. Used at banquets to signal host that one is satisfied.

chutou chuanzi xian lan 出頭椽子先爛, "Exposed rafters are the first to rot," or "He who sticks his neck out bears the brunt."

dage 大哥, "eldest (or elder) brother."

dajie 大姐 , "eldest (or elder) sister."

danwei 單位 , "work unit."

erjie 二姐 , "second elder sister."

fenpei 分配 , literally, to distribute or apportion. To assign, as an individual to a job.

furen 夫人 , an honorific title meaning "Madam;" a wife.

futuanzhang 副團長 , the deputy leader of a delegation.

ganbei 乾杯 , a phrase meaning literally "dry glass," used in toasting. "Bottoms up."

guanxi 關係 , "connections." A system of relationships and reciprocal obligations.

guoyu 國語 , literally, "national language." The term for the Mandarin dialect used in Taiwan and by many Chinese outside of the mainland. Not widely used in the PRC.

guwen 顧問 , "advisor." A senior-ranking member of a Chinese organization or delegation.

he 合 , "harmony." One of the eight Confucian virtues.

hongbao 紅包 , a "red envelope" containing cash, given as a gift, a gratuity, or a bribe.

houmen 後門 , the "back door." The key to delivery of products and services in China through the use of connections.

Huang 黃 , a common Chinese surname.

jiedai danwei 接待單位 , "host organization." The Chinese unit that issues an invitation and takes responsibility for foreign guests during the time they spend in the PRC.

jingli 經理 , "manager."

lao 老 , "old."

laoda 老大 , "eldest child."

lao'er 老二 , "second-born child."

laosan 老三 , "third-born child."

laoyao 老么 , "youngest child."

Li 李 , a common Chinese surname.

li qing, ren yi zhong 禮輕人意重 , "The gift is trifling but the feeling is profound." The Chinese equivalent of "It's the thought that counts."

Lin 林 , a common Chinese surname.

Liu 劉 , a common Chinese surname.

maotai 茅台 , a 106-proof wheat- and sorghum-based liquor frequently served at Chinese banquets.

mianzi 面子, "face." Has both the tangible and intangible meanings of the English word.

nali? 哪裡?, an interrogative meaning "where" that is also used to deflect compliments, meaning "It was nothing."

neibu 內部, "For internal consumption only." Something not to be shown to foreigners.

ni hao ma? 你好嗎?, standard Chinese greeting meaning "How are you?"

ni naiwei? 你哪位?, an expression meaning literally "Who are you?" but often used to mean "What organization do you represent?"

ni nali? 你哪裡?, an expression meaning literally "Where are you?" but actually used to mean "What organization do you represent?"

ni nar? 你哪兒?, an expression meaning literally "Where are you?" but actually meaning "What organization do you represent?"

nüshi 女士, a title meaning "Ms."

ping 平, "peace." One of the eight Confucian virtues.

pinyin 拼音, the system of romanization of Chinese used in the PRC; also the Chinese word for "spelling."

putonghua 普通話, literally, "normal speech." The PRC term for the Mandarin dialect.

qing yong 請用, literally, "Please use." Said by a host at the commencement of a meal to signal guests to begin eating.

qipao 旗袍, a tight-fitting traditional Chinese dress with a high collar and long slits up the legs.

ren 仁, "benevolence." One of the eight Confucian virtues.

ru guo er wen su 入國而問俗, "If you visit a country, ask what its customs are." From *Li Ji*, one of the five Confucian classics.

ru jing er wen jin 入境而問禁, "If you enter a region, ask what its prohibitions are." From *Li Ji*, one of the five Confucian classics.

ru men er wen hui 入門而問諱, "If you cross a family's threshold, ask what its taboos are." From *Li Ji*, one of the five Confucian classics.

ru xiang, sui su 入鄉隨俗, an expression meaning literally "Enter village, follow customs." The rough equivalent of "When in Rome, do as the Romans."

sanjie 三姐 , "third eldest sister."

shengzhang 省長 , governor of a province.

shifu 師傅 , a form of address for waiters, store clerks, hotel staff, and other tradespeople, literally meaning "master."

shizhang 市長 , mayor of a city.

shushu 叔叔 , "uncle."

song zhong 送終 , literally "to attend a dying parent." A homonym of the phrase "to give a clock," and the reason clocks are not traditionally considered acceptable gifts among the Chinese.

suiyi 隨意 , a phrase meaning "at will" used during toasts to exhort someone to drink only as much as he or she wishes.

taitai 太太 , an honorific title meaning "Madam"; a wife.

tie fanwan 鐵飯碗, China's "iron rice bowl" incentive system of lifetime tenure in a job regardless of performance.

tong chuang yi meng 同床異夢 , an expression meaning "divergent interests." Its literal meaning is "two in the same bed dreaming different dreams."

tongzhi 同志 , "comrade."

tuanzhang 團長 , the leader of a delegation.

Wang 王 , a common Chinese surname.

wei 喂, an interjection used to begin and punctuate telephone conversations.

wu jiang si mei 五講四美 , "the five stresses and the four beauties," a 1980s campaign to return to traditional Confucian values.

xiansheng 先生 , an honorific title meaning literally "first born," but most often used to mean "Mister" or a husband.

xiao 小 , "small" or "young."

xiao 孝 , "filial piety." One of the eight Confucian virtues.

xiaodi 小弟 , "youngest brother."

xiaojie 小姐 , an honorific title meaning "Miss"; a young, unmarried female.

xin 信 , "trust." One of the eight Confucian virtues.

xiong 兄 , "elder brother."

yi 義 , "justice." One of the eight Confucian virtues.

Zhang 張 , a common Chinese surname.

Zhao 趙 , a common Chinese surname.

zhong 忠 , "loyalty." One of the eight Confucian virtues.

Zhongguo tong 中國通 , a "China hand." Someone who understands China and the Chinese very well.

Zhongshan zhuang 中山裝 , a loose-fitting, high-collared jacket known popularly in the West as a "Mao jacket," but actually named for Sun Yat-sen (Sun Zhongshan), the father of modern China.

zhuren 主任, "director."

zhuxi 主席, "chairman."

zongjingli 總經理 , president of a company.

zou houmen 走後門 , "to enter through the back door." To obtain products and services in China through the use of connections.

About the Author

A 1973 graduate of Princeton University, Scott Seligman began his study of Chinese in the same year. He served as Sidney D. Gamble Teaching Fellow at Tunghai University in Taichung, Taiwan, for two years, instructing Chinese college students in English composition and introductory psychology. He subsequently earned a master's degree at Harvard University in 1976 and then returned to Princeton for two years as assistant to the Dean of Student Affairs.

In 1978, Mr. Seligman was asked to serve as a legislative assistant on the personal staff of New Jersey Congresswoman Millicent Fenwick, for whom he monitored and drafted legislation in the area of foreign affairs. In late 1979, following U.S. recognition of the People's Republic of China, he joined the staff of the National Council for U.S.-China Trade (now the U.S.-China Business Council), a private, not-for-profit membership organization charged with promoting trade and investment between the United States and the PRC.

Mr. Seligman managed the Council's newly established Beijing office from 1981 to 1982, supervising local and expatriate staff and advising American companies concerning business opportunities, market entry, and positioning in China. He was a founding member of the board of governors of the American Chamber of Commerce in Beijing. After returning to Washington to serve as the Council's Director of Development and Government Relations from 1982 to 1985, he joined the public relations firm of Burson-Marsteller as Coordinator of China Affairs. He has worked in the company's Washington, Chicago, and Hong Kong offices, and is currently Vice President and Creative Director/Asia.

A native of New Jersey, Mr. Seligman is fluent in Mandarin and proficient in written Chinese. He serves on the board of directors of Princeton-in-Asia, a not-for-profit foundation that places young Americans in teaching positions in universities throughout Asia. He is the author of numerous articles in the *Asian Wall Street Journal*, the *China Business Review*, and other publications on subjects related to doing business with

China, and is coauthor of Barron's *Chinese at a Glance*, a Mandarin Chinese phrasebook/dictionary for travelers, and Barron's *Now You're Talking Chinese*, a cassette, microscript, and phrasebook/dictionary kit.

Index

R

Reciprocity, 52–53
  guanxi, 50–52
Red envelope (*hongbao*), 165
Regional differences
  nonverbal communication,
    28
  personal relationships, 81
  tipping, 117
Relationships (Chinese with for-
    eigners)
  business relationships, 76–79
  foreign women, 79–80
  invitation to Chinese home,
    84–87
  personal relationships, 80–83
  sexual relationships, 83
  westerners, view of, 73–76

S

Seating arrangements
  business meetings, 61
  Chinese banquet, 95–99
  visiting Chinese delegation,
    183
Sendoffs, 25–26
Service people
  addressing, 22
  tipping, 117–119
Sexual relationships, 83
Silence, 31
Smoking, 28–29
Spitting, 28, 62
Surnames
  most popular, 20, 23
  position of, 20–21

T

Table manners, Chinese ban-
    quet, 105–107
Taiwan, 6
Telephone, use of, 33–36
  greeting, 34
  initial formalities, 35
  phone system, 33–34
  sound level, 36
Tipping, 117–119
Titles, *See* Chinese names
  regional differences, 117
Toasting, 107–110
Tones, Chinese Language, 193,
    196–197
Translators
  in business meetings, in nego-
    tiation, 129, 133

W

Welcoming party, 24–26, 178–
    179
Westerners, Chinese view of,
    73–76
Women, 79–80
  foreign business women, 79–
    80
  foreign spouses, 80
Work-unit (*danwei*), 40, 42–45
  choosing work-unit, 42–43
  joint-venture unit, 44
  power and influence of, 43–
    45
  switching from, 43